Black Joe and Other Selected Stories

BLACK JOE AND OTHER SELECTED STORIES

ROD MILLER

FIVE STAR
A part of Gale, a Cengage Company

GALE
A Cengage Company

LIBRARY OF CONGRESS CATALOGING-IN-PUBLICATION DATA

Names: Miller, Rod, 1952– author.
Title: Black Joe and other selected stories / Rod Miller.
Description: First Edition. | Waterville, Maine : Five Star, a part of Gale, a Cengage Company, 2023. | Identifiers: LCCN 2022019331 | ISBN 9781432897833 (hardcover)
Subjects: LCGFT: Short stories.
Classification: LCC PS3613.I55264 B53 2023 | DDC 813/.6—dc23
LC record available at https://lccn.loc.gov/2022019331

First Edition. First Printing: January 2023
Find us on Facebook—https://www.facebook.com/FiveStarCengage
Visit our website—http://www.gale.cengage.com/fivestar
Contact Five Star Publishing at FiveStar@cengage.com

Printed in Mexico
Print Number: 1   Print Year: 2023

ACKNOWLEDGEMENTS

"Two Birds in the Bush" is original to this collection.

"Horse Thief Morning" first appeared in *The Death of Delgado and Other Stories,* Pen-L Publishing, 2015.

"Separating the Wheat from the Tares" first appeared in *White Hats,* Berkley Books, 2002.

"The People versus Porter Rockwell" first appeared in *Black Hats,* Berkley Books, 2003.

"Bullwhacker" first appeared in *Contention and Other Frontier Stories,* Five Star, 2019.

"The Death of Delgado" first appeared in *The Traditional West,* Western Fictioneers, 2011.

"Black Joe" first appeared in *Saddlebag Dispatches,* Autumn/Winter 2019–2020.

"The Darkness of the Deep" first appeared in *Westward,* Forge Books, 2003.

"Ben Colton's Downfall" is original to this collection.

"Good Horses" first appeared in *Literally Horses,* Spring/Summer 2000.

"The Turn of a Card" first appeared in *Cactus Country Anthology I,* High Hill Press, 2011.

"The Times of a Sign" first appeared in *Hobnail and Other Frontier Stories,* Five Star, 2019.

"The Nakedness of the Land" first appeared in *Out West* 1, no. 4, Spring 2007, 1018 Press.

"Drowning in Riches" is original to this collection.

Acknowledgements

"A Border Dispute" first appeared in *Lone Star Law*, Pocket Books, 2005.

"Lost and Found" first appeared in *Saddlebag Dispatches*, Spring 2017.

Dedicated to Frank Roderus, Robert Randisi, Dale Walker, Dusty Richards, John Nesbitt, Johnny Boggs, Michael Zimmer, Loren Estleman, and all the other writers who encouraged me to tell stories.

TABLE OF CONTENTS

INTRODUCTION

Over the years I have been fortunate to see ink applied to many short stories, both in anthologies and in periodicals. Some of my favorites are collected here, along with stories appearing for the first time in these pages.

Some of the stories are informed by the history of the American West and adhere to the facts as much as a fictional telling allows. These include a "long" short story, "Two Birds in the Bush," based on the Great Diamond Hoax of 1872. Three stories chronicle some of the many facets of one of my favorite Old West characters, Mormon gunfighter Porter Rockwell: "Horse Thief Morning," "Separating the Wheat from the Tares," and "The People versus Porter Rockwell." Another, "Bullwhacker," tells the story of a pioneer woman, Mary Fielding Smith, who overcame overwhelming obstacles to journey west. "The Death of Delgado," while fictional in its characters, is built from an incident with a horse and a well which is at the story's core. Likewise, "Black Joe," which takes extreme liberties with a true story involving a renegade mustang stud. "The Darkness of the Deep" tells the tale of a murderous outlaw whose fate was unknown for many years. Since the story's original publication, it has been discovered that Rafael López probably made his way to Texas where he was finally dispatched by lawman Frank Hamer, famous for bringing Bonnie and Clyde to heel.

Other stories are figments of my imagination. Even here,

however, I have attempted to stay true to the times. Some are lighthearted in nature, as I have long believed the humorous side of cowboy life has been lost in literature in favor of gunfights. I hope "Ben Colton's Downfall," "Good Horses," and "The Turn of a Card" bring a smile to your face. "The Times of a Sign" imagines a future for some characters from my Five Star novel *A Thousand Dead Horses.* "The Nakedness of the Land" relies on the biblical story of Joseph for its inspiration. "Drowning in Riches" imagines a difficulty of outlaw life not often considered.

"A Border Dispute" and "Lost and Found" violate the limits of Old West frontier fiction. The first features two interwoven stories, one from the past and the other set in the present. "Lost and Found" shows that the modern West in which it is set is every bit as wild as ever.

Finally, I am pleased that a few of these stories have been recognized by various organizations. "Lost and Found" was honored with the Western Writers of America Spur Award; "The Death of Delgado" also won a Spur Award and was a Finalist for the Western Fictioneers Peacemaker Award. "Black Joe" won the Peacemaker Award. "A Border Dispute" was a Finalist for the Spur Award. The no-longer-extant periodical in which "Good Horses" appeared named it the Remuda Award winner for the year.

Thank you for reading. Without you, there would be no reason to write.

TWO BIRDS IN THE BUSH

With more showmanship than necessary, Asbury "Ash" Harpending snapped open the latches on the leather satchel. He peered into the open mouth, shifted his gaze to the men seated around the conference table, and smiled.

"Gentlemen," he said.

With a flourish, he tipped the valise. Gemstones spilled onto the table, clattering and tinkling and rattling and rolling and skipping across the varnished surface, some skidding the table's length. The intake of breath from the assembled men all but relieved the room of oxygen. The men sat dumbfounded, eyes fixed on the jewels. After a time, curious fingers touched stones, sliding them across the tabletop, then picking them up singly to study, closing one eye and holding the gems up to the light. One man did so with the aid of a magnifying eyepiece; a jewelers' loupe he always carried, more for show than practical purpose.

The men, assembled in the conference room of a tony New York City law office, included the man with the loupe, Charles Tiffany, whose considerable wealth had come from precious stones like those spilled onto the table before him. A lawyer and a banker from the city were there. As were three men who had served as generals in the late war: George McClellan, Benjamin Butler, and Benjamin Dodge.

Dodge had traveled to the city from San Francisco with Ash Harpending and William Lent, men with considerable financial interests in western mines. Lent and Dodge were here with an offer to increase the wealth of those assembled—in exchange, of course, for capital—but it was Harpending, a minor partner, more an employee, who did the talking.

"Gentlemen, we all know why we are here. As we have discussed, and as outlined in correspondence you have all received, we—with our partners out West, including Billy Ralston of the Bank of California, who some of you know—are on the verge of establishing what we believe will be the foremost diamond empire on earth. We are in the process of acquiring all rights to a diamond field in the western territories that appears to be richer than any previously known anywhere. In addition to diamonds, the ground also delivers rubies, sapphires, and emeralds for the taking.

"Our syndicate, preliminarily named the San Francisco and New York Mining and Commercial Company, while housed in San Francisco, is incorporating here in New York City, with this office where we are gathered handling the legal niceties. Only a few shareholders are to be involved; we hope you gentlemen will be among them."

The eyes of the New Yorkers turned to Tiffany. McClellan spoke. "Well, Charles?"

Tiffany slipped the eyepiece back into the pocket of his waistcoat and cleared his throat. "Gentlemen, they are the real thing."

Months earlier, two men, bundled in worn coats against the chill of San Francisco's foggy streets, made their way to the offices of the Bank of California. Philip Arnold and John Slack were miners; more prospectors, really, with year upon lonely year of experience trodding the waste places of the American West in search of the one big thing. This time, they believed they had found it.

Arnold took a deep breath and let it out slowly. "Remember, John. Keep your trap shut and let me do the talking. We don't want these nobs to know any more than they need to. And keep your hands on the bag."

Slack nodded and clutched a ragged carpetbag tighter against his chest.

Inside the bank, on the upper floor, William "Billy" Ralston sat behind an oversized desk in a larger-than-necessary office, shuffling a sheaf of papers, the only thing present on the expansive desktop.

A clerk, standing at attention with his hands clasped behind his back, stood before the desk. "They didn't want to say, Mister Ralston. But one of them let it slip they were diamonds."

Ralston's brow furrowed. He tapped the stack of loose pages into alignment, then slid them into a file folder and deposited it in a drawer. He looked at the clerk, his head cocked and forehead still wrinkled. "Diamonds? Where would men like that come up with diamonds?"

"I couldn't say, sir. But, as I am sure you are aware, there's not a day that passes without another rumor of diamond mines in the Southwest deserts."

Ralston leaned back, the swivel chair squeaking. "But why would they come here? Why San Francisco?"

"All I know is, they're closemouthed about the whole thing," the clerk said with a shrug. "If I had to guess, I'd say they're trying to maintain secrecy—they want to stay well away from the source of their diamond mine to avoid discovery."

"Assuming there is a diamond mine."

Again, the clerk shrugged. Ralston told him to fetch the men. Within minutes, the clerk tapped on the door and opened it, ushering the miners into the office. Slack stepped to the side to stand near the door, clutching the carpetbag.

Arnold walked to Ralston's desk and extended a rough hand.

"Philip Arnold's my name. Him there by the door, that's my cousin and partner John Slack."

Ralston stood, eying the man before him. After a pause, he reached out and took the proffered hand. The miner shook, waggling the banker's arm all the way to the shoulder. Ralston withdrew his hand and massaged it with the other, relieving the cramp from Arnold's tight grip. "I am William Ralston, president of the Bank of California. Please call me Billy. Everyone does." He nodded toward the two plush chairs facing the desk. "Have a seat."

Arnold dragged the chair forward and sat. Slack stood where he was.

"I am told you would like us to secure something in our vault."

Arnold and Slack exchanged glances. Neither spoke for a time. Then Arnold scooted his chair closer to the desk and leaned in. "Yes, sir. It's in that bag, there, that John's got."

"We will, of course, be happy to help. However, I must know what is in the bag we are to secure for you."

Again, the prospectors locked eyes. Arnold squirmed in his seat.

"Bank regulations, you see."

Arnold thought for a moment, then nodded to Slack. Slack carried the carpetbag to Arnold. He dropped it on the desk, unlatched it, and removed and set aside some articles of ragged clothing and a tattered journal-type book. Then he reached in and came out with a leather pouch. He untied it and poured out a handful of uncut gemstones.

The banker tried not to react, but his eyes widened at the quantity and size of the stones. Arnold tipped up the bag and shook out the few remaining stones, then, with the side of his hand, scraped the gems into a pile on the desk.

With the release of a held breath, Ralston said, "Oh, my.

When I heard the suggestion of diamonds, I assumed—well, I did not think there would be nearly so many. What are the others? The colored ones?"

"The red ones are rubies; some of them is garnets. The bluish ones is sapphires."

"There are more of those than diamonds."

"Yep. More common, they are. They ain't as high-priced as diamonds, but they're worth picking up when you find them."

"How much do you estimate these stones are worth?"

Arnold said nothing. Slack shifted his weight from one foot to the other, rocking back and forth.

"For insurance purposes for the bank, of course," Ralston said.

Arnold looked at the banker. "Don't rightly know. Enough." He scooped up the stones by the handful and poured them back into the pouch, then stuffed the pouch and other items back into the carpetbag and latched it, handed it to Slack, and stood.

"Gentlemen?"

"Sorry, Mister Ralston—Billy. I believe we'll take our trade somewheres else—where people ain't so nosy."

"Please, Mister Arnold. I assure you, I ask only for your protection. Should our vault be robbed—an eventuality so remote as to be practically impossible—we want to ensure our depositors are fully protected." He cleared his throat. "If you wish, the bank can obtain a rough estimate of their worth. In confidence, of course."

Arnold retrieved the carpetbag from Slack, removed the leather pouch, and handed it to the banker. "I suppose that will be all right. But don't you say nothing to nobody about where they come from."

"I assure you, gentlemen, I cannot disclose what I do not know. In any event, I will hold our conversation in strictest confidence."

"Good enough. We'll keep it that way. The more of you money men that know about this, the more likely we'll get found out."

Again, Ralston's arm convulsed with the intensity of Arnold's handshake, followed by Slack's limp grip. He stopped the miners at the door. "Say, Philip, John. How about you two join me for dinner and a drink this evening? My treat, of course. In appreciation of your trust."

The miners considered the invitation for a moment, Slack looking uncertain. Arnold shrugged, then nodded his approval.

"Occidental Hotel, then? Shall we say eight o'clock?"

Arnold nodded again.

John Slack and Philip Arnold walked slowly through the lobby and into the dining room of the Occidental Hotel. Their escort stopped periodically, hands clasped behind his back, face impassive, but toe tapping as he waited. The miners eyed the polished marble, dark wood, glittering chandeliers, plush furnishings, and well-dressed patrons. Without thinking, Slack brushed at the lapels of his threadbare jacket. Arnold studied the surroundings, but revealed no discomfort.

The host led them to Billy Ralston's table. The banker and the other man at the table stood. Arnold stopped a few feet away. His narrowed eyes shifted from the extra man to the banker. "Who's this? I told you not to spread this around." His lips tightened and his jaws clenched.

A flush climbed Ralston's neck, the only sign of his awareness of the tension. He introduced his companion as Asbury Harpending. "Ash," as he called him, was there as a man experienced in the mining trade.

"Don't seem to me you need no expert in mining to stow a sack in the safe at that bank of yours."

Billy smiled. "You are right of course, Mister Arnold.

However, I believe I can offer services far beyond the safekeeping of your—shall we say, precious stones? But, please, we can discuss that later. Let's enjoy our meal."

The miners had no sooner sat down than servers in starched uniforms appeared, as if unbidden and out of nowhere. Some slid saucers and bowls and plates in front of the men. Others, carrying filled serving dishes or heaping platters or pushing laden carts, ladled and spooned and forked and tonged up food to fill the plates. Still others whisked away the used tableware as soon as the diners lifted the last mouthfuls from its surfaces. And still others hovered nearby with wine bottles, carafes sweating with chilled lemonade, water pitchers, and steaming pots of coffee, keeping the appropriate receptacles filled and ready before the diners. After a time—a longer time than the miners had ever spent at a meal, and more time making meaningless small talk than they had ever before experienced and of which they had little to offer, the meal was down to coffee, brandy, and cigars. In answer to questions, mostly from Ash Harpending, the miners related their stories.

Winding down, Arnold said, "Cousin John, he's been digging for years. We both been at mining a long time. We come out to California in forty-nine. Worked here, the Comstock, New Mexico, Arizona, Utah Territory. I been home to Kentucky a few times, but I always come back West. Worked for a time here in the city for an outfit that makes mining drills. That's how I come to know what a diamond looks like what ain't been cut and polished."

"Other folks, they'll walk right over 'em," Slack said, in an impulsive contribution to the conversation. But there would be more, his tongue loosened by the brandy.

Harpending said, "About this diamond mine of yours. You know, gentlemen, with financial backing you could do much better. Exploit your find more quickly—reap bigger profits before competitors catch on."

Slack sat upright. "Oh, no. Not a chance."

"John's right," Arnold said. "We've had claims before and brought in money men like you-all. Got snookered every time. Ended up us doin' all the work and them gettin' all the money. Ain't goin' to happen this time. This time, it's us what'll get the money, not some 'financiers' nor 'investors' nor other fancy-pants money men with their slick hair and shiny shoes."

Billy Ralston pitched in. "I take your point, Mister Arnold. But it could come down to a choice between your getting all of a very small pie, or a generous slice of a very large pie. If—if, and I emphasize *if*—we agree to a partnership in some form, you could dictate the terms of any arrangement."

"You think so?

"Of course. I have been involved with many, many partners in all manner of financial arrangements. Including mining syndicates. Not all of my investments have paid off, of course. But I have done well for myself. And no one of my partners has ever questioned the fairness of our arrangement. Or my integrity."

"So I am told." Arnold cleared his throat. "Harpending, here, though—now that's another story."

Harpending slammed his drink on the table and stood, leaning across the table toward his accuser. "What are you saying, Arnold?"

Ralston laid a hand on Harpending's sleeve. "Sit down, Ash."

Harpending shook off the hand, tugged at the lapels of his vest and sat, his eyes locked on the miner.

"I ain't sayin' a thing, Harpending—Ash. But I've heard about you. I been told that while you ain't exactly crooked, you bend too easy. Word on the street is that a man ought to keep his other hand on his wallet when he shakes hands on a deal with you."

Harpending sniffed. "You're a fool, Arnold. Both of you. This is your main chance. You'll be a lot richer with our help than without."

Conversation stopped. The men fiddled with their drinks and looked from one to the other.

The silence stretched on uncomfortably until broken by Ralston. "I'll tell you what, gentlemen. As things stand, I am as leery of entering an agreement as you are. I will need more proof. Considerably more. What say you escort a disinterested party to your claim—a trustworthy man of my choosing. He need only verify the existence of your claim. Nothing more.

"I dunno," Slack said. "There ain't nobody seen the place but me and Philip. I'd as soon keep it that way, at least for now."

Harpending snorted. "It's a simple matter."

Arnold leaned over, and with a hand concealing his mouth, whispered to John. John backed away and shook his head. Arnold pulled him back and whispered some more. After a moment, John nodded, unhappy but resigned.

"I don't know," Arnold told the money men. "John ain't in favor of it and I ain't so sure myself. But we'll do what you say. But whoever you-all send, he'll go with us blindfolded so's he won't know where he is or how to get back there."

Billy Ralston sat at his desk in his office, leaned back in his chair, fingers interlaced and hands propped on his stomach. William Lent, a mining magnate whose funds had financed the growth of the Comstock Lode, sat in one of the overstuffed chairs opposite the desk. The identical chair held another man with financial interests in the mining trade, General George Sullivan Dodge, retired from distinguished service in the Quartermaster Department of the Union Army where he served during the War of the Rebellion.

The men in the chairs held coffee cups on saucers, filled from a silver service on a tray on Ralston's desk. Billy's cup sat unused on the tray. Lent swallowed the last of his coffee. The porcelain cup dinged softly as he set it on its saucer. He leaned forward and lowered the cup and saucer with their hand-painted flower pattern onto the desk, again causing a delicate, ringing rattle. Dodge, likewise, set his cup and saucer on the desk, but slid them toward Ralston. Billy sat up, leaned forward, and refilled Dodge's cup from the gleaming pot.

Lent cleared his throat. "Your hospitality is appreciated, Billy. But I'm a busy man. What is it you want?"

Ralston smiled and leaned back in his chair. "I've got a proposition for you, William. You too, General."

Neither man replied. Dodge slurped coffee, still too hot to easily drink, over the rim of the cup. Lent lifted one leg, crossed it over the other, and rested his hands on the arms of the chair.

"You may recall a conversation we had concerning diamonds," Ralston said.

Lent grimaced and shook his head. "Sure I remember, Billy. You did not say much, but you let on this so-called diamond mine was richer than any strike of any kind in all the world. It's been months since you mentioned it. I thought you were blowing smoke at the time, and I still think so."

Ralston smiled. "I can assure you, gentlemen, if I was blowing smoke, it only serves to prove the truism that where there's smoke, there's fire."

Dodge asked what he meant.

"As I told you before, I have a few—a considerable few— gems in hand, and their authenticity has been established. Now, we have verified the existence of the strike. As soon as the season allowed—which was late, given the high country where the claim is located—I had a man go out there and check it out. I have a cable from him stating that everything the miners said is true.

And that the find is even richer than Arnold and Slack represented."

"That's all you've got? A telegram?"

"That's all for now, William. But the miners and my investigator gathered stones while there. A lot of stones. Arnold and Slack and the rocks are on the train and on the way back here as we speak."

"How many stones?"

Billy smiled. "My man figures about a million's worth. Maybe more." He shrugged. "That's just a guess, of course. But it's a lot—a lot of gems, and a lot of money."

"These miners that found the place—are they reliable? And where have they been lately, while you waited until they could get back to the claim with your man?"

"Damned if I know, General. My guess is they probably went down south somewhere for the winter, wandering around in the desert trying to conjure up riches. Arnold and Slack are much like all the other prospectors I've known—the ones you and William have known as well, I'll venture. They're rough as cobs. And suspicious. It took some talking just to get them to agree to take my man out there."

"This man of yours—could he find the place again?"

Ralston laughed. "Not from what he said in the cable. He knows they got off the train somewhere in Wyoming, but they put a bag over his head before the train stopped. They kept him blindfolded the rest of that day, so he has no idea which way they went on horseback. They took off the blinders after that, but he couldn't say where they were or where they ended up after riding, mostly around in circles he thought, for a couple of days. Still in Wyoming, maybe. Could be Utah. Colorado, perhaps."

Lent asked about the man Ralston had sent to investigate the claim.

"He's from Carson City. Engineer. He's worked some of the Comstock mines. But he came out from Duluth, from the iron mines there, back in the fifties to run hydraulic mines in the gold country." Ralston sat forward and poured himself coffee. He held the cup in both hands and propped his elbows on the desktop. "He'll leave Arnold and Slack in Reno. Ash Harpending will meet them there and escort them—and the samples— the rest of the way here on the train. We'll see the stones in a matter of days."

"Harpending? I thought he was in London."

Ralston smiled. "You keep your ear pretty close to the ground, William. You're right, he has been. I sent him there not long after we met Arnold and Slack."

Lent said, "I am surprised he would be welcome there. When he left England last time, I heard he was one step ahead of the law for selling stock in played-out mines."

Again, Ralston smiled. He sipped his coffee and grimaced, set the cup on the saucer and diluted the drink with cream from a pitcher, then added a heaping spoonful of sugar. "Ash bears watching, I'll grant you that. But given his background, he's likely to nose out a con if there is one. So far, he thinks Arnold and Slack are on the up-and-up." He sipped the coffee. "We'll know more when he and the diamonds get back here."

"Well, Billy, we'll wait and see what happens. I can't say I'm persuaded to start writing you checks just yet. Now, I must be going."

"One more thing, before you leave."

"What is it?"

"The reason Ash went to London was to make contact with Baron Rothschild." Billy stretched the tension by pausing for another sip from his cup. "The baron wants in."

Dodge sat upright in his chair. "Rothschild? Rothschild wants to invest?"

"I believe so. I don't have the details yet. I don't know what Ash offered him, or what the baron's intentions are. Regardless, it will soon be time to make a move."

Lent thought for a time. "Right. And the first move ought to be getting those two prospectors—this Arnold and Slack—out of this claim of theirs as soon as possible."

"As soon as we can. But let's not get ahead of ourselves," Ralston said. "If the find proves out—and we don't know yet that it will, although it shows every sign of promise—we will endeavor to buy their claim and get them out of the picture. Prospectors are more trouble than they're worth. Capital doesn't mean a thing to them. They think they're owed all the riches solely on the basis of the discovery."

The general asked what was next. Ralston allowed that he would contact them once Harpending, Arnold, and Slack were back in the city. He would arrange a meeting and allow them to handle the goods.

The train labored up the east slope of the Sierra. Ash Harpending watched out the window as the Truckee River, sparkling below, revealed itself through the pine forest and granite outcrops from time to time. The canyon fell away before him as he sat in a rear-facing seat. John Slack slumped in the seat opposite, fast asleep and snoring. Next to Slack, Philip Arnold sat upright and alert, a rifle butted to the floor in one hand and a bulky leather satchel on his lap. Both miners were dirty and disheveled, apparently shunning any opportunity to bathe or shave or even wash their hands since leaving the diamond field.

"When are you going to give me a look at what's in the case?"

Arnold looked over each shoulder and up and down the coach. "Sure as hell won't be here. Too many eyes to see what don't concern them."

Slack, who had been sleeping even before the stop in Reno,

stirred in his seat with a snort. Without raising his head, he opened his eyes and looked around through a veil of lashes. He fixed his gaze on Harpending. "What the hell you doin' here?" he said, with thick tongue and lips moist with drool.

Harpending smiled. "Billy wanted me to make sure you boys didn't get lost on the way home."

"You come all the way up here from San Francisco for that?"

"Not altogether. As it happens, I'm on my way home as well."

Slack asked where he had been.

"While you boys have been lazing around and off gallivanting God knows where, I have been across the sea."

Arnold asked why.

"Been to London. England. I have been contacting investors there—with some success, I might add—to assess their interest in fronting capital for the development of a diamond mine."

Both men snapped upright, heads swiveling to see if anyone was listening in. Slack stammered, trying to find words. Arnold hissed, "What the hell, Ash? You were supposed to keep this quiet. We told you and Billy we didn't want word of this gettin' out!"

Ash leaned toward the miners with a smile. "Now, boys, calm down. Why do you think Billy brought me in? I'm in on this because I know how to float an offering on a mine."

"That so? Who says there'll be an offering?"

Asbury laughed. "You boys don't really think you can pull this off on your own, do you? It takes money to make a mine pay."

"Not this one," Arnold said. "We can make plenty of money without so much as breakin' a sweat." Then, in a whisper, "Finding the diamonds ain't no harder than gatherin' eggs."

Harpending shrugged. "So you say. You must know it sounds too good to be true. That's another reason Billy and Lent and General Dodge want me in on it—to make sure you're not trying to put one over on them."

Slack said, "Lent? The General? What the hell are you sayin'?"

Ash drew in a deep breath and exhaled slowly. "William Lent. General George Dodge. You boys know both of them, if only by reputation. I guess you don't know Billy has been talking to them. All part of putting together the capital it's going to take to turn your claim into a paying proposition. If you don't get the capital from us, you will have to get it elsewhere."

Arnold leaned forward in his seat, his face stopping inches from Ash's. "You listen to me, Harpending. Me and John has worked too hard on this deal to have you throw a monkey wrench in the works. We aim to make this claim pay how we see fit. If you and Billy and Lent and the General and all your damn Englishmen and whoever else don't like it, you-all can go to the devil."

"No need to get all het up, Philip. They—we—are interested, but that's all. You can't blame us for being just as suspicious of you as you are of our intentions. If what you promised proves out, and you've got what you claim to have in that bag, you've got nothing to worry about."

"It's in there, all right. You ain't got no worries on that account. But me and John's got plenty to worry about. We've seen too many prospectors lose their claims to money men like you-all. It starts out with promises of blue sky and riches. But it somehow turns out to be nothin' but blue sky for honest working men like us, and all our riches ends up goin' into pockets like them in that fancy dandy suit of yours."

Harpending sighed. "Still and all, boys, the simple fact is, if you intend to get rich off this claim of yours—I mean really rich, lifetime rich—you need us."

Arnold chuckled. "So you say. The real fact is, *you* need *us.*"

None of the men spoke for several miles, lost in the din of conversations among other passengers and the click and clack of heavy wheels crossing joints in the steel rails. Slack's chin had just dropped to his chest when he awakened to the sound of Harpending's voice.

"Listen, boys, we can work this out. Say you will at least meet with Billy and the others. You convince them this mine is all you say. Let them try to convince you to allow them to invest in its development. You've got nothing to lose by talking."

Arnold secured his grip on the satchel on his lap. He looked at Slack, then back at Harpending, and nodded.

The meeting was set at Asbury Harpending's home in Oakland. Billy Ralston, William Lent, and General Dodge circled a pool table in the billiard room, taking shots in turn, sipping drinks, and smoking cigars.

"Where the hell is Harpending?" Lent said, stubbing out his cigar in a heavy cut crystal ashtray.

"He'll be here," Billy said. His cue stick met a ball and pushed it gently to its target, tapping that ball toward the side pocket. It missed and bounced softly off the cushion.

Asbury Harpending walked in right then, with long strides and a wide smile. He carried a brass-studded leather sample case, believing, apparently, the prospectors' battered satchel unworthy of the occasion. Arnold and Slack followed him into the room, looking around at the furnishings and fixtures. Both were bathed and barbered and trimmed and decked out in new clothes. While an improvement over their usual attire, the men studying them from across the room could see the outfits were cheap off-the-rack stuff.

After a round of greetings and handshaking, Ash perched the sample case on the edge of the pool table and shoved the balls to the other end. With a big show of undoing the latches on the case, he tipped it onto the table. Some sixty pounds of jewels spilled out onto the green felt. The money men, shocked, stared at the colorful display. But soon, their hands were immersed in the pile, palming up and pouring back the gems, spreading them across the table, and examining them singly and in handfuls.

Hovering in the background, Arnold looked at Slack and smiled.

Later, the men moved to the study and found seats on plush sofas and in overstuffed chairs. Harpending passed around glasses and filled them with whiskey cut with whatever dilution, if any, the guests preferred. As he worked, Slack leaned over and whispered to Arnold, seated next to him on the sofa. "Ol' Ash, he lives pretty high on the hog."

Arnold nodded. "I don't reckon he got that way muckin' around in the dirt. These kind leave all that to grunts like us— then they steal what we find and build fancy houses like this one."

Ash came with the liquor. "Don't cut mine," Slack told him. "Straight whiskey for me."

Billy Ralston offered a lengthy toast to the success of the enterprise, then said, "Just to be clear, men—these gems you showed us represent only half of what you carried away from the mine? How can that be?"

Arnold said, "Well, like that man of yours will tell you, we run into a spot of trouble crossing a river—and don't ask me the name of it. Wasn't no ford or ferry where we was. It was in a canyon, so it weren't too wide, but plenty deep enough, and swift. We swam the horses and pack mules over and strung a rope line, then cobbled together a raft to float the packs—and the stones. See, we'd divided them into two bundles so's each of us could keep one—for safety, you see. Anyhow, we floated 'em over on that raft one at a time, just in case." He stopped for a sip of whiskey. "Good idea, it turned out to be, for somethin' in the water hit the raft on one trip and upset it and we lost one of the packs with some of the stones and a goodly amount of our gear. Your man will tell you it's so."

"He did. But he also told me there was no river to cross on the way to the mine."

Arnold smiled. "Well, we might've got a mite off course, goin' one way or the other. That place ain't so easy to find, you know."

"Never mind that!" William Lent said. "Judging from what's on the pool table, that carelessness cost you upwards of a million dollars!"

"That ain't no skin off your nose, Mister Lent."

"True. But still . . ."

"Be that as it may, gentlemen, we ought to be discussing where to go from here," Billy said. "Mister Arnold—Philip?"

Arnold and Slack exchanged glances, and Arnold shrugged. "I don't know. I reckon me and John'll go back to the mine one more time before winter and bring out some more diamonds."

"You could," General Dodge said. "You certainly could. But doing this piecemeal that way is not the most profitable route."

"He's right, you know, Philip," Ash said.

Arnold looked at Slack again. "We're listening, Ash."

"If that mine is anything at all like you say it is, we have a once-in-a-lifetime opportunity to build an empire."

Billy chimed in. "What we do is form a corporation, funded by a limited and exclusive issue of stock to a short list of select investors. Those in this room, and perhaps a few others. With a well-capitalized organization, we can get the mine into full production quickly."

"That's when the real payoff comes," Lent said.

"What, you mean 'cause we'll be bringin' out more diamonds?"

"No, Philip," Ash said. "Because then we can make a public offering of stock in the mine. We sell shares here, in New York,

30

in Europe. Investors will line up, and with every share sold, we line our pockets."

"Sounds complicated."

"It is. But we have all done it before," Lent said.

"Well, I don't know. Me and John, we just want to make some money on this deal. Ain't no one else ever found a diamond mine like this one. We could just keep on like we're doin' and make out just fine."

General Dodge harrumphed. "Don't be a fool, Arnold. You could do so much better than 'just fine.' "

Slack sat staring into his glass, swirling the dregs of the whiskey slowly around inside. Arnold looked around at the men in the room, his mind churning, his stomach keeping pace. He thought for a time, then said, "Well, gents, as it stands, you've got the money, and John and me's got the diamonds. Long as it's thataway, I can't see anything much changing."

Ash stood from his chair, walked to the sidebar, and refilled his drink. He offered refills for the others. All refused, save John Slack. "Let me make a proposal," Harpending said as he splashed whiskey into Slack's glass. "Let us take a portion of the stones to New York. We'll have Charles Tiffany look them over. I've already been in contact with him, and a few others. Then we'll all have a better idea of what we're dealing with here. While we're there, we can start the wheels turning for an offering. Bring in the lawyers I've talked to, a banker or two perhaps."

"Now, just hold on, you-all!" Arnold said. "Them's my diamonds—John's and mine—and you ain't takin' a-one of them stones nowhere without our say-so."

William Lent asked Arnold what he might suggest.

"Way I see it, you-all have got dollar signs in your eyes and you ain't done a lick of work. John and me, we found the diamonds, and we've done all the work that's been done so far.

31

Every bit of it."

"Well? What is it you want?"

Arnold fixed his gaze on Lent. "What say you give John and me, say, a hundred thousand dollars apiece, and we give you-all and this fancy company you're talkin' about a one-third share of the mine. And, of course, we get a two-thirds cut of whatever you raise in this 'offering' or whatever it is."

The prospectors waited on the sofa while the money men huddled in the corner. The discussion was spirited and at times loud, but the substance of their conversation did not reach the sofa. It took one more refill of Slack's glass—he helped himself this time—before the parley ended.

Billy Ralston spoke. "Here's our offer, gentlemen. We will agree to your terms. We will pay each of you half—fifty thousand now, the remainder due upon verification of the richness of the claim. That verification at the hands of experts of our choosing—and ourselves. Ash will see to the arrangements. You will, of course, make yourselves available at the appropriate time to escort us and our inspector to the mine."

"Now, hold on a minute there, Billy!" Arnold said. "We already took your man out there!"

Ralston shook his head. "That was but a preliminary inspection. It served to verify that the claim exists, and the potential is there. This next will be a much deeper evaluation to determine long-term potential. It could be that the discovery, like many, looks rich initially but is soon played out."

Arnold and Slack huddled for moment, then nodded in agreement.

Handshakes were exchanged all around. When General Dodge had Slack by the hand, he held tight longer than necessary, locked eyes with the miner, then said, "One thing—how do we know you two won't take the money and run?"

All the color drained from Slack's face, but Arnold laughed, then said, "This mine is too rich for me to settle for a measly fifty thousand. I mean to get a lot more money than that out of you-all for this mine before I walk away."

The meeting at the law office in New York City intrigued the men assembled—among them the New York lawyer recruited by Harpending to host the assemblage, a banker, jeweler Charles Tiffany, General George McClellan, and General Benjamin Butler. The delegation from San Francisco fielded questions from the potential investors, as they had been doing for some time.

"This mine, or diamond field if you will—it has been verified?" George McClellan said.

"Only preliminarily." Ash Harpending answered the question, as he had most of the inquiries, given his abilities in salesmanship. "The prospectors who discovered the diamonds are, of course, hesitant as to the location of the claim. They did escort our representative there for a limited inspection and he witnessed vast quantities of stones there for the taking—many of them simply lying on the ground."

McClellan sniffed. "A further, more thorough analysis will be required before you get a penny of my money."

"Of course. Arnold and Slack—the miners—are aware of and agreeable to a detailed survey of the property. That is in the works, we assure you."

Benjamin Butler said, "I'm with George. This inspection, I assume, will be performed by a reliable expert?"

"Absolutely. We have made overtures to Henry Janin. You may know of Henry. He is a respected mining engineer, and his expertise in evaluating mining properties is well known. He has evaluated scores, perhaps hundreds, of properties and word has it that no one has ever lost a dime on one of his recommendations. If he is amenable, he, too, will be invited to invest in the scheme." Ash smiled. "As well as serving as a carrot to encourage his participation, the opportunity to invest will assure a most careful examination on his part. We expect to accompany Janin, with Arnold and Slack, to the site next spring; early summer perhaps."

The New Yorkers mulled that over for a moment. Then Charles Tiffany said, "All this is well and good, gentlemen. But what assurance have you that the stones these men—Arnold and Slack, is it?—have mined are genuine?"

William Lent cleared his throat. "A jeweler in San Francisco has examined a sampling of the gems. He assures us they are as represented."

"That jeweler's qualifications, of course, pale in comparison to yours, Mister Tiffany—Charles, if I may," Ash said with a smile, "and that is why we have invited you here."

In a reprise of his performance on the billiard table at his home, albeit on a smaller scale, Harpending spilled stones out of a satchel and watched the men's eyes light up as the gems danced across the varnished tabletop. "This is only a sampling of the latest haul of stones Arnold and Slack—and our man—gathered from the claim."

The men examined the stones. Tiffany, in particular, gave them the twice-over, holding stones up to the light, turning them, and scrutinizing them carefully through his jeweler's loupe. He slipped the eyepiece back into the pocket of his waistcoat and cleared his throat. "Gentlemen, they are the real thing. Beyond question, these are precious stones."

The next day, out in San Francisco, one of Billy Ralston's clerks tracked down Philip Arnold, finding him in a waterfront saloon. The miner sat at a card table, stacks and piles of poker chips and scattered pasteboards before him, a tumbler of whiskey in hand, a sporting woman on his lap. With much cajoling and the promise of important news, he persuaded Arnold to accompany him to the Bank of California.

Arnold, somewhat less than steady on his feet, walked carefully into the banker's office. Without invitation, he slouched into one of the overstuffed chairs in front of the desk and hung a knee over its arm. "What is it you want, Billy? You've interrupted my festivities."

Ignoring the question, Ralston asked one of his own. "Where's Slack? He should be here to hear this."

Arnold waved him off. "Oh, John's gone off somewhere like he does from time to time. He'll be back when it suits him. It don't matter much—he's authorized me to act for him." The miner paused and tried without success to stifle a belch. "So, what's this news that boy of yours was yammering about?"

Ralston slid open a desk drawer and held up the envelope he took from it. "I've a wire from Asbury Harpending in New York."

"Oh? What's ol' Ash got to say for himself?"

"Tiffany—you know, the jeweler—has checked out your stones. Charles Tiffany himself pronounced them genuine and valuable."

Arnold snorted, scoffed, and chuckled all at once. "Hell, Billy! That ain't exactly news. I told you as much."

"You did, Philip. But Tiffany lends credibility. His word is convincing. But that's not the whole of it. He estimated the value of the gems Ash took to New York at one hundred and fifty thousand dollars. Much higher than anticipated. And that means, Arnold, that your latest haul must be worth at least a million and a half."

Arnold thought for a long moment, then smiled. "Sounds like John and me are due another payday. If you want this to go on, that is."

"Come on, Philip! Don't get greedy on us!"

"Greedy? Me?" Arnold laughed. "The greed's all but drippin'

off your chin, Billy. And unless I miss my guess, it's the same with Ash and Lent and Dodge and them nobs of yours back in New York. I'm tellin' you-all, I ain't the one that's gonna be taken advantage of in this deal."

Ralston sighed. "What have you got in mind, Philip?"

"Oh, say another hundred thousand. Each."

Another long sigh. "I think that can be arranged. Come by the bank tomorrow and we'll have the funds ready."

Arnold smiled and stood up.

Ralston held him there with an upraised hand. "One proviso. The New York investors demand a site inspection—as we have discussed. They, as we do, want a more thorough evaluation. By an expert. We've talked with Henry Janin about having a look. You know Janin?"

"I know who he is."

"So you—and Slack, I suppose—agree to lead the party to the mine?"

Arnold shrugged. "I guess so. But it won't be till next summer. The place could be snowed under already. If it ain't, it will be before we can get there and back."

"Be that as it may, I have your word on it?"

Arnold nodded. "I'll be by the bank tomorrow to collect my money." He smiled. "After that, I feel an urge comin' on to do a little travelin'."

"Just make sure you're back here in plenty of time to show us this mine of yours—ours, I should say."

Arnold delayed the start of the expedition until June, waiting, he said, on the weather and for Slack's return. The miners, along with Henry Janin, Ash Harpending, and General Dodge, boarded the train in Oakland. Arnold assured his guests that the saddle horses, pack mules, supplies, and camp equipment stowed in the cars were sufficient to keep them at the claim as long as necessary.

Days into the journey, the train made an unscheduled stop on a siding somewhere on the Wyoming plains. Arnold shepherded the men off the coach, then hustled back to help Slack and the railroad workers unload the stock and supplies.

The train pulled away, leaving Harpending and the others turning in circles, looking in vain for any sign of civilization in the expanse of dust and brush and bunchgrass.

"Where the hell are we, Philip? Why haven't we stopped at a station?"

Arnold smiled. "Don't worry, Ash. I passed a few dollars to the conductor to let us off here. It'll save us a day's travel."

"Still, where are we?"

"It don't matter none, Ash. All you need to know is that you'll be seein' diamonds soon enough."

For the better part of four days, the party negotiated the broken terrain—up and down ravines and dry washes, over low ridges and across valleys, traversing vast plains and topping broad mesas. The San Francisco men and Janin, more accustomed to desk chairs than saddles, complained of the long days on horseback. The general accused the miners of leading them in circles, an accusation Arnold denied, blaming the lack of landmarks for the sometimes-circuitous route. Late on the fourth day, Arnold signaled the others to join him atop a low ridge.

He pointed out a mesa in the near distance. "That's it, gents. That's where we're a-goin'. Take a good look, 'cause that sandstone ridge and tableland yonder is where the money is."

Harpending wound his bridle reins around the saddle horn and stood in the stirrups, then reached back with both hands to massage his lower spine. "It's about time. What do you think, Janin? Does it look promising?"

"Can't say, Ash. There are no indications of anything unusual over there. But we won't know until we see it up close. Precious metals in their native state have a way of surprising you, sometimes. I suppose it could be the same with gems."

"Don't worry, you-all," Arnold said. "Like I been sayin' all along, there's plenty money to be made over there."

General Dodge cleared his throat. "Let's get there, then. We'll accomplish nothing sitting here talking."

The men pushed on and made camp in the dark. Come morning, even before Slack had breakfast ready, Janin, Dodge, and Harpending gathered picks and shovels and wandered into the brush in the direction Arnold pointed, to scratch around in the dirt. It did not take long before a small furrow Ash had scratched out with his pick revealed a few red stones and a diamond. He dropped his pick, fell to his knees, picked up the diamond and held it aloft. "I've found one!"

Slack, who had abandoned breakfast as a lost cause and joined the diggers, took the diamond from Harpending, licked it, and wiped it on his shirtsleeve. He nodded, verifying it was a diamond. Janin and Dodge hurried over and took turns examining the gem, as well as the red stones Ash had scraped up. Soon, all three investors were finding stones regularly, stuffing them into canvas bags they carried. Their excitement did not diminish. They found diamonds, rubies, garnets, and sapphires under sagebrush, in cracks and creases in sandstone outcrops, in shallow defiles cut by snowmelt runoff, and even sifted out diamonds from disturbed anthills. Slack and Arnold wandered through the brush and pointed out promising places to dig, and dug up stones themselves from time to time. The men, ignoring hunger and thirst, kept at the digging as long as the light allowed.

Slack revived the abandoned breakfast and turned it into a late supper. By firelight, Janin, Dodge, and Harpending knelt and squatted around a canvas sheet. The day's harvest of stones, piled in the middle, made a considerable heap. Dodge asked Janin what he thought.

"Oh, there's no doubt it's a rich find, gentlemen."

"But will it last, do you think?" Harpending said.

"With gems such as these so near the surface, I have no doubt the veins underground must be rich beyond compare. I believe a small crew of workers could mine out many millions of dollars' worth of diamonds well into the foreseeable future." The mining expert shook his head. "I confess it is an unusual find. I don't begin to understand it. Nothing in the surrounding countryside suggests conditions for the formation of diamonds, so far as my understanding goes. But I have to believe the evidence here before my eyes."

Slack and Arnold, perched atop rocks serving as stools, sipped coffee. "I guess they believe us now, Philip."

"Looks like it, John." Arnold stood and spoke to the men pawing through the gemstone pile. "Let's turn in, men. See what tomorrow brings."

The new day dawned to find the investors eager to get back to their work. While still enthusiastic, their excitement diminished somewhat as the stones continued to turn up regularly in the disturbed earth, even appearing on the dusty surface. This day, they stopped when the sun was high and took time to eat.

"I have to say, Arnold, Slack, this place looks to be everything you represented," Dodge said.

Asbury opined it more than fulfilled its promise.

"So, what now?" Arnold said.

Janin swallowed a bite of food. "I don't believe there's much more to accomplish here at this juncture. It seems we're all satisfied. I, for one, am more impressed with the possibilities here than I had imagined."

Dodge nodded in agreement. "I suggest we return and report."

"I concur," Janin said. "However, Arnold and Slack have staked out a fairly modest claim, given the situation. I say we spend the remainder of the day widening the claim to include, say, three thousand acres. That should encompass enough additional territory to cover the extent of the deposits."

Harpending rose and dusted off the seat of his pants. "Let's get at it, then."

Janin divided the men, taking Arnold with himself and pairing up Ash and General Dodge. He rooted around in a pack, came out with two compasses, and handed one to Ash, along with a mallet and bundle of stakes. The teams were to work in opposite directions from a common point, pace off distance at right angles, and plant stakes as they went. Through the afternoon, the men followed their compasses, pounded their stakes, and staked out a claim large enough to satisfy Janin's expectations. For his part, Slack struck camp, packing up everything but what they would need for supper, a short night's sleep, and breakfast.

The next morning, Arnold drained his coffee cup and tossed the dregs into the campfire, then raised a bigger cloud of steam when he dumped the coffeepot onto the dwindling flames. "So, Janin, you think this place is about to pay off big for us."

"Unless I miss my guess, Arnold, I believe it will pay off for us, and many others. Very much so. The potential is enormous."

"Well, I'm damn glad to hear it. Me and John, we've worked our tails off out here. Our whole lives, come to that. It's about time we got what was comin' to us."

"Oh, I believe you will, Arnold. And so, I trust, will the rest of us."

"You will," Arnold said with a smile. "All of you-all will."

Harpending snugged up the cinch on his saddle and looked around the abandoned camp. One horse had not been saddled, and a pack mule was still staked out away from the camp. A saddle and packsaddle, along with a small cache of packs, was set off to one side. He watched Slack drop a bedroll atop the pile. "I say, Slack, what are you doing? What's with the stuff you've set aside there?"

"I'm a-stayin' here. Them's my provisions."

"Staying here? Whatever for?"

Arnold answered. "John and me got to talkin' last night. We figure what with all you-all money men in on this deal, there's too many people knows about this place. Word has a way of gettin' around, you know. So, John's stayin' here to keep an eye on things."

"On his own?"

Slack laughed. "Don't you worry none, Ash. I been on my own out prospectin' in places like this more'n I been with other folks. Besides, I won't be alone—I'll have ol' Henry with me."

The men responded to Slack's statement with quizzical looks. The prospector pulled a lever-action Henry rifle from a saddle scabbard in the pile.

"Here's Henry, right here—my good ol' Henry rifle."

Still holding the rifle, Slack stood in the low morning light as the sun rose and watched the others ride over a ridge in the distance and disappear. He put the packsaddle on the mule and saddled his horse, packed up the remaining camp goods, and loaded the panniers onto the mule. He walked to the still smoking fire and kicked dirt over it. Satisfied after a last look around the camp site, he picked up the pack mule's lead, mounted his horse, and rode off in a different direction than the others had taken.

Harpending, Dodge, and Lent sat at a table in the dining car, enjoying the first meal in days not cooked over a campfire and seasoned with ash and sand. Even more, they enjoyed bottle after bottle of wine, exchanging toast after toast to their good fortune to come.

A man seated at an adjacent table, his back to the festive party, could not help but overhear their talk. The more they talked, the more interested he became. After a while, he rolled up the map on which he had been making notations and left the car. After making his way through the passenger coaches, he knocked on the door of a private compartment.

"Enter."

The man slid open the door and stepped into the crowded compartment. Stacked trunks and cases occupied most of the floor space, rolled maps like the one he carried sprouted from a crate like a bouquet of flowers. Other maps and charts and tables hung on the walls, even obscuring most of the windows. Journals and notebooks and sheaves of loose papers spread across the upper bunk. Perched on the lower berth beside a precarious pile of papers and books sat Clarence King.

King, in the employ of the government of the United States as chief geologist, had just wrapped up six years of tramping across the West with his crews conducting the Fortieth Parallel Survey. Officially known as the Geological Exploration of the Fortieth Parallel, the survey explored a swath of the country roughly following the route of the transcontinental railroad, stretching to include several miles north and south, from eastern California to eastern Wyoming. King and his crew studied and catalogued the geology, paleontology, botany, and ornithology of each region along the route, and recorded timber resources and arable lands. Their reports also identified mineral assets and the practicality of mining.

And so, when the man in the dining car overhead the mention of diamonds in the region just surveyed, it piqued his curiosity.

"Diamonds?" King said.

"Yes, sir. They were celebrating how much money they were

going to make from this find."

"Did they say anything more about this 'find'? Such as where it is located?"

"No, Mister King. I know they came aboard in Rawlins. One of them griped about all the riding. Another said it took them four days to get to it, but only two days back. I got the feeling they didn't altogether trust another of their party—a man sitting off by himself at the other end of the car."

King tapped his lips with the shaft of a pen as he thought. "Two days, you say? Whether north or south of the rail line, that would be within the quadrangles we surveyed. Did they say anything else? Any kind of clue that might locate the place?"

"Not much. One of them did say he would not have expected to find diamonds on an exposed tableland like that. And I believe one of them said something about a sandstone ridge, but I'm not sure he meant the same place—where the diamonds are supposed to be, that is."

"Sandstone ridges and mesas. That sounds like south to me." King leaned back, resting against the wall, tapping his pen on the notebook in his hand. "Diamonds. Can't be anything but utter nonsense, but everybody and their cousins have been hunting diamonds of late. I doubt we'll find anything, but we'd better check it out. Get five or six more of the men together. We'll catch the next train back to Rawlins and set out from there."

King and his men spent days wandering through the wilds, studying maps, reading the landscape, searching as thoroughly as possible while covering as much ground as practical. They determined they were too far to the east, and that the terrain they were looking for lay to the west, most likely in the vicinity north of Brown's Hole, a sheltered Colorado valley reaching into Utah, near the Wyoming border.

Someone said, "But those people boarded the train at Rawlins. Black Butte's a lot closer. Wouldn't it make more sense to get the railroad there?"

"True enough," King said. "But suppose one of them was attempting to conceal the location? Or, at least, mislead the rest?" The others thought it over and nodded approval. "Well, then, we are in agreement. Tomorrow we set our course for the country north of Brown's Hole."

Days later, one of the surveyors came upon a wooden stake planted in the dusty bottom of a shallow dry wash. He stepped up onto the sagebrush plain, whistled, and waved his arms. "King! King! I've found something!"

Philip Arnold closed the door behind him, stepped out into the hallway, and looked back. Set in a double arch on the pebbled glass of the oversized door were the words SAN FRANCISCO & NEW YORK MINING & COMMERCIAL COMPANY. He smiled and unfolded the bank draft, and smiled even wider as he read the amount: $600,000.00. He refolded the paper, tucked it into an inside pocket in his jacket, and started down the hallway. Going down the stairway, he met Billy Ralston coming up. "Billy," he said with a smile, touching a finger to the brim of his hat.

Ralston barely glanced at him, nodded a reply, but did not speak. He went on his way and soon walked through the same door Arnold had lately walked out of. Stopping in the reception area, he looked around. The offices were still under construction, with a few workmen about adding finishing touches. Ralston took a deep breath of air that still smelled of fresh paint and varnish, new carpets and upholstery. Hanging on one wall of the plush and richly furnished lobby was a large map showing the location of the diamond field, but without identifying information. A glass case against another wall showed off a display of diamonds and other gemstones. A secretary at a desk talked with a visitor. A few well-dressed men lingered, studying the map and the gems and reading reports.

Ralston waited. Although an officer and major shareholder in the company, he was a visitor here. Before long, he took a seat across a desk behind which sat Ash Harpending.

"I tell you, Billy, we've struck gold with these diamonds. Thanks to the stories we've 'leaked' to the press, potential investors are standing in line. I hear it's much the same in New York. Rothschild also reports significant interest in London."

"Slow down, Ash. Let's see how far the capitalization from our initial investor group takes us before we start dividing the pie into smaller slices."

"I suppose you're right. I will say that getting Arnold and Slack out of the picture was money well spent to my way of thinking. We'll make back the six hundred thousand it took to buy them out in no time."

"The six hundred thousand plus the two hundred thousand we already fronted them. In any event, let's hope we get it back soon. I'm into this plenty deep, both with bank funds and personally—"

A knock at the door interrupted Ralston's complaint. The door swung open uninvited and an office boy from Ralston's Bank of California rushed in, gasping for breath. "Telegram for you, Mister Ralston. They said at the bank I should get it to you right away."

"Telegram? From where?"

The boy shrugged. "Somewhere in Wyoming Territory, they said. Never heard of it." He handed Ralston the telegram and left as quickly as he had come.

Ralston ripped open the envelope and read the wire.

Harpending watched the color drain from the banker's face. "Billy? What is it?"

Ralston swallowed hard. He cleared his throat. He took a deep, trembling breath. He read aloud, " 'The alleged diamond mines are fraudulent stop they are plainly salted stop.' " He squeezed his eyes shut several times, took deep breath, and read on. " 'The discovery is a gigantic fraud and the company has been pitifully duped stop.' "

Asbury, likewise shocked, sputtered almost to the point of speechlessness. "Wh-wha-what?"

" 'Detailed report to follow stop.' It's signed by Clarence King."

Clarence King, as promised, submitted a detailed report. Billy Ralston assembled as many of the investors as he could in a conference room at the Bank of California to inform them of its contents.

"I still can't believe it," Ash Harpending said. "I can't believe Arnold and Slack could pull off a swindle of this magnitude."

Henry Janin snorted. "I don't believe it at all. There's no way I mistook what I saw out there."

William Lent could only shake his head.

"I have seen men taken in by much less," General Dodge said. "I fear greed is very persuasive. Much more so than care and caution."

"Hell, George—General—it's not like we didn't exercise caution!" Harpending said. "We had the place looked at twice. You saw it. I saw it. Men who know a hell of a lot more about what to look for than we do—like Henry, here—looked at it!"

Dodge shrugged. "And yet here we are."

Billy cleared his throat. "Let me fill you in on King's report. It will shed some light on how we got here." He picked up the stack of papers and tapped the edges into alignment. "I will remind you that Clarence King is a recognized expert in geology—the chief geologist for the federal government, as it happens. His recently completed Fortieth Parallel Survey went far beyond geology, so his knowledge of the region in question is vast.

"The report is in the form of a letter. In the interest of time, I'll not read its entire contents. You will each receive a copy of the letter in its entirety as soon as possible."

After a long swallow of water, Ralston read:

To the Board of Directors of the San Francisco and New York Mining and Commercial Company. Gentlemen:

I have hastened to San Francisco to lay before you the startling fact that the diamond fields on the plains of Colorado, upon which is based such a large investment, and such brilliant hope, are utterly valueless, and yourselves and your engineer, Mister Henry Janin, the victims of an unparalleled fraud. I beg herewith to give a brief statement of my mode of study and its unanswerable results.

After examining the general features of the diamond mesa, my suspicions were aroused and I at once determined to make an exhaustive series of prospects, of which the following are the results.

The gems, in nine cases out of ten, lie directly upon the hard surface of rock, or of an indurated crust of soil. In the exceptional cases where I found them in crevices, there was always ample evidence that the sand and soil had been disturbed and broken up within a year. I selected ground that was more or less strewn with the so-called rubies, carefully shoveled off the surface inch of ground and gravel, and examined by means of sieves and pan washing, all the material down to bedrock. About thirty of these tests were made, and in no instance was a ruby or diamond found where they should have settled through the earth to bedrock through gravity. Examining a gulch leading directly from the gem-bearing surface of sandstone found it to be extremely rich in rubies at its head; but this richness instead of continuing down the bed, as it inevitably must have, not a ruby or diamond was found.

In the midst of thickly sown rubies are certain crevices not opened by your parties. They are filled with soil and pebbles, and more or less overgrown with grass, sagebrush, and small cactus plants. We carefully removed the top inch, dug out the whole crack, finding no trace of diamonds or even rubies. In other crevices which bore unmistakable evidence of having been tampered with, we never failed to find rubies and often small diamonds. Upon raised dome-like portions of table rock, rubies and diamonds lay on the summits and inclined sides, in positions where the storms of one or two winters must inevitably have dislodged them. In the ravines and upon the mesa are numerous anthills, which we found to bear rubies on their surfaces. A closer examination showed artificial holes, broken horizontally with some stick or small implement, easily distinguished from the natural avenues made by the insects themselves. When traced to its end, each hole held one or two rubies. Moreover, about these "salted" anthills were the old, storm-worn footprints of a man. The table rock has produced four distinct types of diamonds, oriental rubies, garnet, sapphires, emeralds, and amethysts. An association of minerals I believe of impossible occurrence in nature.

When altogether satisfied that the gems had been salted, our party set out upon an outside series of prospects all over the mesa and its flanking canyons, until the absolute valuelessness of the property was finally ascertained. The results of these links of proof are that the gems exist in positions where Nature alone could never have placed them; that they do not exist where, had the occurrence been genuine, the inevitable laws of Nature must have carried them; and, finally, that some designing hand has salted them with deliberate, fraudulent intent.

Ralston set the papers aside. "That, gentlemen, is the gist of it."

"Damn," Lent said. He shook his head. "I—like the rest of you—find it hard to believe those two rubes pulled this off."

Janin shook his head. "I feel a complete fool. My reputation is ruined."

Billy took up the pages again, thumbing through them until he found what he was looking for. "King addressed that very thing, here at the end. *This is the work of no common swindler, but of one who has known enough to select a spot where detection must be slow,*' he writes. *'The salting itself is so cunning and artful, the choice of conditions so fatally well made, I can feel no surprise that even so trustworthy an engineer as Mister Janin should have brought home the belief he did. A sense of my duty as a public officer has impelled me to come directly and frankly to you, gentlemen. I am with respect, your obedient servant, Clarence King.*' "

William Lent chuckled without mirth. "So we should all feel good about being hornswoggled by Arnold and Slack." He chuckled again, then sat upright and slapped the table. "The fact is, gentlemen, we are ruined."

No one spoke for some time, each of the men around the table lost in his own thoughts. General Dodge broke the silence. "But what of the stones? Aren't they genuine?"

"Oh, they're diamonds and rubies, all right," Billy said. "Worthless castoffs from gem cutters, and industrial diamonds."

"But Tiffany himself appraised them!" Ash said.

"True. But apparently Mister Tiffany's expertise is in cut stones. He only assigned value based on size and weight and didn't assess their quality."

"But where did Arnold and Slack get the stones? There must be somebody else behind this. Those buffoons couldn't possibly have pulled this off," Janin said.

With a wry smile, Billy said, "Unfortunately, all indications are that those 'buffoons' are sharper than we are. Neither King—nor myself, based on my limited inquiries—found any evidence of other involvement, save the inadvertent assistance of a man Arnold worked with years ago at the diamond drill company. As I said, the stones they brought us were useless industrial diamonds. It seems they got the rubies and other stones from Indians in the Southwest somewhere."

"With our money!" Lent said.

Billy nodded. "With our money. Arnold used our first payment to travel to London and Amsterdam. He spent thousands of dollars buying cheap castoff stones from gem cutters. Bought them practically by the pound. Had the stones been examined more closely, King says we would have found tool marks and indications of preliminary cutting on the surfaces of many of them. In any event, Arnold and Slack salted the field as necessary—just a small area before they took my man out there. Then a wider area to impress Janin."

"Which it did, I am embarrassed to say," Janin said.

General Dodge, still pale, shook his head. "Surely, there must have been some warning, something we missed, some hint that Arnold and Slack weren't on the up and up. I simply refuse to believe I was hoodwinked by those two rubes."

"You might as well get used to the idea. If for no other reason than that it's true," Billy said.

"Still, I see the general's point," Lent said. He waved a hand toward the investors around the table. "We—all of us here, as well as the others in New York and London—are successful men. Men of means. We have all managed to accumulate considerable wealth." He shook his head. "And to think we were taken in by those two . . . those two . . ."

"I understand, William," Billy said. "But all I had is now

gone, or will be soon, owing to nothing more than greed."

"Oh bullshit, Billy. Don't get philosophical, or moralistic, on us!" Harpending said.

Billy shrugged. "You cannot deny, Ash—or any of the rest of you—that we had it. Success. Wealth. Prestige. All that, and more. We had it." He sighed. "I am reminded of the old saw about a bird in the hand. We had it, and it was not enough. We lost it, reaching for two birds in the bush. Two birds named Philip Arnold and John Slack."

HORSE THIEF MORNING

Brown Sal was a darn good horse, even if she was a mare. She could outrun every horse in the valley—leastways every one that ever cared to race against her. She was good to ride, real smooth-like, and could walk out at a right quick pace and do it all the day long. And when I rode out to the far pastures to move the cow herd, I could knot the reins and let them hang on her neck and that horse would handle them cattle without so much as a blink of an eye from me. Why, she'd even submit to the harness and pull Pa's buggy around the streets of Salt Lake when he took a mind to go into the City sporting with Ma.

You can see why Pa thought so much of that horse.

So when that scapegrace Lot Huntington stole her, Pa did not hesitate one minute before sending for his pal Porter Rockwell to get her back. How ol' Port went about it makes for a pretty good story and I will get to it by and by. But first, you got to know about Lot Huntington.

See, Lot was a known rowdy who got into more trouble than his upbringing would lead one to expect. His daddy, Dimick Huntington, was kind of a big deal. He was one who Brigham Young relied on and had answered any number of callings over the years. Mostly, he was the man to see if you wanted to know anything or do anything when it came to the Indians hereabouts. Brother Huntington had been an interpreter with the Utes and the Shoshonis since coming west, and all them Indians trusted him and knew him to be a solid and reliable sort.

His boy Lot, now, he was a different story.

He must have been within two or three years of reaching age thirty when he stole Brown Sal. And already he had been up to more no-good in his life than he ought to have been. Still, Lot was a likeable sort. He always had a friendly smile and a good line of talk, especially when it came to the ladies. I have to say that with all the trouble he was involved in, he never mistreated no women. On the other hand, he was known to defend their honor whenever he saw the occasion required it.

As I said, folks liked Lot. Most men were happy to share a drink with him, whether in one of the saloons or roadhouses, or out of a jug or pocket flask around a campfire. He probably drank more than a Mormon boy ought to, and that might be to blame for some of his misbehavior, but it wasn't uncommon in those days for a man to imbibe. Fact is, they say he had been on a big bender that time he shot Wild Bill Hickman on Christmas day back in '59.

Wild Bill is another interesting story, but I won't go into it just now. Suffice it to say he more than earned the moniker "Wild Bill." He was a sometimes lawman and sometimes outlaw. He rode under orders from Brigham Young from time to time, and other times Brother Brigham would as soon he'd never heard of the man and wished he could be rid of him. For a time, Hickman ran a gang of thieves and rustlers known as Hickman's Hounds, and Lot Huntington was known to have ridden with him now and again. In fact, Hickman kind of took young Huntington under his wing and showed him the ropes of the outlaw trade, according to some.

Anyhow, the way I heard it, some of Hickman's bandit pals, including Lot, stole a herd of horses from one of Wild Bill's friends, who was a freighter. Without Hickman's knowing it, mind you. But Hickman found out who the thieves were and reported it, which resulted in a standoff when a bunch of them thieves caught him out of town one night and threatened to shoot him. Never one to shun a fight, Wild Bill pulled his pistols and faced down all seven of them, and they turned tail and ran, shouting threats as they went. Lot was among them. Must have been they was drunk enough to feel brave but not sloshed sufficient to want to shoot it out with Wild Bill.

Them boys kept drinking and arguing for days, trying to talk one another into taking on their friend. Lot finally got up the courage on Christmas morning and found Wild Bill Hickman outside the Townsend Hotel at the corner of First South and West Temple streets, right in the heart of downtown Salt Lake City.

Lot walked up to Wild Bill, they say, spewing obscenities the like of which ought not come out of any mouth a mother kissed. He drew his pistol, but Wild Bill, being no stranger to shooting scrapes, grabbed Huntington's hand and pushed the gun aside even as he slid a pig sticker out of his belt fixing to gut Lot.

The way Hickman told it, he held up for a second as he didn't want to kill his young friend. One of the men with Lot yelled, "Don't kill him!" and stepped between the two. As Lot backed off, he dropped the hammer and shot Wild Bill, then shot him again whilst Hickman was pulling his own pistol. Lot turned and ran down the alley before Hickman could return fire, which, when he finally did, landed a bullet in Lot's backside. Lot let out a yelp, turned and threw some more lead in Wild Bill's direction, and ran again.

Wild Bill, meantime, was barely able to stand, having been smote by bullets in hip and thigh. Some folks on the way home from Sunday school—not only was it Christmas, it was the Sabbath as well—carried Hickman inside and a couple of sawbones went to work on him, picking chunks of lead out of him. Seems one of the bullets had shattered and ripped him up inside pretty good, even getting some pieces stuck in his bones. Them doctors gave Wild Bill up for dead, but being a contrary sort, he wasn't having it.

He was laid up for weeks and barely breathing. One of Huntington's pals sneaked into Wild Bill's room one night intending to do away with him, but Hickman had Jason Luce there standing guard, and Luce sliced up the intruder pretty good with his Bowie knife—stabbed him a dozen times, they said.

Anyway, thanks to Lot Huntington, Wild Bill Hickman hobbled around on crutches clear through that summer and walked with a limp the rest of his life—every day of which was painful on account of all that lead Lot left in him.

But you got to remember that Lot wasn't drunk all the time, and when he wasn't on a toot he was as nice a fellow as you'd care to meet, even if he was a thief and an outlaw. Fact is, he was the kind of guy that young boys could admire, what with his easy smile and his swagger and the way he wore his hat— cocked at a just a little more of an angle than most men would be comfortable with. And when he had money—probably stolen—he always spread it around, buying drinks for grown men and licorice sticks for kids, which he would pass out in the street to any tike who happened by. Of course, many a mother refused the offer on behalf of their kids, then gathered their skirts and shuffled themselves and their little ones away from the evil influence as quick as they could manage.

But I better get back to my story.

Lot Huntington's theft of Brown Sal didn't just happen on its own. It came near the end of another of his drunken sprees. Let me catch you up on that, then we'll get to the horse steal- ing. And what happened after.

It all starts with Utah's governor at the time. Now, you got to remember that there was no love lost between the United States and Utah Territory in them days. We had barely avoided a shooting war with the government a few years earlier, and they kicked Brigham Young out of the governor's office and put Alfred Cumming in, who didn't know thing one about Utah or Mormons or anything else so far as I could see. Turns out Cumming was a real peach compared to his replacement. But I'll get to that.

Anyway, when the Civil War broke out back East, the army that had come out here to fight us was sent to fight the Southerners—except those who quit the army to join up with the South and fight against their old comrades in arms, which more than a few of them did, including General Albert Sidney Johnston, who had been in command out at Camp Floyd. But no sooner were those soldiers gone than the government sent more soldiers—these from California, under Colonel Patrick Edward Connor—to keep an eye on us Mormons. I guess they was afraid we'd join up with the Confederates, which wasn't all that farfetched a notion seeing as the United States of America had never done the Latter-day Saints any good and had allowed our fellow citizens to do us a good deal of harm when we was back in the States.

Abe Lincoln replaced Cumming with John Dawson—that would have been along about the end of 1861—who was the sorriest excuse for a politician I ever heard of, and that's saying something. First thing, he got up on his soapbox and demanded Utah Territory fork over a passel of money to help the Union fight the Civil War. Which suggestion Brigham Young soon laid to rest, and rightly so.

Most folks wrote that off as politics and didn't pay it much mind. But what Dawson did next got folks stirred up but good. What he did was, he made rude and unwelcome advances of an improper nature towards a woman, whose name I will not mention, who was doing some sewing for him—and he did it right in her own front room, if you can imagine. She told him to leave off and that she planned to report his uncouth behavior to the police. When he offered her a sizeable sum of money to keep quiet, well, that really put a bee in her bonnet and she took up a fireplace shovel and went to work on him; drove him right out the front door, she did.

Once word of that indiscretion got out, Dawson was rightly concerned for his safety so he abandoned his office and absconded for the East. He'd only been governor for maybe three weeks, a term in office that was three weeks too long if you ask me. He made his way up the canyon to Mountain Dell and Ephraim Hanks's stage station to catch an eastbound coach.

But who should find him there in the cold and snow of New Year's Eve but Lot Huntington and half a dozen other yahoos who ran with Lot at times—I can't name them all, but Moroni Clawson was there, as was Wil Luce and Wood Reynolds. Wood Reynolds, by the way, was kin to the woman the governor attempted to compromise and it might have been him who agitated the others to go after Dawson. Not that it took much encouragement, to my way of thinking.

Them boys just hung out at the station drinking and raising a ruckus whilst Dawson cowered in the corner trying to keep warm and out of sight. He came back from visiting the back-house and saw that someone had lifted the fancy beaver robe that had been covering him. He protested, they say, and Wood Reynolds shut his mouth with a balled fist. Knocked him right to the floor, Wood did, and while he was down the rest of the pack lit into him, kicking and punching and giving him what for as a reminder of his lapse of manners. There were rumors that them boys turned Dawson into a steer, but I think that was just a tall tale. Not that I'd put such a mutilation past them boys, if they were drunked up enough. They had the know-how, for certain, having performed that very operation on many a bull calf every spring.

Someone dumped Dawson onto the stagecoach when it came

through and he went back to Washington and raised all manner of uproar for his treatment out here, but so far as I know nothing ever came of it. The courts swore out warrants against Lot and them others, but there wasn't a policeman or sheriff or marshal in the territory inclined to go after the boys, at least for that offense.

Given what happened to Lot Huntington a couple weeks later, it might have been better had he been arrested and lounging in jail. That way, he would not have been accused, right or wrong, of lifting an Overland Mail cashbox with $800 in it from Townsend's Stable and getting another arrest warrant with his name on it for his efforts. Nor would he have stole Brown Sal and got my Pa in a huff, who put Porter Rockwell on his trail.

Here's what happened.

Pa rode Brown Sal into town one evening—not the City, but Jordan Mills, nearest where we lived—to see Bishop Swenson on a tithing matter. He tied the mare to the fence and came out hours later to find her gone—or not find her, I guess I should say. He studied around as well as he could in the dark, but the tracks in the snow and the streets were so muddled he couldn't make any sense of them.

So, it being late, and Pa not being the kind to inconvenience a neighbor by waking them up late at night for the borrow of a horse, he walked on home. Which was no short distance, by the way, and it was darn cold besides, like a January night is likely to get. The trip took him most of what was left of the night and he was in no shape to do anything but take to his bed when he got to the house.

My big brother Sam was right upset with the situation.

"I'm goin' after 'em, Pa," he said as he pulled on his boots.

"Going after who? You don't know who stole Sal any more than I do."

"It won't take me long to find out," Sam said. "Them thieves leave tracks just like anybody else does."

"I told you there was no trail I could make out."

"Well, everybody in the Valley knows Brown Sal, so whoever it was sure ain't stickin' around here or headin' for Salt Lake. That means about the only thing they can do is head south past Point of the Mountain, then west into the desert on the stage road."

"Maybe you're right. But you just leave it be. I'll send for Port."

"You do that, Pa. And get him out here in a hurry. Meantime, I ain't waitin' around."

Pa thought for a minute while Sam threw what cooked food he could scare up into his saddlebags. Pa said, "If you're going south, you'll likely find Port at the Hot Springs. That's where I'd look, anyway."

See, at that time Porter Rockwell owned a roadhouse down at the Point of the Mountain called the Hot Springs Brewery and Hotel. He had a house a little farther on in Lehi, and a big ranch way out west of there at Government Creek. And he had a place in the City as well. Ol' Port's interests were pretty spread out, and you'd likely find him anywhere. But on a cold winter day or night, the Hot Springs Brewery and Hotel was as good a guess as any and better than most.

Sam and me and two of Sam's pals swung into the saddle and headed south. Pa wasn't keen on me going along, but Sam said another gun could make a big difference if it came to shooting. As it happened, I was pretty well-heeled with a .36-caliber Navy Colt percussion-cap revolver that came to me when the army abandoned Camp Floyd. Guns were not among the things they auctioned off to the public when they shut down the fort, so my owning it was not exactly on the up-and-up, but I was not the only one back then in possession of a firearm courtesy of the United States Army.

I could shoot, too. Better than Sam, even. But plinking peach cans off a fence post ain't the same as shooting at a man, so there's no telling how I would do in a gunfight. Truth be told, I was curious about it. But at the same time I was not all that eager to test myself. You know how it is. A young feller like I was is always wondering how he stacks up, if he's fit to be called a man, that sort of thing.

Anyway, when we got to Draperville down at the south end of the valley we found out three men had been through way late the night before, one of them on a horse that matched Brown Sal's description right down to the bulldog tapaderos on Pa's saddle. Which meant Sam was likely right in his notions about where they'd go. And it meant they had the best part of a day's lead on us. But the man we talked to said they didn't seem to be in much of a hurry.

We rode on to Rockwell's roadhouse and found Port there. He'd ridden up from his house in Lehi that morning so did not see the horse thieves when they rode through, but the barkeeper heard them go by in the wee hours and wondered why they didn't stop for the night or at least come in to warm up.

Port was on his way to the City, but did not hesitate half a second to change his plans when we told him Pa wanted his help to get his favorite horse back. Not only did Port favor horses and hate horse thieves, he and Pa were saddle pals from way back and either would most likely do anything the other asked, short of breaking the law. Come to think of it, in Port's case going outside the law wouldn't have mattered much anyway. It was well known he was willing to do darn near anything to accomplish his purposes or fulfill whatever assignment he'd been handed.

"It's Brown Sal they took, you say?" Port said.

"It is," Sam said.

"Damn. That mare's too good a horse for any lowlife horse

thief to have his hands on. You reckon she was took on purpose by someone who knew who she was, or do you suppose they just happened on her?"

"Couldn't say. She was tied to the fence outside the Bishop's house in town. So it could be either way, or both. The thief might have just come by and saw the opportunity. Could be he recognized Sal and that made the chance even harder to pass up."

"How many?"

"Man in Draperville said three."

The barkeep nodded agreement. "Sounded like three horses that went by here. Not much traffic on the road, cold as it was last night. Only that outfit and one wagon came by here all night, and the man in the wagon stopped for a beer and a bowl of beans."

"Were them horsemen in any hurry?"

This time the saloonist's head moved side to side rather than up and down. "Nope. Just walking along."

"That's what they said in town, too," Sam added.

Port thought for minute or two, sipping at a mug of beer and tugging at his beard. "All wheat, boys. It's all wheat. We'll get them."

"Wheat," if you don't know much about Porter Rockwell, is a word he used when he meant everything was fine. Nobody knows for sure why, but some folks think it's because of that Bible story in the Book of Matthew about the wheat and the tares; the wheat, of course, being what was good and the tares what was bad. Not that Port was much on Scripture, mind you. Fact is, the man couldn't read a word, Scripture or otherwise, and if he ever paid attention in Sunday school, you'd never know it. Still and all, even given his lack of observance, Port was as good a man as ever set foot on the earth. Of course, some folks would beg to differ and claim there was never a worse man to walk the earth, but most of them didn't know ol' Port and relied on rumors for their opinions.

We set out from the Hot Springs Brewery and Hotel and once we cleared the gap where the Jordan River cuts through the Point of the Mountain, we started bearing west along the wagon road. That road was well traveled and had been for years, being the route of the Overland Stage and Express, the way to Camp Floyd when the army was out there, and the trail the Pony Express followed. Not that we knew it at the time, but that meant Lot Huntington—who was the one who stole Brown Sal, but which we didn't find out till later—knew the country well, him having been a Pony Express rider and all. Besides, Brown Sal probably wasn't the first stolen horse he had ridden or herded along that road.

We pushed our mounts at a pretty good pace for about twenty miles or so until we got to the Stagecoach Inn. That place, as you might could tell from the name, was a stage station. The big hotel was built a few years earlier when the army pitched their tents at Camp Floyd, which happened to be just across the road.

Wasn't much there anymore, but when the soldiers was at Camp Floyd, Frogtown—what they called the settlement that sprung up—had more than seven thousand folks living in it, they say. Except for Salt Lake, it was about as big a town as you could find anywhere in Utah Territory. Hardly anybody lived there when we went after Brown Sal, but darn near everyone on the Overland Road stopped there. If you were westbound, it was about the last place of any note before setting out into some serious desert, and if you were eastbound, you knew civilization wasn't far off once you got there.

The station agent was a good friend of ol' Port's and he stood us to a hot meal and even hotter coffee. He told us, too, that our quarry was a young man he believed to be Lot Huntington and two others he did not know but had seen around, and they had passed through not so many hours ago, so we knew we were gaining on them. Port figured if we borrowed fresh horses we could catch them at Faust's Station, another twenty miles or so down the road. But the Overland Stage man went him one better, offering Port the use of a coach and driver.

Now, I know you're thinking a man who worked for the Overland Stage wouldn't be giving the loan of a stagecoach to just anybody, but Porter Rockwell wasn't just anybody so far as the Overland Stage was concerned. See, ol' Port, as a deputy United States marshal—did I mention he was a lawman?—had recovered more stolen money and rustled horses for them than they could ever repay him for.

All of us was happy with that development. Having been horseback darn near every minute of a long, long day, sitting in a stagecoach offered a nice respite for our backsides. Besides, the inside of that coach was considerably warmer than what it was outdoors that night.

The driver whoa-ed up the team a ways shy of Faust's Station on account of Port didn't want to alert the outlaws to our presence if they were there. So we stomped the life back into our feet and hoofed it on in to the station while it was still dark. Port sent Sam to look under a shed in one of the corrals to see if Brown Sal was there and he came back and said she sure enough was.

"Wheat," Port said. "Looks like we outguessed them horse thieves."

We backed off a ways and waited while Port figured out how he wanted to handle things. "Here's how this is gonna go down, boys," he finally said. "I don't want any gunplay if we can help it, so check your loads and be ready but don't shoot unless your life is in danger."

I nodded in agreement, and I suppose the others did too,

although I don't guess Port could have seen us much in the dark. But he went on, accustomed as he was to being obeyed in such situations.

"Come the morning, them thieves will walk out the door and when they do, I will be ready for them. With any luck, they'll throw down their guns. I have my doubts about what Lot will do, as that boy don't always use his head as God intended. I don't want to shoot him, or anyone, but if they start burning powder you all jump in and make your aim true. We'll have the advantage on account of we know what we're shooting at and where they are, and they won't."

I nodded again and we all listened as Port told us where to conceal ourselves. He took up the position nearest the station, behind a pile of cedar fence posts stacked end up, sort of like a stubby Indian tepee.

We shivered out there for a good long while, waiting for the sun to rise and take the chill out of the air. But before it did, in the gray light of dawn, things heated up all on their own. First sign of life we noticed was smoke coming out the chimney atop the little log building that served as the stage station and Doc Faust's abode. I don't know what the others thought about that smoke, but it made me wish I was indoors sitting next to that fire, even if it meant horse thieves for company.

After what seemed like a glimpse of eternity, we heard the door rattle, then swing open. Without even meaning to, I took a quick breath, then could not let it out again. My pistol was already in my shooting hand, but I shifted it to the other and flexed my fingers and rubbed them against my pants leg to get the frost out of them and some fresh blood into them. As I passed the Colt back to my shooting hand, I stole a glance to make sure all my caps were seated.

By then we could see it was Doc Faust coming out. Port waited until he closed the door, then stepped out from behind his post pile. Doc's eyes got as big around as coffee saucers. But he hotfooted it right over to where Port waited and the two of them stepped back out of sight of the shack should anyone else happen out the door. From where I sat, I could see Port and Doc talking but could not hear them. Doc talked a lot and waved his hands about and nodded his head up and down and side to side and flapped his hands around some more as he worked his jaw. Port just stood there with his hands in his coat pockets—where, I happened to know, he kept his pistols, their barrels sawed off short so they would fit better—as calm and cool as the morning, his only movement an occasional blink of his eyes.

Port told us later that Doc Faust told him for certain it was Lot Huntington and Moroni Clawson and John Smith who had ridden in the evening before and that just then they were inside eating breakfast. Port told him to go back in and inform the outlaws we had the station surrounded and to toss out their guns and follow them out the door with their hands up.

Doc more than likely passed along the information just like Port said. But those boys in there must have had a different idea, for nothing at all happened for what seemed like the longest time but couldn't have been more than a few minutes.

Then the door opened again and Lot Huntington walked out with a pistol in his hand, him pointing the barrel of it here and there in search of a target. I don't know what kind of gun it was, exactly, but it looked to me to be about the size of a mountain howitzer.

"Throw down that gun and throw up your hands!" Port said.

Huntington looked around but saw nobody.

"Like hell I will," he said to the post pile.

"I don't want to shoot you, Lot. I'd hate to have to explain to your folks why I killed a boy of theirs I'd known since his baby days."

"Shut up, old man! You show your face and I will put a bullet in it."

"C'mon, kid. You ain't got a chance. Nobody has to die here."

Lot kept his pistol pointed at the post pile and walked as calm as you please toward the corral and ducked between the rails.

"Stop right there, Lot!"

"Shut the hell up, old man. I'm leaving here and there ain't you nor nobody else going to stop me."

Port stepped out from behind the pile of posts and stood watching as Huntington rounded the corner of the shed and went out of sight. He walked toward the corral, as if unconcerned or uncaring that at any moment Lot could step out of the shed and shoot him down.

Lot did step out of the shed soon enough. He had Brown Sal by the cheek piece on the bridle and walked her toward the gate so she was between him and Port. I thought at the time that was a pretty cowardly thing to do, hiding behind a horse, but I know it was the smart thing to do and I wouldn't have thought a thing of it had the horse he was hiding behind been any other but Sal.

"Stop!" Port hollered as Lot walked Sal toward the gate.

"I already told you to shut up, Rockwell."

"I'll shoot you, Lot, sure as I'm standin' here."

"You're welcome to try, old man. I ain't afraid of you for one minute. You've outlived your reputation as far as I'm concerned."

Had I been breathing, I imagine the fog of it on that cold morning would have clouded my view of what happened next, but as I was not breathing at the time my view was clear as the winter air. By then, Lot had reached the corral gate, which was nothing more than fence rails like the rest of the corral, except these weren't pegged into place. So, all you had to do was slide them back a ways and let them drop. Which was just what

Huntington was doing, but it was pretty slow going, what with him having to keep his gun and Sal's bridle reins in one hand and both eyes on Rockwell while he nudged the rails along with the other hand.

It looked like Port was just going to watch him do it, and I wondered if I was seeing the last of Brown Sal.

Lot had worked his way up to the top rail by then. As it slipped free, he lost his grip, and it dropped to the ground and bounced into Sal's foreleg. Now, Sal is even-tempered as horses go, but something like that will spook any horse, especially when the tension has got the air so thick you could slice and stack it.

Sal shied, then reared up on her hind legs. Lot Huntington was exposed for those few seconds. But that's all it took for Port to pull the trigger. The horse thief staggered and fell into the fence rails. As he keeled over backwards, his left leg got hung between two of the poles, and that kept all but his head and shoulders from reaching all the way to the ground.

When the gun smoke around Port cleared, I saw he wasn't paying any attention at all to Lot, knowing from experience, I suppose, that there would be no more trouble from that quarter. Instead, his pistol pointed toward the station.

"The rest of you come on out of there," he said. "Send out the guns first."

The door cracked open and a rifle and three revolvers arced out the hole and clattered to the ground. Moroni and John walked out, acting both sheepish and afraid, their wide eyes riveted to the hole in the end of Rockwell's gun barrel, which was still wisping a bit of smoke. Port called the rest of us out of our hidey-holes and had us tie up the two horse thieves.

In the few minutes it took all this to happen, Lot Huntington hung there on the fence rails bleeding out and didn't move an inch. I know, for I cast more than a few glances that way while all this was going on.

There's not much more to say. Rockwell's shooting proved to be as accurate as his legend claimed. The middle of Lot's chest was ripped to shreds by eight balls of double-ought buckshot. I know, because I counted the holes. I suppose it's best to say that Porter Rockwell often charged his pistols with buckshot. He claimed it more forgiving if your aim is a mite off, and more deadly—sort of like hitting a man with six or eight or however many bullets from a .32 caliber pistol, as opposed to one .44 or .45 caliber bullet. Myself, I wouldn't know. But that's what Port said.

There wasn't anything more to do but wrap Lot's body in a canvas sheet and stow it atop the stagecoach, load up the living, and head back toward home. We didn't even stop for a cup of coffee before setting out. The worst part was riding along in that coach as it rocked back and forth, knowing Lot Huntington was riding up top, colder than we were.

Brown Sal didn't seem bothered by his death as she trotted along behind, tied to the back of the stagecoach. When I stuck my head out the window to check on her from time to time, I swear there was a smile on her face.

Separating the Wheat from the Tares

BEING A TRUE ACCOUNT OF THE DEATH
AND LIFE OF ORRIN PORTER ROCKWELL

I am the last man to see Porter Rockwell alive.

In the early hours of the afternoon of 9 June 1878 he passed on to his reward in his office at the Colorado Stables where I am hostler. Since the last words to pass his lips fell upon my ears and mine alone, I feel obliged to set down the events of that day and the night previous, leaving a true and accurate record to refute the rumors and speculations concerning his death.

Having known the man over a number of years it seems my duty, as well, to set straight the facts of his life and rebut the calumny that dogs him even in death. He had not grown cold in his grave when the *Salt Lake Tribune* libeled him in its columns thus:

The gallows was cheated of one of the fittest candidates that ever cut a throat or plundered a traveler. Porter Rockwell is another in the long list of Mormon criminals whose deeds of treachery and blood have reddened the soil of Utah, and who has paid no forfeit to the law. He was commissioned by the Prophet Joseph Smith avenger-in-chief for the Lord when the Latter-day Saints were living a troublous life on the border, and arrived in this Territory where the fanatical leaders of the Church suffered no restraint, and the avenging angels were made bloody instruments of these holy men's will. Porter Rockwell was chosen as a fitting agent to lead in these scenes of blood.

69

The absurdity of these slanders is plain to all familiar with "Port" but painful to his memory even so. The true facts attest that Porter Rockwell was the finest peace officer, bodyguard, bounty hunter, pioneer, tracker, scout, and guide to ever carry sawed-off .36 caliber Navy Colt pistols in his coat pockets.

Allow me, now, to begin my account at the end.

The last words Porter Rockwell spoke came in reply to a question of mine. We had talked off and on since his arrival at the Colorado Stables at about one o'clock in the morning. He kept a small seldom-used office there. Most of his time the past few years was spent at his ranch away out on Government Creek, but he occasionally came to town to visit his family and tend to the remnants of his freighting business. He sometimes slept on a cot in that office, as he did that final night.

Port had escorted his daughter Mary to watch Denham Thompson play the lead in *Joshua Whitcomb* at the Salt Lake Theatre. After seeing her home, he spent a quiet hour at a saloon before walking the three blocks to the stable to retire. He arrived here just after one o'clock. He slept a few hours, then awoke complaining of cold and a sick stomach. We talked off and on as he dozed and thrashed uncomfortably through the remainder of the night and morning. Shortly after midday, he was again taken by chills and vomiting. He struggled to sit up and pulled on his boots.

"Port!" I asked. "How are you?"

"Wheat. All wheat," he replied weakly.

He then lapsed into unconsciousness, never to awaken again in this world—to die, as the saying goes, with his boots on.

Perhaps his final words bear explanation. "Wheat" was a favorite expression of Porter Rockwell's, heard often by those who knew him. Some claim it is of uncertain origin, but I know where it comes from and what it means because Port told me.

It is from the thirtieth verse of the third chapter of *The Gospel According to St. Matthew:* "Gather ye together first the tares, and bind them in bundles to burn them: but gather the wheat into my barn."

So, all that was good was by Port described as "wheat," variously meaning "all is well" or "that is good" or "everything is fine" and such like. His detractors take it further, using the Scripture against him—it is the reason, they say, he killed the forty or eighty or one hundred and more they claim for him; they were but "tares" to be destroyed.

I asked Port one time about the deaths attributed to his hand. His answer was as simple and direct as the man himself: "I never killed anybody that didn't need killing."

On the day of his death, Rockwell was, in fact, awaiting trial for the Aiken affair. In the autumn of 1877 he had been indicted, arrested, and jailed for murder. Only $15,000 bail posted by friends kept him from languishing in a cell awaiting the term of the district court. Anti-Mormon prosecutors obtained from a grand jury with similar leanings a True Bill accusing Port and Sylvanus Collett of murdering John Aiken *twenty years before!* I heard the story from Port himself, and here is the truth of that matter.

Painted by lawyers for the government as innocent and unsuspecting travelers set upon by Brigham Young's Destroying Angels, the Aiken party was, in reality, a band of opportunistic California gamblers. Decked out in Texas hats and riding silver-studded Mexican saddles on fine horses, the party of six, led by John Aiken and his brother Tom, arrived in the Territory in late fall, 1857. Hearing that the United States Army was marching to attack and occupy Utah Territory, they had set out from southern California with a considerable stake and a gambling outfit including playing cards and dice and a faro layout, intending to pick the soldiers clean.

The bunch was arrested before even reaching Great Salt Lake City. Jailed in Ogden and later transferred to the territorial capital, the Aiken party was held for two weeks or so while authorities decided what to do with them. They determined to release the Californians and escort them from the Territory on the southern route to prevent any possible contact with the approaching army. Port was assigned to lead the escort party, duly authorized by law.

"Four of us took four of them south, two of the gamblers being allowed to stay at large in the City until spring," Port said. "We was camped on the Sevier River when I was woke up by some commotion, which was our charges attempting an escape. One of them fancy men had the best of Collett and so I shot him, but he run off through the bushes with a bullet of mine in his back. Them two Aikens and the other'n was down and I figured them dead, so we dumped the bodies in the river. Come dawn we rode north, considering the job a bad one, but a finished one just the same."

The next afternoon, the wounded outlaw stumbled barefoot into the town of Nephi bleeding from his head and the bullet wound in his back. The local sawbones probed for the bullet, and, sure enough, it was the same caliber as Port's Colts. Later in the day, the townsfolk were surprised by the arrival of another of the outlaws—this one John Aiken, obviously not as dead as believed—apparently revived by the cold water of the Sevier River. He, too, was barefoot and bleeding from head wounds. Four or five days later, the pair had healed enough to travel and asked to be driven to Great Salt Lake City. Two young men volunteered for the job.

Eight miles north of Nephi, the party stopped to water the team at Willow Creek when the door of the sheepherder's shack there flew open and blasts from a shotgun cut down the wounded gamblers. The boys lit out of there and Aiken and his traveling companion were never seen again, dead or alive.

Twenty years after the fact, Port and Sylvanus Collett were blamed in the mysterious Aiken affair on the flimsiest of evidence—or a complete lack thereof if you ask me. Port refused even to cooperate in his defense, "Wheat" being his only reply to questions from his lawyers.

Laying the blame on Porter Rockwell is not a recent development. As far back as the thirties, when the Mormons were abused and mobbed by Missouri Pukes, Port was accused of being chief of the "Danite" bands that retaliated against the mobs. Then, when Governor Lilburn Boggs ordered the Mormons evicted from Missouri *or exterminated* and an assassin attempted his life in reply, that, too, was attributed to Rockwell.

There was no credible evidence in either case, and I believe that if Port had set out to kill Boggs, the governor would be dead today. Whether with pistol, rifle, or shotgun, Port's skills as a marksman were the stuff of legend—as you will see from the facts behind another of his more famous escapades, as related to me by the legend himself.

The year was 1845, and the place was Hancock County in Illinois, not far from the city of Nauvoo and not long after a mob had jailed and murdered the Mormon prophet Joseph Smith and his brother Hyrum.

Port was a favorite of Joseph Smith's, appointed by him in his capacity as mayor of Nauvoo as a deputy marshal and personal bodyguard. In fact, Rockwell's long, flowing locks were the result of his association with Smith, who prophesied, "Orrin Porter Rockwell—so long as ye remain loyal and true to thy faith, ye need fear no enemy. Cut not thy hair and no bullet or blade can harm thee." A true prophecy as it turned out. But I digress.

The other characters in the incident at hand were Frank Worrell, leader of the Carthage Grays, a so-called militia unit that murdered the incarcerated Smiths; and county sheriff Jacob Backenstos, unpopular in the area because the mobocrats accused him of sympathy with the Mormons.

Rockwell tells the tale:

"I was watering my horse alongside the Warsaw Road when I spies Backenstos whipping up his horses and flying down the road towards me in a carriage. Coming over the rise a ways behind was two men a-horseback. Jacob hauled in the lines in a cloud of dust and hollered to me, 'Rockwell, in the name of the State of Illinois, County of Hancock, I order you to protect me from the mob at my heels!' I had my pistols and a rifle so I told the sheriff not to worry. I didn't know so at the time, but five other men was behind the riders, coming on hard in a rig and a light wagon.

"One horseman was well ahead of the other. Backenstos hails him and orders him to halt. Instead, he pulls out a pistol. By now I seen I was facing that sonofabitch Frank Worrell so I shot him."

The sheriff later said in official reports that the rifle bullet, fired from a distance of 100 to 150 yards, tore through Worrell's chest and launched him from the saddle. The other rider, and the men in the two outfits that had by now arrived on the scene, lost heart at the sight of their leader bleeding in the dirt. After loading the dying body in the wagon, they turned tail.

" 'Well, I got him, Jacob,' I says to the sheriff. 'I was afraid my rifle couldn't reach him, but it did. Only missed a little bit.' 'What do you mean?' he asks me, and I says, 'I aimed for his belt buckle.' "

Another silent witness to Port's long-distance accuracy with his weapons was the unidentified scapegrace behind the Great Bullion Robbery of 1868. The Overland Stage, eastbound out of California, was held up in the Utah desert and relieved of some $40,000 in gold. The driver pushed on to Faust Station, next along the line, where Port was to board the stage as a Wells Fargo shotgun guard for the run to Fort Bridger. Instead, he mounted up and rode off on the stage's backtrail in pursuit of the thief.

"He was a wily one," Port told me one time, "taking care to cover his tracks and otherwise confuse his movements. But I catched him up on Cherry Creek, two days after taking up the trail. The gold was in the ground, I figure, so I lay low keeping an eye on him. After a week or so of skulkin' around out there, he's sure he's not being followed so he sneaks off and digs up the gold. About the time the last bar comes out of the hole, I draw down on him and make the arrest without incident.

"Me, that gold, and the outlaw make our way to my place on Government Creek where I has Hat Shurtliff keep an eye on him while I gets some sleep, which I had been missing a lot of, you see. Ol' Hat, though, he fell asleep on the job and wakes up just as the prisoner clears the corral gate on one of my horses. I stagger outside whilst trying to peel back my eyelids and blink out the blur just in time to see him skyline on a little ridge east of the cabin. Them stubby Colts of mine ain't much for distance, but I fired all the same.

"Well, I figures I missed since I didn't see no evidence to say otherwise. So's I finishes up my sleeping and gets things in shape at the ranch, then hauls the gold on into the Wells Fargo office in Great Salt Lake City, where there's a report of a dead man found propped up agin a telegraph pole. Seems his horse had wandered off, leaving the poor soul to bleed to death from a bullet wound in the back. I never saw the body. But I suspect I'd of recognized him."

★ ★ ★ ★ ★

The infamous Lot Huntington felt the effect of Porter Rockwell's marksmanship from a range close enough to look the fearsome lawman in his pale blue eyes.

The cause of the whole affair was The Honorable John W. Dawson, vacating Utah in the dead of night following a glorious three-week term as governor of the Territory, during which time he had managed to aggravate enough folks high and low with his debauched behavior that he feared for his life. Which, by the way, would have been no great loss.

While waiting at the stage station, the disgraced Dawson was set upon and pistol whipped by a half dozen drunken cowboys who left him for dead and rode off into the windy winter night. Dawson survived and identified one Lot Huntington, a known petty outlaw and rustler, as leader of the gang. Local police had no success in locating the accused after two weeks of searching, at which time the story takes a curious turn.

A strongbox containing $800 cash belonging to the Overland Mail disappeared from the Townsend Stable, along with Brown Sal, one of the finest horses in the Territory. Suspicion again centered on Lot Huntington and his crowd, who were seen leaving the vicinity and heading west. A posse was formed to take up the chase, with Porter Rockwell in the lead. The posse passed through Camp Floyd some several hours behind the bandits and rode hard through the night to Faust Station, where Port spotted Brown Sal under a shed in the corral. He takes up the tale from there, as best I remember his telling it.

"It was coming on morning and we was cold and tired and the wind was hard and bitter. But, wanting to avoid any unnecessary gunplay, I elected to surround the station and wait and see. Along about sunup, Faust himself comes out of the inn to do his chorin' and I beckons him over to where I was hidden.

He tells me Huntington is in there with two others eating their breakfast.

"So I sends Faust back inside to explain the situation, figuring they'd see the hopelessness of their plight and come out with hands up as instructed. Well, lo and behold, next thing I know Lot Huntington comes strollin' out pretty as you please with a big ol' .44 caliber cap-and-ball pistol in his fist. I calls out a warning and shoots in the air but he walks on over to them corrals like he ain't got a care in the world. I rushes over to the shed just as he's swingin' onto Brown Sal bareback and I hollers out another warning. Lot aims that pistol at me but before he could fire, I unloaded eight balls of buckshot from my Colt into his belly. He gets all tangled up in the fence rails fallin' off that horse and made a strange picture danglin' there and dyin'."

The other two surrendered without further violence, and Port and the posse delivered the corpse, the prisoners, the strongbox, and Brown Sal to the authorities back in the City. While unsaddling his horse minutes later, Port hears gunfire.

"With pistols in hand I ran back to where I left the prisoners with the police. 'What happened?' I asks the constable and he says all matter-of-fact, 'Tried to escape.' But I looked at them bodies close, and both was powder-burnt and one shot in the face. How the hell that happened I couldn't discern, less'n he was runnin' away backwards."

A final incident, selected from many, must suffice as testimony to Porter Rockwell's skills as a horseman and tracker. Known far and wide for his ability to handle horses no other could master and getting more miles from a mount than possible as a practical matter—with no ill effects on the animal—Port was sometimes accused of thinking more like a horse than a horse did. The upshot was a relentlessness on the trail that, combined

with seeing sign where there wasn't any, made Port the first one
called upon when there were rustlers to be caught.

One story, as I say, will serve. It was told to me, not by Rockwell, but by letter from Frank Karrick, a freighter who hauled
goods between Sacramento and Great Salt Lake City and was
the beneficiary of Port's services in recovering a herd of stolen
mules. I quote his missive at some length:

I was 70 miles south of Great Salt Lake City back in '61
when several valuable mules disappeared in the night.
Upon discovering my loss in the morning, I left the
teamsters to guard the wagons, goods, animals &c while I
went off in pursuit, but soon lost the trail in a confusion of
hoofprints. Knowing no other recourse, I reported the
crime in Great Salt Lake City where B. Young himself suggested I enlist the support of Orrin Porter Rockwell. Upon
retaining his services, we repaired to the place I lost the
trail, now three days cold. Rockwell examined the ground
for a time and pointed out the track we were to follow.
Asked how he knew, he answered, "Never mind. They've
only taken the shoes off the mules. We'll just stay on this
trail."

About dusk the trail again became entangled, having
been crossed by a large herd of cattle. Rockwell expressed
no dismay and followed up the herd. After dark, we approached the drovers' camp, unnoticed until reaching the
edge of the firelight where Rockwell reined up. Soon we
were looking down the barrels of several firearms in the
hands of the startled men in the camp, one of whom hollered, "Stay right where you are or the shooting starts!"
Rockwell answered in his squeaky voice, "Wheat, fellers,
wheat." Either the voice or the term had meaning in the

camp, as the reply came back, "Port! Step down and join us! Supper's soon ready and the coffee's hot."

(Note: Perhaps I neglected to mention that, rough and tough though he was, Porter Rockwell's voice did not match; it being rather high-pitched and tending to break higher when excited. This fact was not to his liking. Likewise, his hands were small and well formed, almost feminine in appearance and not at all in keeping with what one might expect in a so-called "rough character." Continuing now with Karrick's report.)

After sharing the warmth of the fire through the night and a hot breakfast, both courtesy of the men moving the cattle, we rode out ahead of the cowboys as they were lining out the herd at first light. As if he never doubted their course or destination, Rockwell soon pointed out the tracks of my stolen mules. We pushed hard through the day. Near sunset, we trotted up a rise and saw a faint trace of dust in the far distance. Rockwell rustled about in his saddlebags and produced a telescope. "Two men . . . some horses . . . and mules—come on!" he said. And go on we did, with haste.

For the second time in as many evenings, we rode up on men hunched around a campfire. This time Rockwell did not wait to be noticed, but instead rode right into the rustlers' camp (there can be no doubt on this point—my mules were clearly visible in the fading light, grazing on the banks of a nearby stream) with snub-nosed Colt revolver in hand.

I regret my tale lacks the excitement of a shootout (although I did not regret it at the time), but the fact is the two were visibly frightened of Rockwell and offered no resistance. They were soon behind bars, my mules back in harness, and Rockwell gone home richer by $500 worth of my gratitude. On reaching my destination in California, I rewarded him further with the shipment of a hand-tooled saddle and a demijohn of fine whisky. I heard later he was vastly more interested in the whisky than in the saddle.

In all my years of freighting, never once did I have the pleasure of meeting a better man than Porter Rockwell. His ability as a tracker I have never seen equaled. Nor have I seen another who commanded such presence among men, as demonstrated by the gladness and the fear I saw in the faces of the cowboys and the outlaws, respectively, we encountered during our brief expedition. My gifts did not begin to repay Porter Rockwell and I consider myself ever in his debt.

Respectfully,
(signed) Frank Karrick
Sacramento, Calif.

By now it ought to be clear to even the most skeptical that Orrin Porter Rockwell was a credit to his people and a force for law and order. I could tell more. But I fear the lies and venom would yet outweigh any further words I could put to paper.

The reports of his death by poison or by bullets or by a beating administered by various people he is said to have wronged are likewise false. He died, as I have said, in his office at the Colorado Stables in my presence. The coroner's jury, influenced by the testimony of four physicians, determined there was "no evidence of injury, nor any symptoms of poisoning" and the death a result of the "failure of the heart's action, caused by a suspension of the nervous power."

If that description is correct, it is the only time Porter Rockwell ever lost his nerve.

THE PEOPLE VERSUS PORTER ROCKWELL

Now comes V. Harmon Haight, District Attorney in the First District Court in and for the Territory of Utah, appearing for the People of the United States of America, Plaintiff, seeking from this duly summoned and sworn Grand Jury a True Bill against Orrin Porter Rockwell, Defendant.

"Thank you, Mister Secretary. Gentlemen of the jury, the oath you have taken requires you to evaluate the evidence The People will present in this matter. Your duty is to determine whether or not probable cause exists to believe the accused committed a crime. If the evidence establishes such a probability, you must return a True Bill and, thus indicted, Porter Rockwell will stand trial to determine guilt or innocence. You may also, of course, refuse to indict—but after hearing the quantity of evidence The People will present before the Grand Jury, I doubt it.

"The crime for which Rockwell stands accused is murder. Now, gentlemen, this crime is not a recent one. The victim, one John Aiken, was last seen alive on the earth in October of 1857, just one month shy of twenty years ago. The details of the crime appear dim through the dust of passing years and the evidence obscured. And, even though you will hear from witnesses who place the defendant at or near the scene of the crime those many years ago, The People will not ask you to reach your decision in this matter on testimony of those long-ago events alone. No, gentlemen, you will be allowed to evaluate the man Porter

Rockwell as a whole—to determine his role in this affair within the context of a life of bloodshed and carnage. But, since it is the murder of John Aiken for which the man stands accused, the evidence in that crime shall first be presented to the Grand Jury."

"Guy Foote, do you understand the oath you have taken?"

"Yessir."

"Very well. Tell the jury, please, your place of residence in October of 1857."

"Nephi."

"And do you recall the events that are the subject of this inquiry?"

"Yessir. I'm told you're looking into what happened to them Aikens who came through there in chains."

"What did happen?"

"Well sir, as I said, they came through as prisoners, under the charge of Porter Rockwell and some other men. I didn't know them then and I don't recall them now—"

"But you do recall Porter Rockwell. Why is that?"

"Oh, everyone knows Port. All us kids back then held him up as a hero."

"Do you still?"

"I can't rightly say as I do."

"What changed your mind, Mister Foote?"

"It was this affair with them Aikens I'm trying to tell you about."

"Go on, then. I apologize for the interruption. Tell the jury the course of events."

"Port and his posse passed through town in the afternoon and we all turned out to see. They rode on by and, I was told later, stopped a few hours farther on and camped by the river out there, the Sevier River.

"Late in the night I was woke up by some folks talking in the public room—my folks ran a sort of hotel, see, putting up boarders and travelers. I heard Porter Rockwell say, kind of mad-like, 'We made a bad job of it, boys—one of them got away.' "

"Did you *see* it was Rockwell?"

"No sir. But it was his voice, kind of high and squeaky-like. Anyhow, they was gone when I woke up and I didn't think much of it. Later on, though, one of them prisoners, Tom Aiken he was, came back to town afoot with a bloodied head and a bullet in his back. He hadn't his shoes nor shirt, and was pretty thoroughly chilled. His story was that the posse had fallen on them in the night, hollering about an Indian attack, and whacking them over their heads. He managed to get to his feet, he said, and run off but was shot in the back—by Porter Rockwell, he believed, as he had seen Port with a pistol in his hand— before he could make his escape. But he managed to get away in the dark and the willows, and hid out all night. Them others was killed and dumped in the river, he says. Ma and Pa put him up in a bed and Doc fished a bullet out of his back.

"Along about evening, another one of them men showed up—John Aiken this time—him, too, with a nasty gash on his topknot and barely half-dressed hisself. He didn't remember nothing but waking up when he hit that cold river, and managed to stay out of sight until he thought it safe. He took to a bed at our hotel too."

"Moving along, Mister Foote, we understand from other testimony that the local authorities opted to escort the two 'prisoners' back to Great Salt Lake City once they were sufficiently recovered. You had a role in that?"

"Yessir. Me and Billy Skeen offered to make the trip. There wasn't much on that time of year, and us being about fourteen years old, thought it would make a fine adventure."

"You weren't afraid?"

"Nah. Them two was pretty used up. They was barely in shape to travel, so no one figured they'd try anything. They was outfitted by folks in town—I remember Pa gave John Aiken an old coat he had—and we set out. About eight miles or so north of Nephi there's this place called Willow Creek; nothing there but a spring and a sheepherder's cabin, but it's a convenient watering hole where most folks stopped, as did we. While I saw to the team, Billy and them others was stretching their legs. I heard that cabin door bust open and considerable gunfire, and turned and saw both them Aikens fall, one of 'em near torn in two from shotgun balls. Someone in that shack hollers out for me and Billy to just climb in the wagon and get on home."

"Do you know who it was?"

"No, Mister Haight, I can't say as I did then or do now."

"Could it have been Porter Rockwell?"

"He might of been in there, but it wasn't him hollering. I would of recognized his voice. So I guess I can't say he was there."

"How does the story end?"

"We lit out of there as ordered and went back to Nephi. Some folks went back out to Willow Creek after we said what happened, but nobody ever saw them Aiken fellas again, nor even their bodies. They figured whoever had shot them dumped them in the spring.

"That evening, Rockwell and another man rode into town and spent the night at the hotel. A day or two later I found Pa's old coat hanging in a lean-to we had over the back door. It was stained with blood and I counted eight holes in it. Billy Skeen saw it, too. I showed him."

"Mister Secretary and gentlemen of the jury, I would like now, if you please, to read into the record a correspondence from one Albert D. Richardson of the *New York Tribune*, who visited

Utah Territory in 1865 in the company of the eminent Schuyler Colfax, then Speaker of the House of Representatives in the United States Congress."

"What is your purpose in doing so, Mister Haight?"

"Merely to show, Mister Foreman, another aspect of Rockwell's character—to further establish a ready disposition toward violence, if you will."

"Go on, then."

"Thank you. This, from Richardson's published accounts in the *Tribune:*

" 'While abroad on the streets of Great Salt Lake City yesterday I encountered the notorious Mormon assassin Porter Rockwell. The chance meeting was a frightful one, as Rockwell had me confused with Fitz Hugh Ludlow, another reporter, whom I am said to resemble, and who passed through Utah Territory some time earlier and had written in the *Atlantic Monthly* an unflattering description of Rockwell. He believed it was I who had characterized him as the murderer of one hundred and fifty men; and he significantly remarked that if I had said it, he believed he would make it one hundred and fifty-one!' "

"State your name and rank, please."

"Patrick Edward Connor, Colonel, Third Regiment, California Volunteers, retired."

"Colonel, how did you come to know Orrin Porter Rockwell?"

"In 1862, I was ordered by the President and Commander-in-Chief to move seven companies of my command to Utah Territory to protect the Overland Mail route against Indian depredations. And, it was understood, to keep an eye on the Mormons whose loyalty to the Union was suspect.

"I had heard of Rockwell. He enjoyed a certain notoriety throughout the West. I had even heard tales of his exploits in

California in the gold rush years. But my first direct experience of the man came in the form of a report that he was riding through the streets of Great Salt Lake City as my command approached, offering any and all a five hundred dollar bet that my soldiers would never cross the Jordan River. We did, of course, and marched through the heart of the City with loaded rifles, fixed bayonets, and shotted cannon. We pitched our tents on benchland overlooking the city and established Fort Douglas among the Mormons."

"Fine, Colonel. Had you any direct dealings with Rockwell after that?"

"Considerable. If you have read your history, you know of the Battle of Bear River. I shall spare this assembly the details; suffice it to say that in the dead of winter, my California Volunteers located and attacked a camp of hostile Shoshoni Indians in Cache Valley, killing more than two hundred, destroying their camp and supplies, and recovering property stolen from settlers.

"Rockwell was instrumental in this effort. He guided us to the savages and offered valuable strategic advice for overtaking the camp. He participated bravely in the fight as well. But his greatest value came after the battle. I daresay that without his valiant service in obtaining teams and wagons to transport our wounded and unhorsed troops back to Fort Douglas, most of my command would have died in the cold and the storms."

"What is your opinion of the man?"

"Over time, I came to consider him a friend, Mister Haight. One whom I admire greatly. I know of no better guide or frontiersman. He is, in my opinion, to use his own words in describing good things, 'all wheat.' "

"You say you became his friend, Colonel. Would you describe yourself, also, a confidant?"

"I suppose so. We have talked a good deal about his life.

Given all I had heard about him, I was curious about the facts of his history."

"You're aware, I'm sure, that Rockwell was accused of the attempted murder of Lilburn W. Boggs, ex-governor, at the time of the assassination attempt, of Missouri."

"Yes. I questioned Rockwell closely about that incident one evening after we had shared a number of what he called 'squar whiskies.' "

"Would you relate to the members of the Grand Jury, please, his answer."

"He said, 'I shot through the window, and I thought I had killed him, but I had only wounded him; I was damned sorry I had not killed the son of a bitch.' "

"Madam, we sincerely appreciate your appearance before this Grand Jury to relate a difficult incident that must still grieve a mother's soul. If you will, state again your name for the members of the Grand Jury."

"I am Eliza Scott McRae."

"Missus McRae, I need not remind you that you are under oath. Relate, please, the events of your life in late July and early August of the year 1861 in which Porter Rockwell played a role."

"Well, Mister Haight, my two sons, Kenneth and Alexander McRae, were accused at that time of robbing an emigrant. I don't know but what they might have done it—they were young men and full of themselves, and had been given to occasional mischief. But this crime was more serious, so I don't know.

"At any rate, Porter Rockwell and a police officer set out to track them down and, as it was told to me, they caught my boys a ways up Emigration Canyon."

"Were your sons then jailed and brought before the court?"

"No, sir. At an out-of-the-way place there in the canyon, they were gunned down with a double-barreled shotgun in the hands, I believe, of Porter Rockwell."

"Were there witnesses to this fact, Missus McRae?"

"None that could or would talk."

"Then why do you attribute the atrocious act to Rockwell?"

"On account of what happened next. Rockwell and that police officer rode up to my house with the boys toes up in the back of a buckboard. Port dumped the bodies into the dirt of my door yard. Then he spoke to me. He said, 'Mizz McRae, had you done your duty when raising these boys, I would not have been forced to do mine.' "

"Gentlemen of the jury, in my hand I hold reports from numerous investigations The People have conducted into the affairs of Mister Rockwell. As you see, it is a stack of considerable thickness. I will not burden you nor the record of these proceedings with a full account. It is available for your perusal should you so choose. I must remind you, gentlemen, that Porter Rockwell stands accused—formally—only of the murder of John Aiken. We do not seek an indictment for all these crimes. But allow me, gentlemen, to read out to you a few of the more notorious incidents attributed to Rockwell. And recall the old saw, gentlemen: Where there's smoke, there's fire.

"July, 1850; Rockwell, upon orders from Mormon leaders, cured the sick old woman Alice Beardsley of the disease of 'apostasy' by slitting her throat.

"August, 1850; an unidentified argonaut on the trail to California was decapitated by Rockwell, Mister Scott the sheriff, and another man, merely on the suspicion that he had been a member of the Illinois mob that killed Mormon leaders Joseph and Hyrum Smith in 1844.

"April, 1851; Rockwell, leading a posse that captured four Ute Indians suspected of horse thievery, ordered the prisoners shot rather than returned for trial.

"October, 1853; a government surveying party under the command of Captain John W. Gunnison is wiped out by a band of Indians led by Kanosh. It is believed that Rockwell inspired or participated in the atrocity.

"April, 1856; the bullet-riddled bodies of Almon W. Babbit and his teamsters are found dead on the prairie near Fort Kearney, relieved of twenty thousand dollars in government funds en route to Utah for the construction of the Territorial Capitol. Papers belonging to Babbit and stock carrying his brand are found in the possession of Porter Rockwell days later at Fort Laramie.

"September, 1857; Rockwell initiates aggression against troops of the United States Army marching to quell rebellion in Utah. Raiders, under Rockwell's command, burn forage, stampede livestock, and destroy food and stores, thus endangering the lives of some 2,500 soldiers forced to winter on the high plains with insufficient supplies.

"February, 1858; Henry Jones and his mother, accused of an incestuous relationship, are mutilated and murdered at their home in Payson. It is widely known that Rockwell was dispatched by authorities to dispense this 'justice.'

"September, 1859; the sound of gunshots in downtown Great Salt Lake City led to the discovery of John Gheen, stretched out on the sidewalk with blood and brains oozing from two gunshot wounds to the head. Again, Porter Rockwell is widely believed to have been responsible for this 'apparent suicide' of a man troublesome to Church authorities.

"May, 1860; two known outlaws, Joachim Johnston and Myron Brewer, staggering drunkenly from a saloon toward a boarding house, are gunned down on the streets by an unseen assassin. Porter Rockwell is believed to have been responsible for saving the City the expense of a trial.

"December, 1866; the body of a black man, Thomas Colbourn, also known as Thomas Coleman, was found with throat slit from ear to ear. Rockwell, in this instance, the leader of a group enforcing the laws against miscegenation.

"Gentlemen of the Grand Jury, I could continue. While much of the evidence is sketchy and covered up by those who have been in *de facto* authority in the Utah Territory these past thirty years, there is no doubt that this carnage occurred. And, I submit, there is little doubt that Orrin Porter Rockwell was involved in these, and other, events attributed to his bloody hand. The most conservative estimate of the bodies in his wake runs to forty. Others place the tally much higher.

"The People ask you, as duly sworn members of this Grand Jury, to return a True Bill against this killer in one case and one case only—the murder of John Aiken. This indictment, alone, will be sufficient to bring Porter Rockwell to trial and justice; to rid our society of this scourge. Gentlemen, do your duty."

We the members of the Grand Jury currently seated in the First District Court in and for the Territory of Utah, believe, according to the evidence laid before us, that sufficient cause exists to suppose that he did commit the crime and do herewith return a True Bill against Orrin Porter Rockwell and order that, thus indicted, he be tried in court to determine his guilt or innocence in the murder of John Aiken.

Addendum: Let the record show that on 29 September 1877, Orrin Porter Rockwell was arrested by the United States Marshal for the murder of John Aiken and delivered to the penitentiary for safekeeping.

Addendum: Orrin Porter Rockwell did appear on 6 October 1877 before Associate Judge Phillip H. Emerson, where he was admitted to bail in the amount of $15,000, released from custody, and ordered to stand trial for murder during the October 1878 term of the First District Court.

Addendum: 9 June 1878; Orrin Porter Rockwell, awaiting trial for murder, died this day in his office at the Colorado Stables. Autopsy and inquest ordered.

Addendum: 11 June 1878; Upon physician testimony and autopsy results, the Coroner's Jury investigating the demise of Orrin Porter Rockwell today brought a verdict of death by natural causes due to failure of the heart's action, finding no evidence of injury or poisoning. The body was released for burial.

BULLWHACKER

The woman muttered under her breath, using words she would never say aloud. She cursed the oxen that had wandered off in the night. She cursed the rain that made the trail up Little Mountain a boggy mire, more stream than road. She cursed the tattered wagon sheets through which water seeped and dripped, fouling the scant supplies that must see her through the winter in the valley she hoped to reach this day, and cursed again the storm hindering that arrival.

And she cursed the man who, months ago, way back on the Elk-horn River, had done his best to prevent her joining the migration, declaring her wagons unfit for the road, her oxen not up to the trail, and a widow woman with a passel of children a burden on the company.

In a fit of ire, she had told the wagon master she would not only make the trip to the distant valley without his help, she would get there ahead of him. But now, the storm, the scattered stock, the muddy trail gave lie to her promise.

June 1848, Elkhorn River, Unorganized Territory
Cornelius Lott tugged the seat of his pants out of his backside cleavage. He wadded his floppy felt hat and raked his fingers through scant hair. He scuffed a foot through the dust, walked over to the biggest of the animals, and slapped it on the shoulder.

"Ain't no way, Mary," he said. "These here critters is the sorriest bunch of cattle I've ever seen. This one here's the onliest one looks like he can pull his own weight, and that not far. Rest of these ain't no good. How do you expect to get these wagons across the plains when you ain't got but four oxen barely worthy of the name yoked to half-growed steers and a cow?"

Mary Smith said nothing.

Lott slapped the ox on the rump in disgust. "And speaking of wagons. These of yours ain't in no better shape than the cattle. 'Specially this farm wagon. Damn thing'll fall apart 'fore you've gone half a mile. And what about that rattletrap ambulance hitched to the back of it? Which of these useless cattle you expect to pull *two* wagons? And that other'n ain't much better— looks ready to collapse just standin' there."

The sorry state of her means of conveyance was not news to Mary. The twenty-seven-mile trip from Winter Quarters to the Elkhorn where the wagon trains were assembling revealed the weakness of her preparation. Already, a wagon axle had cracked climbing a creek bank, a bow on a yoke had split, and a spoke had shattered on a wobbly wheel. And it was true the teams were mismatched and poorly trained. Even the loose stock—two milk cows with calves, and half a dozen sheep—seemed more prone to wander than submit to herding.

"Land sakes, Mary! You ain't even got a man to run this outfit!" Lott blustered, tucking plump thumbs behind his braces and giving them a tug.

John, at fifteen the oldest male in Mary's "family," stepped forward. Nine-year-old Joey threw his hat to the ground and, with doubled fists and red face, started for Lott. Mary grabbed the back of his collar with one hand and placed the other on John's chest.

With another tug at his galluses, the wagon master blustered on. "That there pimply boy ain't growed up enough to lead, and that hot-headed runt ain't worth a mention."

The boys strained forward, but Mary kept them in check.

"Them, and them three girls, that half-witted woman, and them two old women you brung along ain't gonna be nothin' but trouble. Never mind what the brethren say, I'm damned if I'll let you-all hold this company back."

Now it was Mary's face that flushed red. She studied the small crowd gathered to see what the commotion was about, then spoke.

"I will have you know, Cornelius Lott, that me and mine will be no burden to you. How do you suppose my Hyrum and I got from Kirtland to Far West? How do you suppose I got from Far West to Nauvoo, with Hyrum locked in jail? And how do you suppose I got from Nauvoo to Winter Quarters with Hyrum dead in his grave?"

Mary punctuated every sentence with a determined step in Lott's direction. She stopped a scant foot from the man and raised a pointed finger to within an inch of his nose.

"Do not be attempting to school me in the ways of wagon travel, Cornelius Lott. You are not to worry one iota about me or my family or my wagons or my livestock. And if what you mean by a 'man' to take charge is anything like the likes of you, I will happily take my chances with me and mine alone."

She emphasized the point with a thrust of her finger into the man's chest, then turned on her heel and walked away. Lott, flushed and flustered, sputtered for a response but found none.

Mary turned again to face him. "Know this. I will make the trip to Great Salt Lake City with this company, and I shall do it without your help. Not only will I arrive there in good order, I shall do so ahead of you!" She stood her ground and the crowd parted as Lott walked away.

The family Mary spoke of was no family in the traditional sense of the word. Joseph—Joey—was her son by Hyrum, and Martha Ann, just turned seven, also resulted from their all-too-brief marriage. The other children, John and his younger sisters,

Jerusha and Sarah, were the three youngest of Hyrum's children from his first wife, who died from complications following Sarah's birth. Two older girls from that union were married and gone.

In addition to the children, Mary had inherited three other women upon marrying Hyrum. "Aunty" Grinnels and Maggie Brysen, spinsters in their fifties, were part of the Smith household before Mary's arrival, helping to care for the children. The third woman, Jane Wilson, was a distressed soul, prone to fits. Hyrum, being a charitable sort, had taken responsibility for her care.

Now that responsibility was Mary's. And, later on the emigrant trail, that obligation would give Cornelius Lott yet another reason to confront Mary.

Jane was fond of taking snuff. And, noticing her supply diminished late one afternoon as the wagons circled for camp along the Platte River, she walked the mile or two up the trail to another wagon camp in the expedition to visit a friend and replenish her snuff box. Jane told Mary she would spend the night there, and rejoin her come morning.

Lott walked among his charges in the gray light of dawn, assuring all was in order before giving the command to roll out. After his customary dismay at the state of Mary's stock and equipment, he asked if all was well.

"That it is, Mister Lott."

With a snort, he grabbed his galluses and leaned toward the woman. "All well? You tell a lie, Mary Smith. I have it on good authority that a woman of your party is missing! Jane Wilson is gone, likely wandering alone in the wilderness. And who can say what tragedy may have befallen the poor woman? No thanks to you, this train will be delayed until she—or what remains of her—can be found!"

In his ire, he chose not to hear Mary's explanation.

"Well, then, Mister Lott, you may stay and search to your heart's content. But as for me and mine, we shall take to the trail and Miss Jane will join us in good time."

With a poke from her prod, Mary the bullwhacker "hawed" her team around the parked wagons waiting ahead of her. John and Joey followed with the farm wagon and trailer hitched behind, and the girls shepherded the loose stock along after. No one paid any attention to the florid-faced wagon master's hollering and stomping—save a few members of the company who turned to tightening the lashings on wagon sheets, checking the keys on oxbows, and finding other mundane tasks behind which they could conceal their amusement.

As Mary predicted, Jane rejoined the train and plodded along the Platte Valley with the rest of the Smith caravan as the days stretched into weeks.

It was somewhere in sight of Chimney Rock that one of Mary's uncertain draft animals finally failed her. But it was not a cow called to service under the yoke that faltered, nor one of the half-grown steers. For no apparent reason, one of the strongest of her oxen, the offside wheeler on her lead wagon, staggered and collapsed. The hulking beast gasped its last, tumbling to its side, and Mary watched in horror as the reflected sun faded in its glazed-over eye.

The woman dropped to her knees and sat with head bowed, whether in prayer or despair the members of her family could not say as they gathered. The other wagons in the train creaked to a stop and the circle of onlookers grew. Barely a breath was drawn among the bystanders until the wagon master elbowed his way through.

Lott pulled off his misshapen felt hat, wiped a palm over sweaty forehead and pate, then dried the damp hand on the seat of his pants.

"Mary Smith, I warned you about this very thing. Here we

sit idle on account of your poor preparation. That we have made it this far before you fulfilled my prophecy is the only surprise here."

Mary rose to her feet and brushed the dust from the skirt of her dress.

Lott pitched in. "Now, woman, unless you have a better idea, drag this animal out of the way and yoke up a milk cow, or one of those sheep if you'd rather. Be quick about it and you may catch up to our camp by nightfall. But we'll not wait."

No member of the company spoke up, but Lott heard much mumbling and muttering as his charges shuffled and scuffed.

"Well?" he hollered. "Get a move on!"

"Wait," Mary said. Her voice was soft, but reached every ear.

"What is it, woman?"

Mary studied the faces in the circle. She stepped closer to Lott. "I have a better idea."

Lott's only response was a furrowed forehead and arched eyebrows.

"You said, 'unless I have a better idea.' Well, I do," Mary said.

The furrows in Lott's forehead deepened and his lips tightened and turned down.

Mary's eyes locked on Lott's without blinking. "I want this ox healed."

The wagon master's eyes widened and his jaw worked at a reply, but none came.

"You hold yourself up as a pious man, *Brother* Lott. Lay hands on that ox and command him to rise."

Lott stammered and stuttered and sputtered and spit as crimson crept upward from his collar, coloring his entire visage. "I will not!" he finally managed. "It is sacrilege! It is blasphemous!"

"It is the Lord's will." Mary looked around at the stunned faces around her. "Does He not say, 'Ask, and it shall be given you'?" She again fixed her gaze on Lott. "I believe you will find that in Matthew, *Elder* Lott. And does not James tell us, 'Is any sick among you? Let him call for the elders of the church; and let them pray over him'? And does he not go on to say, 'The prayer of faith shall save the sick, and the Lord shall raise him up'?"

"It don't say nothing about no ox! It is an outrage to even suggest it. Besides, that critter ain't sick, he's dead!"

"Do you lack faith, Mister Lott? Surely the Lord's mercy extends to animals. I cannot quote chapter and verse, but there is a Proverb that reads, 'A righteous man regardeth the life of his beast.' Are you not a righteous man?"

Lott's hat hit the ground. "Enough of your spouting Scripture, Mary Smith. We're burning daylight here. Now, the rest of you, get a move on!"

Nobody moved.

Mary again scanned the faces in the crowd. "Josiah Fielding," she said, settling on the face of her cousin. "You are the closest this family has to a man at present. Will you lay hands on my ox?"

Josiah hemmed and hawed, nodded sheepishly, and looked to a friend who likewise signified his willingness.

"I forbid it!" Lott said.

The men ignored the wagon master and walked slowly toward the ox, removing their hats as they went. Lott followed, tugging at their shoulders and remonstrating at them with every step. The crowd drew closer, forming a tight semicircle around the fallen ox, shushing Lott. Fielding and his friend knelt beside the prostrate animal, laid hands on its horny head, and prayed fervently for the Lord's blessing. The prayer ended with a command to the ox to rise and walk and an "amen" repeated by the onlookers.

Only Lott failed to voice the benediction, instead emitting a derisive snort.

The ox responded with a snort of its own, drew in a long wheezing breath, rolled to its stomach and tucked its legs, hiked up its hind end, then the front, rattled the draw chain with a shake of its head, and looked for all the world ready to pull.

Mary, a smile teasing the corners of her mouth, said, "Well, why are you people standing around? You heard Mister Lott— get these wagons rolling."

Never mind Cornelius Lott's difficulties with Mary Smith. The man enjoyed a long—and deserved—reputation as a competent, capable leader. His assignment as wagon master of this train in the larger migration was neither surprising nor undeserved. Almost without question, the emigrants in his charge valued his leadership, followed his orders, and held to his advice. His malice toward Mary Smith was viewed as a curious and atypical oddity.

Given Lott's orderly approach to things and attention to detail, it was a wonderment to all that while Mary's inferior draft cattle slogged along day after day and mile after mile, it was Lott's oxen that next delayed the train.

It happened in the gray light of dawn one morning along the Sweetwater as the company approached Independence Rock. When the cattle were roused from their bed grounds and herded into camp to commence the day's work, several of the wagon master's oxen were not among them.

Expecting his teams had wandered away in search of greener grass, Lott assembled a party to search the surrounding plains. The oxen were soon located, dead on the ground.

No clue as to the cause of their demise was evident. Perhaps it was a bellyful of alkali-tainted water. More likely, the bull-whackers thought, in their grazing through the night the animals happened onto a patch of poisonous plants.

Lott was having none of it.

"Mary Smith!" Lott hollered as his mount slid to a stop next to her wagons. "What have you done, you infernal woman?"

Wide-eyed and open-mouthed, Mary had no answer, and could only shake her head.

"Well?"

She slid the kitchen box the rest of the way into the wagon and dusted off her hands. "Pray tell, Mister Lott, whatever are you talking about?"

"You know good and well what I'm talking about! What I want to know is how you did it."

Lott dismounted and moved toward Mary with long strides. She backed away, but bumped against the back of the wagon. John and Joey heard the ruction and came running, but Mary signaled them to stop short. Others halted their chores and gathered round. With little attempt to contain his anger, Lott told how his oxen—and only his oxen—had died in the night under circumstances he saw as suspicious.

"How, Mary?" he said. "Was it you, or did you send these boys of yours to do it?"

"I ask you again, what do you think we have done?"

"Don't play the innocent with me! What did you-all do to my cattle?"

Mary only stared at him. She looked to the boys, but both looked bewildered. She looked back at Lott and shook her head.

"Dammit, woman! My patience is wearing thi—"

"I will thank you to bridle your tongue, Mister Lott," Mary said as her ire rose along with the flush in her face. "We did nothing to your animals. To even think so is absurd. If no oxen belonging to others were so afflicted, it must be that they had better care in herding."

Mary paused to catch her breath, then, in a voice so soft most strained to hear it, she offered Mister Lott the use of some of her cattle, poor and trail-weary and unfit for service though they might be.

The wagon master shook a finger in Mary's face, but despite his working jaw, he could find no words. He turned and strode away, stopped to again waggle his finger at Mary from a distance, then walked away again. Realizing he had left his horse, he hove to and ordered a boy standing nearby to fetch it. Jerking the reins from the boy's hand, he yanked on the bit and dragged the startled horse away with him.

Winding up the trail toward South Pass, the company, following Lott's wagons, which were drawn by the few oxen he had left yoked to animals borrowed and bought from fellow travelers, plodded through meadows, sand dunes, rocky ridges, and sage-covered plains, and crossed, time and time and time again, the Sweetwater River. All along the way, the trail was littered with castoff goods from earlier emigrants, with dead cattle ranging from bloated corpses to whitened bones, and with graves—a seemingly endless parade of graves lining the wagon road. Some were covered with heaps of stone to keep varmints at bay; some displayed headboards pulled from wagon boxes and crudely carved with a name and date; some were marked only with sticks lashed together to form a cross. Others were unmarked, their presence made known only by disturbed earth; still other, older, graves by a depression where the ground subsided as the corpse beneath moldered away.

The presence of trailside graves was so common an occurrence by then that they went all but unnoticed; as ever-present as the dust and the wind. But the reality of it all came home to Mary one evening as she watched Jane Wilson perched upon a wagon tongue writing in her journal. This, too, was commonplace, but this evening it piqued Mary's curiosity.

She gathered her skirts and sat beside Jane on the tongue.

"You are a staunch keeper of records, Miss Wilson."

Jane nodded and closed the book, her place marked with her stub of a pencil.

"I do not mean to pry, but what is it you write?"

The woman blushed, and, head bowed, looked upward at Mary. "It is nothing," she said. "Just a few notes. Numbers, mostly."

"Numbers?"

Jane nodded. "I keep track of things. Keep count."

"May I see?"

Jane's flush increased as she handed the book to Mary. Mary paged backward through the entries. The notations were much the same.

July 19—14 miles, passed 2 graves
July 18—16 miles, 4 graves
July 16—made 15 miles, 7 graves passed
July 12—15 miles, 5 graves
July 11—13 miles, 15 graves
July 6—9 miles, passed 6 graves
July 5—18 miles, 9 graves
July 4—12 miles, passed 2 graves
July 1—16 miles, 3 graves
June 30—14 miles, 3 graves

And so on, all the way back to the Elkhorn River.

"You have a lovely hand, Miss Wilson."

"Thank you."

"But why keep such a dismal count?"

Jane again bowed her head, and Mary waited for an answer.

"If I . . . without someone . . . if no one takes note of those who died on this trail, I fear they will be forgotten. If their passing goes unnoticed by those who followed them, will they have died in vain?"

Mary gently closed the book and handed it back to Jane.

When the Oregon and California trails diverged from the Mormon Trail at Fort Bridger, the Utah-bound emigrants knew they were on the home stretch of their thousand-mile trek from Winter Quarters to Great Salt Lake City. The wagons crossed the Bear River and creaked and crawled down Echo Canyon before facing their last obstacle to reaching home.

Although Big Mountain was a barely noticeable ridge among the peaks of the Wasatch range, climbing it put the train at its most elevated point on the entire trip. A scant twenty miles from their new home, the Salt Lake Valley was within sight from the summit. But getting down off the top of Big Mountain proved one of the toughest trials on the trail.

Mary, John, and Joey unyoked the lead teams on their wagons and rough-locked the rear wheels by chaining them together. The wagons slipped and slid and skidded one at a time down the hill as John poked, prodded, geed, and hawed the wheelers around the stumps of cut trees frequenting the track. After getting the Smith wagons down safely, he did the same a dozen times more, helping other wagons in the train negotiate the steep course. At the bottom, with wheels unlocked and lead teams back under yoke, the wagons traveled another mile or two along the road to make camp on the banks of Brown's Creek.

"A long day for you, John," Mary said when the boy plopped down in the dusk on a log. Where his ragged clothing wasn't sweat-stained it was saturated with dust. "And this your sixteenth birthday."

John shrugged. "Wagons all down safe," he said between mouthfuls of boiled rice and raisins. "Should be out of these mountains by tomorrow."

"So they say. But the ridge we have yet to cross—Little Mountain, they call it—to reach the canyon down to the valley looks much the same as the one we crossed today. The climb is steep, and the descent as well, they tell us." Mary dusted flour off her apron as she studied the fading sky. "I do not like the look of the weather. I fear there is a storm in the offing."

"Joey out with the critters?"

"That he is. Off there in the woods somewhere," Mary said, pointing with her chin in the direction the boy had taken, as she hefted an oven of biscuits from the fire and set it aside to cool. "I expect he will have them bedded and be back soon."

And so he was. The fire burned low and glowed to ashes as the Smith camp slept. With the ribbon of dawn barely discernible in the east, Mary shook the girls and women awake, and rousted out the boys to fetch the stock.

But someone—Cornelius Lott, they expected, or someone under his orders—had been there before them. None of the Smith cattle were anywhere in sight. After reporting the loss, the boys set out to search farther afield.

Mary stood forlorn beside her packed wagons. Lined up beside her like so many tenpins were Jane Wilson, Aunty Grinnels, Maggie Brysen, and the girls—Jerusha, Sarah, and Martha Ann.

The wagon master did not bother to tell Mary the train would not be waiting for her. Lott merely looked back and smiled as his lead wagon, first in the caravan on this last day of the journey, rolled past.

In keeping with Mary's prediction, the sky had clouded up overnight. Rather than the morning brightening as it should, it dimmed as heavy black clouds rolled over the crest of the Wasatch, threatening to boil over. And they did. With wagons strung out along the steep trail up the ridge, oxen bearing down under the load and bullwhackers urging them on, the storm broke.

Lightning flashed, the bolts raining down in overlapping arcs. Thunder cracked and rolled and boomed and echoed off the mountainsides. Rain fell in sheets, pouring onto the dusty road up the ridge and turning it into a quagmire. Panicked oxen thrashed and kicked and bucked and bolted, threatening to overturn wagons as the wheels slipped and slid and sank into the mud.

Fetching logs and rocks in a near terror, men, women, and children chocked wheels so the wagons wouldn't roll backward down the mountain. Drovers tugged and wrenched and jerked on draw chains and clevises and oxbows and yokes to free the panicked animals in an attempt to keep the wagons on their wheels, rather than toppled and tipped over. Once free, the uncontrollable cattle stampeded down the ridge and disappeared into the tempest.

The storm passed, the clouds thinned, and rays of sunlight sliced through, illuminating the chaos on the ridge. Curses, wailing, and cries of despair tumbled down the hill to where Mary and her charges crawled out from under dripping wagon covers.

They did not wait long before John and Joey, soaked and sodden, followed the Smith cattle and livestock out of the woods and into the campsite. Sheltered somewhat in groves of quaking aspen and patches of scrub oak, the animals had weathered the storm better than the hitched oxen exposed on the bare ridge.

"The brindle milk cow and her calf are missing, Miz Mary," John said, hat in hand. "And two of the sheep."

"That is as it may be. Once we reach the valley, we will come back to find them. Are these animals fit to work?" Mary said with a nod toward the cattle, ready to resume her duties as a bullwhacker on the emigrant trail.

"Yes'm," John said, and they set about the business of yoking the draft cattle to the wagons.

The oxen, the young steers, and the unlikely cow, long since accustomed to the yoke, huffed and grunted their way up Little Mountain, finding enough firm ground beside the rutted track to ease past the mired wagons.

Reaching the head of the train and Cornelius Lott's conveyances, disabled and helpless, Mary Smith did not return the wagon master's loathsome stare. She marched on by with all the dignity an unfit widow woman could muster, leading her unsuitable wagons, useless animals, and hodgepodge of a family, her eyes fixed on the trail ahead, the end of which she would reach by nightfall.

THE DEATH OF DELGADO

I came face to face with my future the day Christian Delgado rode onto our ranch. At least I hoped—dreamed—I had.

Delgado was a cowboy.

Oh, there were plenty of cowboys in our part of the county. But Delgado was a different sort. Flashy isn't the right word, but there was a certain amount of sparkle to the man and his trappings. He was some strange crossbreed of what nowadays we'd call Californio, buckaroo, and vaquero. Heavy-roweled Mexican spurs, high-topped boots with tall, underslung heels, short chaps that covered his lower legs with nothing but leather fringe, wool vest up top.

His saddle was especially eye-catching. Unlike the plain and practical kacks around our place, his slickfork was silver mounted with conchos, buckles, and bands; his other tack and horse jewelry likewise festooned.

As I said, I was enthralled the minute I saw him. He filled the dreamy eyes of this eleven-year-old Idaho ranch kid with a near-perfect vision of what a cowboy ought to look like.

Mind you, he wasn't anything outside of ordinary from a physical standpoint. He wasn't tall, maybe seven inches above five feet, hung on an average frame that was neither slender nor stocky. Not particularly handsome, I'd say, but neither was he hard to look at. His face, save for a sharp-trimmed mustache, was so clean-shaven it always looked as if he'd just now toweled off the last flecks of lather. He was, I suppose, in his twenty-third or -fourth year that summer.

Even though Christian Delgado had never seen the south side of the Rio Grande, he was, to folks hereabouts, a Mexican. (Some called him a greaser, but never within his hearing.) But he claimed descent direct from the Spaniards of old, and offered deep green eyes and the pale skin on the inside of his forearms as proof of his genealogy. And, to this fascinated boy, he did carry himself with the elegance of a conquistador, a caballero, a don. There's no doubt he was the kind of man folks paid attention to—the focus of attention in most every crowd, with the quiet confidence of one accustomed to that attention.

He showed up in the Curlew Valley because he heard that Dad had horses that needed rode. He'd heard right.

Dad and Uncle Evan had a sizeable ranch and raised a good many horses for sale. Nothing fancy, mind you, just good solid cow horses and some heavier stock for driving. We also put up a considerable amount of winter feed cut from hay meadows, and ran cattle on range that required the beef to graze at a fast walk just to get to enough grass to work up a cud of a size worth chewing.

And so, Delgado went to work. Most of the time he spent horseback, either tending the cow herd or breaking horses. His means of training was simple: a good horse is the result of a lot of wet saddle blankets. When he wasn't sweating the edge off green-broke colts on long trails up and down the hills and canyons of our rocky, brush-covered country, you'd find him starting even greener colts in the round pen. He'd sometimes have half a dozen tied up outside waiting their turn.

Every chance that summer, you'd find me hanging by my elbows from the top rail, eyeing his every move. On a lucky day, I'd ride beside him through the brush, doing my best to handle one of his graduating students like a real hand—like Delgado—would. While abroad on the range we'd see to the cattle; doctoring any that needed it and drifting them back toward home if they wandered too far. Lucky days, for sure, for a kid with cowboy dreams.

But I wasn't all that lucky all that often that summer.

Dad, you see, was digging a well up in the corner of the south pasture. Water was scarce in Curlew Valley, and the stream through that end of our place, while wet enough in springtime, flowed only shallow dust by late summer. A reliable water supply was always to be desired, and always to be realized when chance presented itself. So when Dad watched a forked willow stick in the hands of an itinerant water witch take a nosedive, he dedicated his summer to digging a well.

Digging a well in those days and in that place wasn't a complicated job—you just grabbed the handle of a shovel and put the business end of it to work. The only thing you needed to worry about, Dad always said, was to fill up the back half of the shovel—the front half would take care of itself, he said.

He also told me that when you stood in the deep bottom of the long hole the well was becoming, you could look up at the narrow opening and see stars shining in the middle of the brightest day. But all I could see those long days helping out at the well was lost opportunities—squandered time, wasted time, time I wanted to be with Delgado.

Instead, I spent my time daydreaming about what I was missing. Now and then, in answer to Dad's call echoing up the hole, I'd pull the well rope off the stake it was anchored to and knot it to the clevis on the singletree, then kiss ol' Socks into a shuffling walk, watching the rope feed its way through the squeaky hand-carved wooden block lashed to the top of the cedar pole tripod over the hole. When the heavy bucket cleared the hole, I'd whoa-up Socks, swing the laden tub over to solid ground, and call the horse back to slack the rope until the bucket landed.

Ol' Socks didn't even need a jerk line to control, just voice commands.

Bucket settled, I'd walk over to the horse, unhook the rope out of the clevis, walk back and two-hand-heft-and-grunt the bucket over to the pile and dump out the hole it held. Hand-over-hand all along the length of the rope, I'd lower the bucket back down the well, careful not to let it fall too fast for Dad to grab before it beaned him, then take another hitch to the anchor stake. As Dad commenced putting more of the hole in the bucket, I'd bring Socks around and back him up close to the hole so we'd be ready to haul up the next load.

Mostly, the big bucket would be heaped with dirt and rocks, but for a few days now it had been showing more and wetter mud, so Dad was feeling like the bottom of the well couldn't be far off.

A couple of times a day, besides the trip up for dinner and the one at the end of the day, Dad would ride the bucket up for a rest and some fresh air. Sometimes the air down there would get pretty thick, he said, and that meant more trips up the hole and longer stretches in daylight before going back down.

From time to time he would fashion a bundle of grass hay about the size of the hole, tie it to the rope, and plunger it up and down the well to force the heavy air out. A trick he learned, he said, from an old "Cousin Jack" miner who lived in town.

Dad sensed my fascination with Christian Delgado, and knew I saw in the young man the realization of my cowboy yearnings. And, of a normal summer, he would not have objected to my making of myself a full-time apprentice to the horseman. But he needed my help at the well, what with Uncle Evan and the hired hands busy with haying from dark to dark those long hot days. And he often enough made me realize he appreciated my help, and promised there'd be a time for cowboying.

Truth be told, Dad wished he could be out cowboying too,

for he was a man who loved horses and cattle. I knew, too, that he admired the touch Delgado had with horses. Not as much as I admired him, maybe, but even through eyes wrinkled with experience Dad saw something beyond the ordinary in that cowboy's ways.

The day Delgado died dawned like any other.

He haltered and tied that day's mounts to the rail outside the round corral. Uncle Evan and the hay hands hitched up a team and hayrack and rolled out for the meadow. And Dad and I and ol' Socks shuffled slow toward the hole in the far corner of the south pasture.

"It's getting pretty boggy down there, son," Dad said.

"How much deeper you gonna have to go," I asked through a wide yawn as I fisted some of the sleep out of my eyes.

"Can't say. The mud makes for a messier job, but the water does cool it down some."

The past day or two he'd been coming out of the hole muddy above his knees, and he'd said the bottom got softer with every shovelful he hefted out of it. We were threading a good sixty feet of rope down the hole by then.

"I hope, in another day or three, to have to tread water down there. Then I'll know it's a good well. If it draws water enough in the dead of summer, it ought to serve year round. And, near as I can tell after straining the mud through my teeth, it's going to be good, sweet water."

Being a kid, and lacking proper appreciation for such things, I answered with another yawn.

We soon settled into the day's routine, and it did not appear anything would be along to break it. As usual, a breeze kicked up as the day warmed then grew gusty and dusty as the air got hotter. A dust devil whipped up out on the flat and I watched tumbleweeds spin around and around and up and up and eventually peel off to roll back to earth.

"Up!" Dad hollered from down the hole, but his call hardly registered.

"Up!" he said again, louder, jolting me back into the present.

I worked the rope off the stake, knotted it through the clevis, and kissed Socks into motion. Unlike me, he'd paid attention to Dad's call and was ready to lean into the harness. By now, the both of us could practically do the job in our sleep and I was soon back on the powder box I used for a seat with barely any recollection of having left it.

This time it was the wind that woke me from my daydreams—heavy, hot gusts peppering me with dirt and debris. I squinted over my shoulder to see that dust devil right there and bearing down on us. With arms wrapped around the top of my head, I fell to my knees and made myself small.

Through the blow I could hear, barely, rattling harness and ol' Socks snorting and blowing. I peeked past a bent elbow in time to see the horse sidestep then shy backward, haunches down and head up as he tried to back away from the swirling wind.

It was gone in an instant, but by then Socks was caving off the raw rim of the well, raining dirt and pebbles down the hole. Upset all the more, he kept snorting and shuffling until his hind legs slipped and he rolled onto his back and into the shaft.

He couldn't fall far—he wedged tight against the sides no more than six or eight feet down, all the while thrashing and screaming. He skidded another few feet and settled there.

"Dad?" I squawked with what little voice I could find. Socks blocked the echo I was used to hearing in the hole, and I thought maybe he blocked my voice as well. Beyond the horse there was nothing to see but darkness. The falling dirt must have broken Dad's coal oil lantern or knocked it into the slop.

"Dad?" Again, louder this time.

I didn't even realize I'd been holding my breath until it

rushed out with relief when I heard Dad's reply.

"Honey?" he yelled. "What happened up there?"

"Socks fell in the well!"

"I see that. Think you can help him out?"

Our yelling upset the horse again, and his scratching and thrashing sent another rain of dirt and stones rattling down on Dad.

"I don't think so," I said. "He's too far down. And he's upside down."

"Damn!" I heard Dad say—the first foul word I'd ever heard out of his mouth, the hearing of which shocked me almost as much as the mess we were in.

"We'd best be quiet so's not to spook him any worse than he is," he said. "Check the rope, see that it's tied off tight."

I hustled over to the stake and took another double half hitch around it just to make sure.

"Is it all right?"

"I think so."

"Now, son, you just sit tight." I heard him working the shovel as he chinked a ledge in the shaft where he set the bucket to get it out of the way. "What I'm going to do is try to climb out of here. Think there's room for me to squeeze past ol' Socks if I can get up there?"

"Maybe," I said. "I don't think so."

The horse took another fit, and in the squirming and straining slipped another foot or two. The block lashed to the tripod started to sway and rattle, the rope jerking rhythmically as Dad pulled himself steadily upward. Dirt and rocks splashing in the bottom said he was using his feet to help claw his way out of the well.

The rope stopped jerking from time to time as he wedged himself against the sides to rest. Soon, the pulse of his grasping hands would travel up the rope again and before long I could hear his breathing, and the strain in it.

Then the horse must have sensed Dad's presence beneath him, and not known what to make of it. In a renewed bout of heaving and clawing, twisting and straining, ol' Socks came loose of a sudden and slid down the well, scraping rocks, dirt, and Dad off the sides and taking it all down with him. They bottomed out with a thick splash and heavy thud that reverberated all the way to the surface. A few more pebbles and dirt clods trickled down, falling into silence along with the fading echo.

I wasn't there to hear the quiet.

After crossing the pasture at a dead run, I stumbled to a stop, the rails of the round corral the only thing keeping me from tumbling all the way down.

Delgado had seen me coming and waited quietly across the fence atop one of the colts, which shied and scrambled backward when I hit the fence. When the colt stopped, Delgado flexed his hips and kissed his lips to urge it forward, finally touching it with the spurs. A soft haul on the hackamore reins stopped the colt's sudden lunge and Delgado settled down into the saddle as I struggled for breath.

"It's, it's Daddy," I said. "He's down. The well. Socks fell in. On top. Of him."

The corral gate was already swinging open. Delgado had dismounted in an instant and already he and the colt were on my side of the fence. Without a word, he grabbed me by the waist and swung me aboard the skittish colt.

"You hurry. Tell Evan to bring the team and his men to the well. They are unloading. Tell him to bring the derrick cable. Hurry. I will go to your father."

That horse was only half under my control, if that, on the run to the hay yard. Once or twice he kicked up his heels and tried to bog his head, but by sawing on the reins I was able to

114

prevent a come-apart or complete runaway.

He didn't want to stop when we tore out of the hay meadow and into the stackyard. I cranked his head to one side until it was practically in my lap and he finally came around in a circle and stopped as Uncle Evan and the three workers looked on.

Before the story was half told, Uncle Evan had scrambled down off the stack of loose hay, chopped the derrick cable in two with a hay knife, and was pulling it screaming through the pulleys on the derrick. The hay hands lit into the load like windmills, forking it off every side of the wagon. They kept at it even as Uncle Evan heaved heavy coils of derrick cable over the rack on the front of the wagon and then climbed up, hooked a leg over and whipped up the team with the lines.

As the hay wagon clattered and bounced out of the stack-yard, I tapped my heels to the colt's sides and hoped he'd do something other than go to pitching. He snorted some and flung his head around, but another soft kick in the belly convinced him to line out and walk. Once he settled in, I urged him into a long trot and figured to let it go at that.

Delgado was just clearing the lip of the well when I rode up. Any hope I had for Dad washed away in the tears streaming down his muddy face.

He'd stopped only long enough to grab a lantern from the milking stall and an ax and shovel and pry bar from the tool shed—whatever was at hand, I guess. By the time Uncle Evan arrived, Delgado was already at the bottom of the well, having slid down the rope with the lit lantern in his teeth. But all he could find to do was pull the bucket out of the mess, tie it to the rope, and ask Evan to haul him up—which he did, by hand, with help from the three men on his hay crew.

The cowboy stepped out of the bucket as it reached the surface and plopped down on my box.

"I cannot find him," he said as he absent-mindedly scratched with a fingernail at the mud that covered his chaps, then unbuckled and peeled them off. "The hole is full of nothing but broken horse and mud. I felt around as much as I could. Nothing." He unbuttoned and pulled off his vest, then tugged his shirt over his head.

Delgado unsheathed his knife and went to whittling on the ax handle. It seemed a poor choice of activities in the circumstances. I said "What—"

"There is no room to work the ax in the hole," he said, cutting off my question. Although his voice was quiet, anger, frustration maybe, was as evident as if he had shouted. "It is too tight."

Still unsure what he was doing, I thought it best to keep my peace.

He snapped off the handle and shaved the raw edge to smooth the splinters as best he could. To Uncle Evan, he said, "I guess we won't be needing that cable. There is no way we'll lift that horse out of there without caving in the sides. He will have to come up in the bucket. Lower me down, then get your team ready. It will be too much lifting to do by hand."

Evan and at least one of his hay hands were years older than Delgado. It didn't occur to me at the time, but I have since wondered why it was the younger man giving orders in that tense situation, and why the others complied without question or comment.

It did not dawn on me, either, what Delgado was doing down there until the first bucket came up. Blood sloshed over the sides as Uncle Evan swung it away from the well. The horse's head hung over the rim, muzzle stained scarlet and nostrils dripping gore.

I hit my knees as that red mess splashed to the ground and I heaved up what was left of breakfast and kept heaving until there was nothing left to come up and then I heaved some more.

And even after that, the sound of Delgado and his ax at work down the well would set me to gagging all over again.

One front quarter, then another, came out of the hole in poorly butchered pieces. Then Delgado came up. Blood-spattered and gasping, he sat flat to the ground and sucked in air.

"Anything?" Evan asked.

"No. Nothing."

Uncle Evan asked no more questions, simply stared vacantly at the hired man on the ground.

"You're spent. I'll go down," he finally said.

"No. There is no room. I can hardly get any leverage myself, and I am smaller than you. I will finish the job."

He said the lantern kept flickering out from lack of air, so he gave up trying to keep it burning and did his awful work in the dark. Worst of all, worse than the dark, worse than the heat, worse than the mud, he told us, was the stink. Even in the open air the stench of blood and torn flesh was overpowering when the wind swirled it your direction. It got worse when broken entrails and smashed organs topped the pile.

Finally, the second hind leg, broken at an odd angle, plopped out of the bucket and onto the pile dripping mud and blood and that was the end of ol' Socks.

Standing with hands grasping spread knees, Uncle Evan bent over the lip of the well awaiting word from Delgado. From time to time he would hear him sloshing around down there, or the occasional splash.

Finally, "I have found a hand."

Later, "I have freed as much of him as I can, but he is stuck fast. You will have to send down the cable."

From the hay wagon, Uncle Evan fetched a steel pulley and short length of chain and hooked it to the tripod next to the wooden block through which the well rope was threaded. As he tested the strength of his work, his men stretched the kinks out of the cable. He threaded it through the pulley, quickly clamped a clevis to the end, and shoved the wire rope down the shaft an arm's length at a time.

It seemed an eternity until Delgado asked to be lifted up in the bucket. He stepped out, cut the well rope from the bail, then pulled the end through the block and tossed it out of the way so it would not tangle with the cable.

"I don't know. He is stuck pretty tight. I got a loop around him but I don't know," he told Evan as they watched the hands hitch the cable to the doubletree harnessed to the team. "I never could feel his feet. Too deep."

As the slack slowly came out of the cable he said, "I hope he doesn't come up like that horse."

Uncle Evan took over the team, and with his easy hands at the lines they leaned slowly into the load.

Nothing.

He urged the horses on—tugs creaked, singletrees cracked. The cable hummed, the pulley trembled. The heavy cedar posts in the tripod groaned and their thick bottoms pushed up ridges in the dirt as they tried to spread wider, threatening collapse.

The team grunted and strained and leaned harder into their collars as Uncle Evan, in desperation, slapped one horse then the other on the rump with the lines. Slowly, almost imperceptibly, they moved ahead. Half the length of a hoof. Another. And then, with a release felt deep in the belly of every one of us, the team was walking free.

The pulley from the hay derrick squealed as it slowly rotated. Uncle Evan handed the lines to another of the men as the team's distance from the hole increased and he quickly followed the cable back to the well to stand beside me and Delgado.

Dad came up belt buckle first. Uncle Evan collapsed in a heap when he saw his broken brother, bent double, backwards, swinging slowly from the derrick cable.

I stared, uncomprehending. I guess my day's ration of distress was long since used up, to be replaced by shock and resignation.

Like I had done so many times, Delgado swung the load away from the hole as the team backed slack into the cable and settled it to solid ground. He pulled the pin out of the clevis and cast it aside and carefully, gently, gathered Dad's limp body in his arms and carried him to the hay wagon. Then he turned for the house and walked away.

Delgado did not die that day.

At least not like Dad was dead.

But the spirit was gone out of him as surely as if it had been his body we pulled out of that temporary grave at the bottom of the well.

In a way, I guess it was.

He didn't stop at the bunkhouse any longer than it took to stuff his few belongings into his war bag. I don't know what he wore on his feet when he left our place. His soggy high-topped boots with the blood-and-mud-encrusted Mexican spurs still strapped to them were left standing outside the door, abandoned to the well as surely as Dad's were; his sucked off in the muck in the bottom of that hole where, I suppose, they still are.

So far as I know, ol' Socks was the last horse Delgado ever touched.

For years, he stayed around these parts setting his hand to a variety of jobs—sacking wheat at the feed and seed, clerking at a grocery store, tending bar, that sort of thing. Last I heard, he was somewhere off in Wyoming pushing folks around in wheelchairs in a convalescent hospital.

I led that green-broke colt he'd mounted me on that day back to the yard and pulled off Delgado's silver-mounted saddle

and hauled it inside the tack shed. It has been there ever since,
hanging from a rafter on a rawhide tether.

BLACK JOE

The dun horse trotted in with flecks of foam floating off its shoulders like snowflakes. Sweat runnelled from under the skirts of the empty saddle down the flanks, dripping away with the horse's every footfall. Thin streams of blood glowed red on the left hind leg, and a patch of hide the size of a five-dollar bill flapped and dangled above, peeled from the thigh. The horse slowed to a walk, favoring the right foreleg, the knee of which showed a slight swelling. Stopping at the corral fence, the gelding hung its head between spraddled front legs, sucking air and quaking like an aspen leaf.

"Sonofabitch," Andy Hill muttered under his breath. The other cowhands in the pen watched as Andy climbed the rails. The horse flinched when he dropped to the ground, his boots spitting out puffs of dust as he lit. He spoke low to the trembling animal as he grasped the cheek piece on the bridle. The other hand came back smeared with blood when he stroked the neck, the horse half-heartedly shying backward a step at the touch.

"Sonofabitch," Andy mumbled again. The blood staining his hand came from a long abrasion along the neck. He pushed clumps of mane away, revealing droplets of blood oozing from flesh relieved of its hair and layers of skin, as if grazed by a farrier's rasp.

Andy sidled along the left side of the horse. Dangling askew in its leathers hung a crushed oxbow stirrup. Higher up, the saddle horn was smashed, leather was skinned off the swells, and skirts and fenders were barked and scratched. Crusted blood trimmed a gouge on the horse's rump still leaking and clotting fresh gore.

"What the hell happened, you think?"

Andy heard, but did not comprehend the question. He turned back toward the corral and saw Brenn Nelson, leaning against the top rail with his elbows hitched over.

"Huh?"

Brenn cleared his throat and spat. "What do you suppose happened to that horse? Better still, where's Mister Kirkwood?"

Andy shook his head. "Don't know."

"Six bits says it's that damn Black Joe."

"You're probably right. But we best be finding out."

Andy told the other hands to tend to Kirkwood's horse and saddle a fresh one, then get on with the branding. He led his own horse out of the pen with Brenn trailing. Following a brief stop at the bunkhouse, rifles rode in scabbards hanging from their saddles and pistols nestled in belted holsters—Brenn's at his waist, Andy's secured to the saddle bow—as the men spurred their mounts into a long trot, the led horse following, onto the sage plain in the direction from which the battered horse had come.

Duncan Kirkwood owned the ranch where Brenn Nelson cowboyed and Andy Hill worked as straw boss. The spread held title to only a few hundred acres along the broad banks of the river bottom as it meandered between bluffs cut into the high desert, but claimed grazing rights on a hundred square miles of sage-covered plains, juniper-studded hills, rock-strewn canyons, eroded arroyos, and dusty playas.

It took a lot of acres to feed a cow in this country. Cattle scattered far and wide across the expanse, chasing grass a day's distance from the occasional seeps and springs and thin streams that offered scant refreshment. The stock willingly shared the water and grass with roving pronghorns and wandering mule deer. Now and then a Basque or Mexican herder and his sheep might encroach on Kirkwood's claim, but the woolly flocks soon caught the notice of Kirkwood's cowboys, and were driven off under threat of gunfire.

Also rustling for a living on the range was a band of mustangs. Wilier than the deer and warier than the antelope, the herd wandered unseen most of the time. The cowhands knew they were always out there—hoofprints around waterholes, hair clinging to thorn bushes, decaying carcasses, and dry bones all spoke of their presence. But the horses themselves were seldom seen, and even then the glimpse was fleeting, often nothing more than flashes of color in a distant cloud of retreating dust, or a brief appearance of the band's stud silhouetted on a ridge on the far horizon.

Sightings often led to the laying of plans among the cowboys to run down the herd and rope out the best-looking of the horses. But mustanging was forbidden on the ranch. "No sense ruining good horses just to catch worse ones," was the excuse Kirkwood gave for the order.

But Andy knew the real reason Kirkwood ordered his hands to stay away from the wild band. And that reason was Black Joe.

One day last summer, Andy and Brenn were working outlying ridges on Kirkwood's range, pushing cows and calves back toward the river. Shaded up from the afternoon sun in the shadow of a cedar tree, the men were sipping from canteens and gnawing on bacon-stuffed biscuits when their ground-tied mounts started in to snorting, ears pointed across the draw toward the opposite ridge. A black horse appeared atop the slope, trumpeting his presence and then scratching at the air as he reared up on his hind legs.

"That's that Black Joe stud," Andy told Brenn.

"Well, I'll be damned," Brenn said. "Black Joe. I've heard

some of the boys mention him. Say he runs a band of mares out here. Say they've wanted to round 'em up but boss don't allow it."

"He sure don't."

"Why is that?"

Andy studied his partner's face as Brenn studied the stud horse still making their mounts nervous as he paraded back and forth against the clear blue sky. When finally he spoke, Andy repeated the oft-told reason. "Well, Mister Kirkwood, he don't think them mustangs amount to much in the way of horseflesh. Ain't worth the wear and tear on ranch horses to run them down."

Brenn laughed. "Aw, hell, ever'body knows that. But that don't stop nobody from chasin' 'em now and then, if only for the sport of it. I've rode for outfits that made mustangin' a regular deal—even caught some half-decent horses from time to time."

"Well, that's what Mister Kirkwood says, just the same," Andy said after a long pause.

"I take it you don't believe him."

Andy paused even longer as they watched Black Joe paw, snort, toss his head, turn tail, and trot away with tail and snout held high. Then, "It ain't that I don't believe him. It's just that I know there's more to it."

After another long pause and a sip of water, he spun the story.

As Andy told it, Kirkwood had been out riding one distant summer day with his daughter. Fiona was eight, maybe nine, years old at the time, as Andy recalled. She rode a palomino mare Kirkwood had found for her, the girl in love with the idea of golden horses with silvery manes—a notion likely picked up from reading about palomino ponies in books she devoured.

They often rode together because the rancher doted on the

girl. An only child, and a late arrival in a marriage that had long since despaired of the blessing of children, Fiona was a pleasant surprise. The very thought of the girl brought a smile to Duncan Kirkwood's lined and furrowed face. Saddling the palomino mare and a mount for himself was a welcome chore for the rancher; one he took up at her every request.

"Don't know exactly why they went ridin' that day," Andy said, "but it don't really matter. That girl liked to ride and the boss was always happy to oblige. The thing was, that little mare was in season. Mister Kirkwood didn't know it at the time, but he found out soon enough when the trouble started . . ."

Andy drifted away on his thoughts, munching slowly on a bite of biscuit. Brenn held his peace, sipping water and flicking biscuit crumbs from his shirtfront. After a moment, Andy flinched, gave his head a shake, and blinked awareness back into his eyes. "Sorry. My mind drifted off the trail for a minute there."

He cleared his throat, then swallowed another mouthful of water from his canteen. "Anyhow, Kirkwood and the girl reined up atop them low bluffs above the river out by Twin Cedars. Them mustangs was feeding down in the bottoms. The horses hadn't smelled them coming on account of the way the wind was blowing, but then that mare of Fiona's whinnied. That stirred up the band, and the lead mare bolted and the bangtails followed her up the trail on the opposite bluffs. But that Black Joe stud pinned his ears back and came at the boss and the girl.

"Kirkwood told Fiona, 'Ride hard for the ranch!' and slapped that palomino mare on the rump with his bridle reins, and watched her whippin' up that little horse through the brush. She likely didn't know what all the fuss was about, but she could see her daddy was scared and kept bangin' that pony's belly with her bootheels.

"Meantime, Black Joe was clawin' his way up that bluff and

Mister Kirkwood met him when he reached the top—he rode hell-for-leather broadside right into that stud horse, knockin' him back off the ledge and tumblin' his own horse down after him.

"The boss said that stud would find his feet now and then as they slid and tumbled downslope, and when he did, he'd come after him. He managed to get his lass rope unstrung from the saddle by the time they made the river bottom, and he used it to beat off Black Joe as much as he could.

"Said he fought that stud horse for what seemed like an hour—sometimes from horseback, sometimes on the ground.

"I guess Black Joe finally got tired of that rawhide reata larrupin' him, or that sorrel horse kickin' at him, 'cause he finally left off and hit the river. He kicked up dust along the trail his mares took earlier. Mister Kirkwood said he stopped on top of the bluff up there, turned around, and give him one last look, then trotted off out of sight.

"When Mister Kirkwood got back to the ranch, first thing he wanted to know was if Fiona made it back safe. Then he unsaddled his horse, stitched up the worst of the cuts, and rubbed the horse's legs down good with liniment.

"All this, he done in a shirt shredded in the back and missin' one sleeve, and a hat with half the brim tore loose from the crown. Had a hoof scrape down the middle of his back that was oozin' blood in places, and his neck and shoulders was all bloody from a gash on his head—but he wouldn't take no help for hisself till he knowed his girl was all right and his horse was tended to."

Brenn could only shake his head at the story.

Andy took a minute to catch his breath from more talking than he usually accomplished in a day's time. Then, "Well, I guess you can see why the boss don't want us messin' with them wild horses."

The old story rolled around in Brenn's memory as they followed the backtrail through the brush. "You reckon the old man might have a different idea about chasin' mustangs now?"

"Maybe so."

"I'm willin' to bet that when we find him, first thing he'll want to do is get on the hunt for Black Joe."

"Maybe so—if it is Black Joe that he tangled with."

"Ah, hell, Andy. You know damn well it was. Ain't nothin' else out here could lay that kind of hurt on a saddle horse. Lord only knows what he did to Mister Kirkwood."

The men rode on in silence, each painting his own picture of what they would find when they came to the end of the faint trail left by Kirkwood's saddle horse. The track of the injured animal had traced a more-or-less beeline to ranch headquarters, maintaining the general direction as it flowed between low ridges, veered around outcrops, descended arroyos, and climbed out of ravines.

A dry cow, three cows with calves, and a yearling steer loosely scattered and grazing the shady side of a low ridge told the cowboys they were near where Kirkwood had been, for the assortment of stock must have been gathered and driven there, or somewhere nearby, and left only recently to wander. These had to be strays Kirkwood meant to trail back to headquarters when interrupted in the chore.

Andy and Brenn stopped and studied the cattle for minute.

"Well, what do you think?"

Andy did not answer at once, sitting with his hands stacked on the saddle horn, watching the cows watching them. Then, "Flat Rock Spring ain't far from here—just over that ridge. Was I Mister Kirkwood and unhorsed out here, I believe that's where you'd find me."

"Could be. Could be he couldn't of got there if he was hurt bad."

Andy thought on that for a time. "Maybe so. Still and all, I say we ride for the spring and if he ain't there, we come back here and pick up the trail."

The cattle rattled off through the brush and cedar trees as the cowboys started up the low ridge. They topped out and the horses slid down the other side's steeper slope on their hocks, the riders at times reining them into switchbacks down the face of the ridge, barren on this slope save for bunch grass and sagebrush.

A narrow, wandering watercourse, flowing only with sand and pebbles, threaded the base of the ridge. They followed it upstream as it gradually widened. Oak brush sprouted along the course, growing thicker and more tangled as they went. The horses' hooves cut through the surface sand, overturning moist, darker sand beneath, and soon there were wet spots, then stagnant puddles, then a thin stream of flowing water that disappeared into the sand.

They followed the meager but widening stream until they reached a shallow pool, no bigger than a saddle blanket, nestled in the shade of the oak brush. Water seeping out of a patch of green on the sidehill dripped off a flat rock overhanging the edge of the puddle, the source of the moisture as well as the name given the place.

Duncan Kirkwood looked to be sleeping, head on chest, back propped against a shallow rock ledge beside the spring, legs stretched before him. His right hand lay on the ground, grasping a wet and bloodstained bandanna he usually wore around his throat. The blood likely came from his left shoulder, which showed a seeping wound through the ripped shirt. The left arm, cradled in his lap, was swollen and bent at an odd angle.

Andy squatted next to his boss. "Mister Kirkwood?"

There was no response, so Andy reached out and gave the shoulder that wasn't bloody a gentle shake. Kirkwood flinched and groaned. His head wagged slowly back and forth, then raised to look around, eyes blinking.

"Andy . . ."

"What happened, Mister Kirkwood? Where're you hurt?"

Kirkwood winced as he shifted his seat. "I am pretty sure my arm's busted. Got a knot on the back of my head." He grimaced and swallowed hard. "Ribs are pretty sore, and I don't think the boot will come off my left foot. Ankle and leg are all swolled up in there."

Brenn stood by, looking the area over. There was no sign of disturbance around the spring save the usual assortment of cow tracks, those left by deer and antelope and various small animals and birds, and hoofprints of unshod horses. He did see drag marks in the ravine above the spring, left, he assumed, by Kirkwood. "Lord a'mighty, Boss. How'd you get here?"

Kirkwood raised his head to look at Brenn, but said nothing.

"I can see you dragged yourself here. What I mean is, where'd you come from? And what the hell happened? It was that Black Joe stud, wasn't it."

Kirkwood dipped the wadded bandanna into the puddle, squeezed the water out of it, and mopped his brow. He dipped it and wrung it out again, and wiped at the wound on his shoulder, cringing. "One question at a time, son."

The old man allowed as how he'd limped, then crawled, his way to the spring from the point of the low ridge his hands had just crossed. He told how he'd gathered a few strays—the cattle Andy and Brenn had encountered—and was starting for the ranch.

"That Black Joe stud came down that ridge, neck flat and ears pinned back and teeth bared, and barreled into the side of my horse without even breaking stride." Kirkwood said it was a surprise, as there had been no sign of the stud's band of mares.

"Knocked my horse plumb off its feet and sent us flyin'. I hit the ground and my horse come down atop me amongst the rocks and brush—I reckon that's what put most of the hurt on me. But Black Joe was not finished. He wheeled around and came for us, reared up and came down scratching with his hooves. My horse had just got his front legs under him, but Black Joe took him down again, spun around and kicked him with both hind legs, then took another turn and come for me. He liked to have stomped me into mud, but I rolled away and got enough of me under a cedar tree to where he couldn't get at me much—still, them hooves of his found me now and then, doin' more of what damage you see.

"That black devil finally left off and trotted away. My horse had long since quit the country. Don't know how bad off he was or where he went off to, but I did not figure I could find him. I knowed this little spring wasn't far away, so I hobbled along dragging this damn leg long as I could, then crawled the rest of the way."

"Lord above, Mister Kirkwood! That must be half a mile if it's a yard!" Brenn said.

"Maybe so. It took a while, that's for certain."

Andy slid the rancher's vest off, then peeled the tattered shirt from Kirkwood's back and tossed it to Brenn, telling him to stitch up the worst of the tears with mane or tail hair from the horses. While Brenn poked holes with the point of his knife blade and knotted stiff lengths of hair to close the gaps, Andy poked and prodded at his boss's wounds. He used his own bandanna to wash the dried blood and dirt and grit from the cuts and scrapes beyond Kirkwood's reach. His fingertips pressed along the boss's collar bone and found a ridge that should not be there. The old man winced when he touched it.

That his forearm held a broken bone or two was clearly visible, given the kink in its length.

Brenn tossed the roughly repaired shirt to Andy. "Here. Won't win any ribbons at the county fair, but it'll keep the sun off him till we get back to the ranch."

"We won't be going back to the ranch," Kirkwood said, grimacing as Andy worked the shirt into position. "We'll be going after Black Joe."

Andy stopped what he was doing to stare at the boss. "If you don't mind my sayin' so, Mister Kirkwood, you ain't in any condition to be goin' anywhere but to bed."

"My bed will still be there when we're done. Just get me on that horse you brought. Tie me on, if you have to. But I'll be trailing that black devil all the way to hell if I have to. You boys can come along if you like. If not, go on back to the ranch and fluff my pillow so it will be ready for me. But before you go, I'll borrow one of those rifles you're carrying. Pistol, too, if you don't mind. Black Joe has fought me twice. There will not be a third time."

Brenn grinned. "Reckon I'll ride along. Always had a hankerin' to chase wild horses."

Andy shook his head, resigned. He took Kirkwood's bandanna and knotted it to his own and looped them around the boss's neck to make a sling for his injured arm. "I guess it's best to leave your leg be. I'd likely have to cut the boot off and we wouldn't never get it back on."

Kirkwood nodded. "Leave it be. Long as it's in the stirrup, it will be all right. Now, help me up and get me horseback."

Andy took Kirkwood by the right hand and pulled him to his feet. He wrapped the man's arm around his shoulder and supported the boss's weight as he hobbled his way to the horse. "Don't know how the hell we'll get you in the saddle."

After debating the issue for a time, the men agreed on a

method. Brenn stationed himself on the right side of the mount, holding the reins snug in case the horse shied in the unfamiliar circumstances. On the left side, Andy propped Kirkwood against the horse and the old man grasped the cantle on the saddle with his mobile right hand.

"Here goes nothin'," Andy said. He squatted behind Kirkwood, wrapped his arms around the boss's legs, and stood, lifting the old man. Once he had him high enough, he shifted his hands to Kirkwood's buttocks and twisted him as he lifted some more. Brenn steadied the old man from the opposite side as he swung his right leg across the horse's rump. It took two tries and some extra hefting from Andy, but Kirkwood somehow managed to grab the saddle horn, get his leg across, and land gotch-eyed in the seat. For a moment he lolled in the saddle as his body sought balance and equilibrium, like a man who had too much to drink. The sight only added to the cowboys' amusement.

"Quit your damn laughing," Kirkwood said through gritted teeth.

"Sorry, Boss," Brenn said between snickers. "It's just that I ain't never seen no one get aboard a horse in that fashion before."

"Andy, see if you can get me into that damn stirrup."

Shoulders shuddering with stifled laughter, Andy shoved Kirkwood's rump into the center of the seat then ducked his head and fitted the injured foot into the stirrup. "Someday you'll laugh about this, Mister Kirkwood." His smile held as he watched the boss heel the horse into motion with his good leg.

"Maybe so. But just now it doesn't seem the least bit amusing. Hurts like hell, for a fact."

The cowboys hustled to get mounted, then followed the rancher up the draw through the rocks and brush, along a narrow trail worn by cattle and wild animals on the way to drink at the Flat Rock Spring.

They hadn't traveled far when a pair of mourning doves burst out of the brush, thumping and clattering and churring skyward and away. Kirkwood's horse spooked at the outburst, shying sideways. A desperate grasp of his right hand found the saddle horn, barely keeping him seated, his all-but-useless left leg offering no support in the stirrup.

Andy rode up beside him and studied the man slumping in the saddle. "You all right, Mister Kirkwood?"

Slowly, Kirkwood raised his head and met his foreman's eyes. "I'll survive." He shifted in the saddle, seeking a less painful seat. "I surely could use something to ease the hurt." He looked at Brenn, a few yards behind, then back to Andy. "I don't suppose either of you boys have anything in the way of whiskey in your saddlebags—for medicinal use, of course."

Andy shook his head. "Strong drink ain't allowed on the ranch outside the bunkhouse. You know that, Mister Kirkwood."

Kirkwood nodded his head, then, "Brenn?"

The cowboy's face reddened, and he seemed at a loss for words as Andy watched him. Then he touched his spurs to his horse's belly and rode up beside the rancher. "Well, sir, I do sometimes carry a small bottle of spirits—but only to treat cuts I might find on the cattle, you understand . . ." he managed to say among hems and haws.

"Uncork it, son. As I said, it's for medicinal use, which is in keeping with your purpose."

Brenn pulled a wad of sacking from a saddlebag and produced a half-pint bottle of whiskey from among its folds. He passed it along to Kirkwood, who fumbled around uncorking the bottle, took a small sip, grimaced, then tipped up the bottle and drained a good share of the liquid down his throat.

He squinted and shook his head like a dog after watering, then held the bottle up and studied its contents. "If you've no objection, young man, I'll keep this should the need once again arise." Without waiting for an answer, Kirkwood stuffed the flask in his vest pocket and, with his good leg, spurred his horse into motion.

Just around the point of the ridge, the riders reached the place of Black Joe's attack. From the tracks, Andy could see the stud had come off the ridge at a run. His hoofprints then stirred into a soup of tracks left by the cattle Kirkwood was driving and the tracks of Kirkwood's shod horse. The soil was disturbed over a wide area. Drops of blood darkened the dirt and scattered rocks showed crimson patches. A bloodstain under the low limbs of a cedar tree showed where the rancher found refuge from the striking hooves and snapping teeth of the mad stallion.

Andy followed the trail of the stampeded cattle for a few rods, then veered off and started a semicircle back around the site of the skirmish. He stopped when he found the track of Black Joe's leaving. "That stud came this way," he said. After studying the landscape in the direction of the trail for a few minutes, he completed his round and rejoined Kirkwood and Brenn.

"Can't see no trace of his mares out there anywhere, nor no tracks. Did you see them, Mister Kirkwood?"

"Nary a trace. Had I seen the mustangs, I would have kept watch for Black Joe. But I tell you, he came out of nowhere. He was on me before I knew it." Kirkwood took another sip of whiskey and pushed the bottle back into his vest pocket. "You say he went that way, do you?" he said with a nod of his head in the direction of the trail. "We'd best be after him."

They rode for miles through rolling, brush-covered country strewn with outcrops of black lava rock and rugged, protruding hills that forced their path to meander some. At sunset, they stopped, lit a fire fed by sagebrush and dead cedar limbs, and settled in for the night. Kirkwood needed help dismounting, and then Brenn's support as he hopped to a seat on the ground. His saddle served as a backrest and, later, as a pillow—the same accommodations available to Andy and Brenn.

From greasy sacks in his saddlebags, Andy shared now-stale biscuits and cold, sliced roast beef he'd gathered at the bunkhouse kitchen on the way out the door earlier that day. The men had no blankets against the cold of the night and the chill crept up through the hip holes they wallowed in the stony ground seeking comfort. There was little talk that night, but when Kirkwood rousted his cowboys in the pale light of early dawn, he shared with them a plan devised between brief bouts of fitful sleep.

"That horse can't be far from here, and he doesn't seem to be in a hurry to get anywhere."

"I ain't seen any sign of the rest of them mustangs," Andy said.

Kirkwood nodded agreement. "I have been thinking on that. Could be he's not looking for them. That Black Joe is pretty long in the tooth. A younger stud may well have driven him off, and that harem is no longer his. No matter. Unless I miss my guess, we'll be upon him soon, and here's what we'll do."

He pointed in the direction the stud horse's trail had been leading. "Diablo Gorge ain't but a few miles farther along. I figure if we separate, say put a quarter mile betwixt us, and ride on toward the gorge, we'll push that devil horse to the rim. Then he won't have but two ways he can go on the rim, and at least one of us should be positioned to head him, either way he chooses. If we hold him there against the rim, one of us ought to be able to get off a shot."

"Sounds good," Brenn said, "except for one thing."

Kirkwood studied the cowboy. "And what might that be?"

"There ain't only them two directions—there's three. He could cut back and try to slip between us."

"That's true enough, I suppose. My hope is that we will surprise him, and dispatch him before he has the chance."

Andy laughed. "You think he don't already know we're here?"

After considering the question, Kirkwood allowed as how the horse probably was aware of their presence. "Still and all, it's the best plan I can come up with. And unless one or the other of you has a better one, it's what we will do."

The cowboys had nothing to offer. Kirkwood's foot and ankle were less painful than before, able to bear his weight long enough for him to lift his right foot into the off-side stirrup and get mounted unassisted. With the most-likely-broken arm still in a sling below the injured collar bone, he realized a long gun would be less than useless, so he borrowed a pistol each from Brenn and Andy. Kirkwood advised the cowboys to keep a sharp lookout and sent them on. After spreading out as directed, the men exchanged waves, and the boss motioned the thin line forward toward the canyon.

Diablo Gorge confined the same river that flowed through Kirkwood's ranch headquarters several miles downstream. There, it was a lazy stream meandering along a wide flood plain bordered by low bluffs. Here, the river flowed fast and deep at the bottom of a narrow chasm cut through lava rock and sandstone over time beyond measure. For miles in either direction, the defile denied all hope of crossing.

And, Kirkwood hoped, Diablo Gorge would prevent the escape of the devil mustang.

The riders reached the lip of the gorge at more or less the same time. No one saw Black Joe, nor had anyone seen any trace of any horses, save the ones they rode. All three sat horseback near the rim, scanning the plain for any sign of the stud horse.

A bugling, squealing whinny split the air. Black Joe trotted out of a shallow coulee—not deep enough to conceal a horse,

Kirkwood had thought—and stood, head high and tail arched, less than two hundred yards from the rim. The rancher's trail had taken him no more than a stone's throw from the sly stud as he passed.

Trumpeting again, then rearing and pawing at the air, Black Joe lunged into a furious gallop, eyes and course riveted on Kirkwood.

The rancher slid off his saddle horse. Shock waves of pain shuddered through Kirkwood's body when his feet hit the ground. Using the saddle seat as a rest, he unleashed shot after shot until he emptied one pistol. He threw it aside and thumbed back the hammer on the revolver borrowed from Brenn. Whether all the shots went wild or some found their mark, they had no effect on the charging stud.

Along the rim in either direction, the cowboys could only watch. Brenn slid his saddle gun from its sheath, but knew it was useless at this range. Andy's spurs gouged his horse's belly and Brenn smacked his mount's rump with the rifle barrel as the men set out in a futile race to reach their boss. Even at distance, even over the sound of pounding hooves and streaming air, both cowboys heard the crash. Even more, they felt it deep inside.

Black Joe never slowed. At a dead run, he smashed into Kirkwood's mount. The force of the collision carried the mustang stud over the edge, pushing the saddle horse and the man before him.

Andy and Brenn slid to a stop in the ravaged soil where Kirkwood took flight. The men's breathing as labored as that of their horses, they could only stare at one another. After what seemed an eternity, Andy shook his head and stepped out of the saddle. Brenn followed suit, and the men edged to the lip of the canyon. With hands gripping knees, they leaned into the gorge.

Nothing, not even a ripple in the roiling river, betrayed the presence of Kirkwood or the horses. Andy thought he saw a hint of black horsehide roll to the surface and disappear, but he could not say for sure.

The cowboys stood for long minutes without speaking, searching the water as it flowed away, scanning the rocks below for any trace of Kirkwood.

Eventually, Andy spoke. "Sonofabitch," he whispered.

After a time, he shook his head slowly. "Sonofabitch." He led his horse away from the gorge and snugged up the cinch. He looked at Brenn and again shook his head.

The two cowboys swung into their saddles and sat, staring at one another.

"I guess we'd just as well head back to the ranch," Brenn said.

"I guess so."

"Ain't nothin' else to be done."

Andy shook his head yet again. He sat in the saddle for a few more eternal minutes. Then, "On the way back, we'll pick up those stray cows Mister Kirkwood gathered."

THE DARKNESS OF THE DEEP

I fear darkness. At times it wrings sweat and squeezes the breath out of me as I lie abed wishing for the illumination of dreams. It has not always been so. I can trace the origin of my fright to a precise time and place: twenty-three years, seven months, thirteen days ago; the Alta Incline in the Minnie Mine. I shall relate how I came to be at that place at that time.

The year was 1913. The "Wild West" was but a faded memory in most locales, but the narrow defile of Bingham Canyon was as raucous and rowdy as ever was any town at the end of the trail or the end of the rails. As you might have surmised, Bingham Canyon was mining country, a mountain filled with treasure but trapped in ore so low in grade that only large mining syndicates could afford the machinery and manpower required to extract paying quantities of metal. The mines needed men, so the town was awash in men. A regular stewpot, it was—Cousin Jacks, Chinks, Micks, Bohunks, Canucks, Greasers, Scandahoovians—every kind of man you can think of. Too many men, and too few women. Therein lies the beginning of this tale.

Rafael López, they say, was at the end of his one day off in the week. A day spent swilling what passed for liquor in the town's saloons. He stumbled and staggered through stupor and snowstorm uphill to the shack where his "sweetheart" lived and met a friend making his exit through the door López planned to enter. They argued. They fought. López pulled a pistol from his pocket and shot the man dead.

Now comes Police Chief J. W. Grant. "Dub," he was called. By the time he arrived at the crime scene, López was long gone. But there was no shortage of witnesses to the fact that the killer, sobered by his deed, had gone to his own quarters, loaded up with firearms and ammunition, and hightailed it out of town afoot.

Standing in fresh-fallen snow at the edge of town, Dub shivered as he eyed the trail.

"Well. He ain't likely to get too far too fast," he said. "I suppose mornin's soon enough to start after him. Sorenson!"

"Yeah, Dub," answered Jules Sorenson, deputy sheriff assigned by the county to the Canyon.

"Gather up Otto Witbeck and Nels Jensen and meet me here at first light."

Dub and the deputies followed the clear trail across the divide into Utah Valley, surprised as the sun climbed higher how much of the country López had covered. Crowding the western shore of Utah Lake, the Mexican led them all the way south into Goshen Valley. After spotting from his saddle some fresh footprints, Dub, keeping Sorenson at his side, sent two of the deputies on a small circle to attempt to corner the fugitive. He warned all to stay alert.

Too late. Rifle shots rang out from the willows.

"Dub, I'm a dead man!" Sorenson said. He looked surprised as he slid from the saddle.

The other riders, still a short distance away, spurred up to ride to the defense of the police chief, whose horse was pitching and milling in the hail of bullets. Otto took a bullet just under the hat brim and rolled backward off his mount. Another shot hit Nels in the shirt pocket. With half his force shot out of the saddle and half of what was left mortally wounded, Dub controlled his horse, grasped the reins of the horse Nels was clinging to, and fled the field with appropriate haste.

Now begins my part in the hunt for Rafael López.

By the following morning, Dub had gathered a considerably larger posse for the pursuit. I was a member, one of twenty or so down from Bingham Canyon. While sincere in my intention to aid in the capture of the desperado, I confess a secondary ambition—to capture the excitement of the event for the readers of the *Canyon Chronicle*, for which I was employed as a reporter and typesetter. In spite of the mostly indoor nature of my vocation, I was not unfamiliar with the outdoor life, the squeak of saddle leather, or the use of arms. As the fourth son of the third wife of a polygamous Mormon father, my prospects of maintaining a livelihood in my family's livestock operations were nil. Being bookish by nature, I opted for a college education and the literary life. The education, at least, had panned out. Authorial success beyond the newspaper page was yet some distance into the future.

But I digress. Our posse was joined that morning by another dozen men from the nearby burg of Lehi, with small groups from elsewhere swelling our ranks as the day passed. We found nothing of López, despite scouring the shores of the lake in ever-growing circles radiating from the scene of the fugitive's ambush of Dub and the deputies. The snow had somewhat melted away and drifted so no trail was apparent. An uneventful day, all told. The next day started the same, save that there were now in excess of a hundred men in our camp, the perceived excitement of the chase having spread from village to town.

"Men, this Rafael López we're after is a bad hombre," Dub announced to the assembled mass. "He knows how to shoot and he's not afeared to pull the trigger. Most of you know by now that he's killed three good lawmen and a no-account Mick miner already. So be sharp. Don't do nothin' stupid. We don't need no dead heroes."

We rode out in contingents of twenty riders, directed by Dub to various parts of the lakeside mountains as if on a gather. Late in the afternoon, shooting broke out somewhere north of our location. We hastened over the intervening ridges until we reached the dry canyon whence the shooting originated.

López had ensconced himself in a jumble of boulders at the top of a steep draw that offered no access from any direction save below, due to surrounding cliffs and shale-covered slopes. From his eagle's nest, he could hold off an army, which is exactly what he was doing when we arrived. After the initial flurry, the noise of which had attracted virtually the entire posse to the area, those in pursuit realized they could not get a clear shot at the pursued, who, with a few well-placed shots, kept us at bay until nightfall.

Morning brought renewed attempts on our part to infiltrate the Mexican's lair. It soon was apparent that the site was undefended, our quarry having disappeared into thin air. Shell casings revealed that López had expended all available ammunition for his discarded rifle, and his use of pistols the evening before had been of necessity rather than choice. Finding no clue as to his current whereabouts despite hours of casting about for sign, the posse disbanded. Those of us from Bingham Canyon turned our mounts north.

"Dub, where do you suppose he's gone to?" one of our party asked the police chief.

"Well, I reckon he's on the way to California. There's a whole lot of nothin' between here and there, but if anyone can make it, and plenty have, that pepper belly can sure do it."

"So you're not going after him?"

"Nope. Not unless someone reports seein' him somewheres. Like I said, there's a whole lot of nothin' out there."

"But Dub," I chimed in, "what can I tell readers of the *Chronicle* about the disposition of the case?"

"Hell, I don't know. You're the newspaperman, not me. But I guess you can say we got rid of López. Maybe it's not all neat and tidy like a trial and a hangin' but he's gone all the same."

Life in the Canyon had settled back into its routine of changing shifts, clanging hoist bells, the felt but not heard thump of blasting deep underground, and the ring of ore car wheels rolling on steel tracks when word reached the police that Rafael López was back in town.

"Bullshit!" Dub sprayed into the pale face of the store clerk standing before him. "You're nuts!"

"N-n-no sir," the clerk managed to force through rattling jaws. "It was h-him. He's carried an account at the company store since I been there. I've waited on L-López a dozen times at least."

"Well, what the hell did he want this time?"

"B-b-bullets. He wanted bullets for a rifle and two kinds of pistols. And s-some food. You know, canned stuff. Stuff that would keep."

"And you gave it to him?" Dub asked.

"No sir. I didn't give it to him. I sold it to him on account. Like I s-said, he's on the books."

"Damn. A cold-blooded killer and known fugitive waltzes into the store pretty as you please for supplies and gets them, just like that. Lemme guess what happens next—he invited you up to his shack for supper in appreciation of your cooperation."

"No, D-Dub—ch-chief—sir. He didn't. He didn't go home. He went into the Minnie," the clerk said.

An interesting turn of events, I thought. I'd overheard the greater part of the conversation after beating a quick trail to the police station upon getting the news from a street urchin we pay to keep us informed of events.

So here we have Rafael López on the lam in a vast network of drifts, stopes, shafts, winzes, and inclines deep in the dark bowels of the earth. Knowing the Minnie mine well from his employment there, he would likely be able to elude capture for quite some time—or at least as long as provisions allowed. Dub, seeing no other course, opted to wait him out. Guards were posted at every point of egress from the Minnie, with simple instructions to be especially vigilant during shift changes, and to arrest López when he surfaced to replenish his supplies.

But he never resurfaced. Plenty of miners reported encountering him in the depths of the mine. Some claimed he robbed them of lunch buckets at gunpoint. Others reported food and water pilfered from places they had stowed it while working. As time passed, Dub was convinced the Mexican had accomplices—willingly or under threat—carrying supplies into the mine.

Finally giving up on his ineffectual siege strategy, Dub decided to smoke out the fugitive. Literally. He as much as ordered the mining syndicate to shut down operations for a shift at tremendous expense. Engineers closed off certain ventilation shafts to control airflow through the mine and Dub had huge bonfires built at all the intake vents. Additional guards were posted at every point of escape from the mine. Then piles of wet straw, moldy hay, and green juniper boughs were heaped on the fires. Clouds of greasy, acrid smoke poured into the mine and eventually found the outlets. Dub ordered the crews to keep the fires smoking and the sentries to keep a sharp eye. But, in the end, smoke was the only thing that came out of the mine.

"Well, hell. There's no way he's still in there," Dub opined. "If he ever was."

"But there have been eyewitness reports. Besides," I asked, "if López isn't in the Minnie where is he?"

"You ever been in a mine, copy cub?"

"No. I've never had occasion."

144

"Well, let me tell you somethin'. It's dark down there. Real dark. So dark it can make you see things that ain't there. And you hear things. Hell, I don't have any idea what them witnesses thought they saw."

"But what about the stolen dinner buckets?"

"That's easy enough explained. Come the day after payday, a lot of them miners down that hole ain't got two nickels to rub together. I don't suppose chowin' down on somebody else's lunch would weigh too heavy on their minds. As for your other question, I can't even guess where López is—but I don't intend to lay awake nights worryin' about it. There's plenty enough misbehavior out in plain sight in this canyon to keep me busy."

So, once again, the routine of changing shifts, clanging hoist bells, the thump of blasting deep underground, and the ring of ore car wheels on steel rails held sway. But not for long. One day a visibly shaken miner rushed into the police station. By happenstance, I was there checking arrest records for anything that might prove newsworthy.

"I have a message for the police chief," the miner said.

"And who might you be?" Dub said.

"My name is Gustav Mueller. They call me Dutchy. I am a timberman at the Minnie."

Dub perked up at the mention of the mine. "What's the message and who's it from?"

"The man, he said his name is Rafael López. He said to ask about the deputy he met by the lakeshore—if the deputy has a bad headache."

Dub mulled that one over, realizing that while it was no secret Otto Witbeck had been shot and killed, not many knew or cared that his death resulted from a bullet placed dead center in his forehead. The chief's interest heightened.

"What else?"

"This López, he seems very angry. He said he wishes to meet

Dub Grant at the Alta Incline in the Minnie between shifts tonight. He said he will kill Dub Grant."

"He says that, does he," Dub said. "Well, here's what we'll do, Mister Dutchy. You're goin' to keep my appointment with Rafael López."

"Oh no, sir! I do not care to see this man ever again."

"But you'll do it Dutchy, or you'll find yourself behind bars for aidin' and abettin' a fugitive or whatever other reasons I can come up with to put you there. And by the time I decide to let you out on account of the whole thing being a big mistake, your sorry life will have passed you by. Now pay attention, and tell López this—tell him that headache ain't botherin' that deputy no more, but it's still likely to cause him—López—plenty of pain and sufferin'."

The reluctant miner attempted to deliver the message, he claimed, but the Mexican failed to show at the appointed time and place. Despite the futility of the previous attempt to smoke the renegade out, Dub considered another try to be a smarter approach than sending men into the Minnie to poke their noses into all the dark corners to see if López would shoot them off. So the miners showing up for morning shift were sent home and the fires were kindled again. Again, the result was a disappointment. As the final wisps of smoke vacated the mine, Dub decided to comb the Minnie despite the difficulty and danger.

Dub lined up a reluctant posse, recruiting as many miners familiar with the Minnie as possible to serve as guides or deputies or both. At each of the mine's several levels, teams trooped outward from the shafts, breaking into ever smaller groups, following branching drifts toward working faces and raises that led to overhead stopes. I obtained permission to accompany Dub. Guided by Dutchy, we hiked directly to the place of the miner's reported encounter with López.

The Alta Incline is, in the jargon of the mining trade, a

winze—a tunnel that angles upward from the 825-foot level to the 700 level. Dutchy led our parade upward by the light of a miner's torch he carried; our only light, as Dub and I had our hands full of armaments. We had proceeded maybe a third of the way up the Incline when a rifle roared, effectively deafening us with its initial report as well as its echoes in that confined space. Dutchy pitched face downward and the lantern shattered, plunging us into instant and complete darkness save for the bright spots burned behind my eyes by the muzzle flash.

I could see nothing. I could barely sense my own presence in the pitch black let alone that of Dub, Dutchy, or our attacker. And while the feeling of isolation was frightening, the fact that I knew I was not alone was even more disconcerting. I did not know what had become of Dub. Perhaps the shot that downed Dutchy had taken the police chief out of action as well. I dared not speak, fearing my voice would betray my location and provide an effective, if unseen, target for the assassin. So I waited.

The blackness was so overwhelming that my very senses failed. Although I hugged a rock wall, I had no sensation of being upright. For all I knew, I may have been lying down or even upside down. I know not how long I sat in fear and silence. It seemed an eternity, but may have been mere moments—my ability to sense the passage of time no longer functional. There were sounds. Small sounds, strange and unfamiliar; their source or location indecipherable. And the occasional rattle of pebbles falling, or rolling.

"You there, scribbler?"

Had I known up from down I would have jumped a foot in the air. The voice of Dub Grant boomed out of the silence, although he spoke barely above a whisper.

"I am here. Are you wounded?"

"Nah, I'm fine. You?"

"I have not been shot. But I am not fine."

"I know what you mean," Dub said. "This is a strange fix I find myself in."

"At least you can find yourself. I am not even sure I am me."

Dub did not respond. The darkness that had seemed to lift with our conversation once again weighed on me.

"Dub?"

"Yeah?"

"Do you think he's still here? López?"

"Can't say for sure, but I don't think so," he said. "I've been listenin' and I can only hear the two of us breathin'."

"I guess that means Dutchy is dead."

"I fear so. The last thing I saw was the back of his head turnin' inside out."

Having no response, I allowed silence to descend. I heard nothing except my own breathing, unable even to detect the sound of Dub's, though he could mine, he had claimed. After an interval that seemed interminable came the sound of pebbles dribbling down.

"What does that noise mean, Dub?" I asked.

"Beats the hell out of me. Rats, maybe. Might just be the ground shiftin' a bit and shakin' things loose. I've heard miners tell stories about tommyknockers. Maybe it's them."

"How are we going to get out of here?"

"We ain't—at least until someone misses us and hunts us up. We try walkin' around blind down here, we'll be bumpin' our heads and bouncin' off walls or fallin' down holes. We had best just stay put. I do believe a smoke will help pass the time."

Dub rustled about a bit, rolling a cigarette, I assumed.

"Aren't you worried that you will betray our position?"

"Nah. I'm pretty sure that pepper belly has crawled back in his hole. Care for the makin's?" Dub asked as he scratched a match against the wall.

"No, thank you. I don't—

The explosion of rifle fire would have drowned out my next words, had there been any. The sound of the shot reverberated up and down the Incline as I watched Dub's toes turn upward in the feeble light of the dropped match fizzling out. I heard deliberate footsteps retreat; whether up or down the Incline I cannot say. Then, only darkness.

Later—how much later I do not know, but had it been much later than it was, it would have been too late—I heard voices and detected a faint glow. Then I could see three men, two carrying lights, standing above—I assumed at the point where the Alta Incline connected with the 700 level.

"Dub!" someone shouted. "Dub?"

"Down here!" I replied. "Be careful! López was here—but I believe he has gone."

"We heard shooting. Anyone hurt?"

"Dutchy is dead. And Dub is shot. He may be killed."

No one found Rafael López that day. No one has found Rafael López since. Reports drift in from time to time of sightings in other mining regions—Colorado, Idaho, California, Nevada—reports carried by gyppo miners who claim to have known him in those parts.

And there were—and still are, from time to time—sightings of the Mexican in the Minnie. He is blamed yet for stolen dinner buckets, misplaced tools, misfired rounds, and any number of other misdeeds. For a time, I followed up every report, and can say without equivocation that the whereabouts of Rafael López are unknown. Perhaps he did escape from the Minnie and departed for parts unknown. Maybe he remained underground, victim of an unknown accident—blown apart in a powder blast, I like to think, mucked up with the ore and burned away as dross in the mills; a refiner's fire, of sorts.

As it turned out, I was in the darkness in the Minnie that day for a mere forty minutes, more or less. Just long enough for other searchers, who had heard both shots, to track down their source. Forty minutes from which I have yet to recover. Sometimes my dreams are illuminated by the sight of the toes of Dub's boots turning upward as he died. But, always, the light fades and there is only darkness.

It is the darkness that haunts me.

BEN COLTON'S DOWNFALL

Ben Colton might as well have been nailed to the bench in the bunkhouse. Day after day, he sat. He sat there night after night, head sometimes pillowed on folded forearms atop the table. He must have left his seat from time to time to visit the backhouse, but no one ever caught him at it. The other cowboys in residence wondered at his sluggishness, discussed his stagnation, conferred about his stupor.

Something must have happened to cause Ben's fall from grace. Something big. Something bad.

But no one knew what it was.

Only weeks ago, Ben had been a better-than-average cowboy on the place. A top hand, for that matter. A real ranahan. As a bronc peeler, he topped off a lot of horses that left the other hands eating dirt. As a roper, he could thread his twine into places most cowboys could not even contemplate, then reel it in with a bawling bovine caught in the loop. He saddled the mounts no one else wanted and turned them into quality cow horses. He ferreted out the deepest holes and thickest tangles where cattle shaded up and rounded them up and moved them out.

Ben had always kept his saddle well-soaped, his ropes limber and lively, his spur rowels spinning freely, and his chaps buckled snug. The brim of his hat always carried a handsome curl, his pants were always tucked neatly into his boot tops, and his shirt buttons never missed a buttonhole.

Saturday nights in town, Ben was more likely than not, and more likely than most, to buy a round for the house. A barn dance would find him coursing the boards with the prettiest girl present on his arm. Sunday morning would find him in the pews taking on a weekly load of religion. At Sunday dinner, Ben displayed a healthy appetite but never took more than his share and always left the last biscuit on the platter or the last slice of pie in the pan for others to enjoy. And he never, ever missed the spittoon when indulging his tobacco habit.

Back then, before it happened—whatever *had* happened— even an ordinary evening in the bunkhouse would find Ben delightful. While he never lorded his knowledge over others, he was well read and erudite. He could, and would, contribute to any discussion on any subject, and offer insight that edified the occasion. The mouth harp he always carried in his pocket emitted rich tunes worthy of a pipe organ, and his musical repertoire was widespread; seldom would a request for a song—any song—go unanswered. When his mouth was free, Ben could sing with a voice that stirred souls, recite endless verse penned by the masters, and spin yarns with entertainment in the warp and enchantment in the weft.

In a word, he was a man to ride the river with.

But something, whatever it was, had taken the life out of Ben Colton. Sapped his strength. Eliminated his energy. It was as if, the cowboys said, he had folded the poker hand that held his give-a-shit card.

And so he sat. And sat. As if nailed to the bench in bunkhouse, as it were. Steaming cups of coffee placed before him turned tepid, then cold. Dinner plates, served up by other cowboys concerned for his nutrition—or lack of same—sat untouched through the meal and long afterward. Most jarring of all to his saddle pals, Ben had altogether ceased and desisted honoring the time-honored cowboy practice of carrying one's own soiled tableware to the wreck pan.

Something was wrong with Ben Colton. Seriously wrong.

But what?

His once ruddy complexion had turned wan. His once supple skin and meaty musculature sagged from a skeletal rack increasingly evident to the onlooker, unhidden despite a cover of limp and unlaundered clothing. Ben's normally lustrous hair had turned lank and lifeless; the beard he had kept tame and well-trimmed now sprouted whiskers wild and woolly and in want of bridling.

One at a time in turn, in pairs and in threesomes, in bunches and in clusters, his compadres quizzed Ben Colton. They questioned and queried, poked and prodded, grilled and interrogated, asked and inquired as to the cause of his complaint or condition, his malaise and malady, his ailment or affliction.

All for naught.

Ben held his silence. He spoke not. His lips were sealed. He did not meet their eyes, save in passing, and then with absence of awareness. He did not so much as acknowledge their existence. In a word, he ignored them. Still and all, they did not sense any unkindness or ill intent in Ben's lack of regard for them. It seemed to them that their friend was not even there, in spite of the indisputable fact that he—at least his shell, his carapace if you will—sat before them on the bunkhouse bench, a clear physical presence, yet absent by any other measure.

Wanting answers despite a lack of input from the source, the cowboys conjectured. They mined their minds in search of some event or incident, some episode or experience in the recent past that might be responsible for the downfall of Ben Colton.

"You know," one offered, "the boss brought in them broncs from off the mountain. Could it be that Ben didn't feel up to the task of toppin' 'em off? Them horses don't know what fences is, ain't never been in no kind of a pen, and ain't never even

153

seen a human being before now. You don't suppose ol' Ben figured they was too much for him, do you?"

The suggestion spurred scorn, scoffs, sneers, rejection, and ridicule.

"Bullshit," someone said. "You know as well as I do that Ben can—could—ride anything with four legs and hair. You heard him say his own self, more than once, 'There never was a horse that couldn't be rode.' "

"Sure, I heard him say it. But you know as well as I do that there's another part to that saying—'There never was a cowboy that couldn't be throwed.' "

The other cowboys remained unconvinced. That might be true most times, in most places, with most people, but it simply did not apply to Ben Colton, they said. The man never considered the odds, never counted the cost when it came to taming cayuses. He was overstuffed with try and knew not the meaning of quit. And he sure as hell held no fear of horses.

No, they opined, it couldn't be that.

"Is he just plain trail weary?" one man wondered. "As you-all know, fall works ain't that far off. Has Ben rid his last roundup? Could it be that he has just plumb had his fill of beatin' the bushes, ridin' the ridges, ramblin' up and down canyons and coulees and scourin' the sage to scare out cow critters, that if they had their druthers, would just as soon be left where they are? Has his love affair with ridin' circle fizzled? Has he gone and lost his taste for the gather? Don't he care no more 'bout runnin' after bunch quitters and cuttin' out slicks and draggin' calves to the hot iron? Has he breathed the smoke of his last brandin' fire and smelled his last burnin' hair?" The man shook his head and a tear cut a trail down his cheek. "Is Ben Colton—our Ben—bound to sell his saddle?"

Again, the crowd refused to concur. They allowed that love of the cowboy life flowed too thick in Ben Colton's veins to be thinned out at the mere prospect of work. After all, they claimed, Ben lived to be horseback. Was invigorated anew every time he stepped into the stirrup and swung into the saddle. No. A man whose heart pounded at the prospect of riding after cattle could not possibly lose his taste—nay, his dedication, his devotion, his ardor, his passion—for doing cow work, owing only to the prospect of more of it to come in the form of fall works. If anything, such a forecast would stir his soul, warm the cockles of his heart, and inflame his fervor for the work he loved and lived for.

"Besides," someone said, "if it was anything like that, he'd likely just light out for other ranges, not sull up like he has."

It must be something else.

Someone asked if Ben had received any letters of late. "Y'know, anytime you open an envelope that's come through the post, there's a better-than-even chance it'll be bad news inside."

"What? What kind of bad news?"

"Oh, y'know—could be anything."

"Like what?"

"Hell, I don't know. Maybe his faithful ol' dog back home died. Or his grandma."

"Did Ben have a dog?"

"How would I know? It's just a thought, that's all!"

"Well, it ain't much of one."

"Maybe he got a letter sayin' the crops failed. Or a sow got out and rooted up the kitchen garden. Or maybe it said his little sister ran off with a medicine show."

"Oh, for hell's sake! You don't even know if Ben got a letter!"

"Well, he could've."

By common consent, all the other cowboys concurred that that particular bone had been picked clean, and found the notion of bad news by the post unlikely, lacking any evidence that such had arrived.

"Well, maybe it was a telegram . . ."

"Shut up."

Through it all, Ben sat unaware and unresponsive on the bench by the table in the bunkhouse. He did not stir. The talk neither agitated nor aroused him from his torpor. If he was even aware of the debate and discussion, he made nary a sign to indicate such. Whatever ailed him, it seemed, was deep-seated and firmly entrenched.

But what ailed Ben? What was behind this apathy, this idleness, this impassivity?

What, indeed.

As the days passed, the colloquy grew more intense, the questions more acute. The cowboys went about their work in a fog, the worry and concern overwhelming their ability to make a hand. Some even feared the entire cowboy crew might be falling into whatever it was that afflicted their friend Ben.

But can any friends worthy of the name ignore such tragedy as that which had befallen Ben—whatever it was? They thought not. So, they thought and thought and thought until their minds turned to mush. And still they found no answer.

One night, one man sent the discussion down the path of love. A path that led to lost love, to be more precise.

"Does anyone know if Ben has—had—a sweetheart?"

While Ben was a favorite of the ladies whenever the opportunity to be in mixed company arose, no one in the bunkhouse could recall his being attached to any one young woman in particular.

"There was that girl in the red-checkered dress two barn dances back. I saw Ben fetch her a cup of punch."

"Aw, hell, that ain't nothin'. Ol' Ben, he'd do the same for anybody."

"I guess that's true. But it sure did make that gal show her pearly whites when he done it."

"Y'know, that one girl—you know that one I mean, her daddy owns the Bar-Y—she sure lights up like a coal oil lantern whenever she sees Ben."

"I know the one you mean. And I'll admit that Ben's right nice to her. But, then again, ain't he—wasn't he—nice to everyone?"

"There's that yeller-haired girl. The one he give ridin' lessons to. They spent a lot of time out on the range a-horseback."

"They did at that—but you forget, her little brother always went along. So it ain't likely they got up to nothin' but equitation on them rides."

"I guess you're right."

"The thing is, fellers," the voice of reason said, "there ain't none of that that matters. Sure, Ben was nice to the ladies. And sure, the ladies all liked Ben. But that ain't the kind of thing that would bring a man down to the lowly state we find our friend in. That could only happen if Ben took a shine to a particular filly and she led him on long enough to where he was a goner, then she went and pulled the rug right out from under him and plumb broke his heart. And we all know there ain't a woman within three days' ride of this here ranch that would do any such a thing to our Ben 'thout us havin' some inkling of its occurrence."

"Yeah, I guess you're right."

"Makes sense."

"Maybe some girl wrote him one of them 'Dear John' letters . . ."

"Shut up. Besides, his name's Ben, not John."

On another evening, one falling at the end of the month as it happens, when the men received their pay packets, the questions turned to those concerned with cash—the acquisition of it, the want of it, the need for it, the lack of it, the owing of it, and other such related matters.

"Anybody know anything of Ben's financial situation?"

"Nah. He never seemed to have much money, but never seemed to want for any. I reckon he was plenty enough frugal and set a little aside for a rainy day. But he weren't no miser. You-all know as well as I do that Ben spared no expense when it come to havin' a good time—and seein' that his friends came along for the ride."

"Anybody know if he was in hock to the bank on a loan or a debt or some such?"

"Wouldn't think so. I went into the bank with him from time to time, and all he ever done was put a few dollars into his account for safekeeping. But it ain't like they treated him like he was one of their big investors or anything."

"Far as I know, he weren't in no trouble at the store. Sure, he kept an account on the books there. For tobacco, and cartridges, and maybe a can of peaches now and again, or some penny candy if he saw a kid on the street that looked like he had a sweet tooth. And, of course, all them town kids knew it and word would spread quick-like whenever he come to town. But he always paid up his account, right to the penny, every payday. And there weren't never no complaints from the storekeep that I ever heard of him bein' in arrears or anything like that."

"How 'bout the doc? He into that ol' sawbones on a debt?"

That question spawned laughter. Ben Colton had never been hurt, never mind how many horse and cow wrecks he had survived. His bones were unbreakable, his hide tough and impenetrable, and his blood stayed where it belonged. And, of course, Ben had never been sick a day in his life.

That last thought, of Ben's dependable good health, stopped the conversation, and all the men turned to thoughts of their own. And they all, each and every one, thought the same thought: *Until now, that is.* Now, Ben was sure enough sick. Or something. But what?

Soon enough, a universal desire to help their friend started up the investigation anew.

"He ain't into one of them card sharps in town at the saloon for a debt, is he?"

"Naw. Ben, he never gambled none. Oh, he might sit in for a hand or two of poker at the Occidental now and then, but it ain't like it was gamblin' with him; not really. He didn't never bet but a dollar or two and always quit when it was gone or when it come back to him. He only played cards for fun, and if a game got too serious-like or too rich for his blood, he'd always cash in his chips and turn his attentions elsewhere for entertainment."

The night lengthened. Eyes tired. Brains fatigued. Bodies numbed. The men turned in, vowing one to another that come the morrow, with renewed energy, they would once again pursue, with vim and vigor, the recovery of their friend, Ben.

And so they did.

And still Ben sat, as if nailed to the bench by the table in the bunkhouse, uncaring—unaware, even—of the world around him or the people in it.

"Mayhap some bad man is after Ben."

"Maybe you're right! Maybe someone we ain't heard nothin' about is threatenin' violence against our Ben for some reason!"

"You don't suppose Ben got up to no good sometime, somewhere, and now there's a bounty hunter or lawman after him?"

"That could be it! Maybe he's been on the lam all this time and now it's caught up with him!"

The men paused in their probing, surprised at themselves for thinking such a thing.

"Nah. It couldn't be that. Ben, he's as honest as the day is long. I just can't feature him goin' astray of the law like that."

"Could it be there's a bad man, a gun hand on his trail? Some pistoleer who's been huntin' for him and has finally found him, and now is comin' for him?"

"You mean like some quick-draw artist who's carryin' a grudge for some reason, fixin' to brace Ben in a showdown in the street?"

"Maybe so. You know, that feller might've wrote him a letter warnin' him that he was comin'!"

"Will you shut up about them damn letters!"

Again, the voice of reason intervened. "Now, boys, you know that can't be so. None of it. Not a word. I ain't sayin' there couldn't be somebody with a grudge against Ben for some reason. But think about what you're sayin! We all know he ain't a violent man. Ben's a peaceable sort. But that ain't to say he can't handle himself."

The men all nodded in agreement, and some voiced similar sentiments.

"That's right. Ben ain't afraid of a fight. He don't prefer it that way, but if it comes down to it, he can sure enough hold his own."

"In about any situation, I'd say."

"And if trouble was comin', Ben sure as hell wouldn't cower in the corner like some snivelin' coward. He'd stand tall and face it—whatever it was—head on."

The cowboys agreed they would have to look elsewhere for an explanation. At the same time, they lamented the fact that other untried avenues of inquiry were hard to come by. If not injury, if not love, if not money, if not the threat of violence, what could possibly explain the state of Ben Colton?

Still, there was a sense of urgency surrounding the affair. To put it simply, Ben Colton was wasting away. Hollow eyes in a sunken face made the man almost unrecognizable. And when one noted the dissipated frame upon which a vital, robust, vigorous, rugged human being once hung, one could not help but fear for the continued existence of the ragged remnants of the now diminished man. The situation teetered between life and death. An answer must, *must,* be found.

But how to find an answer when every avenue of inquiry, every investigative line, every path probed in search of a solution proved empty, unproductive, futile, fruitless?

And then one day there came a knock at the bunkhouse door. Timid, tentative taps. A muted series of three short strikes of bare knuckles against the boards, barely worthy of the word "knock."

The cowboys inside were reluctant to answer the appeal; as uncertain as the hesitant hand that offered it. But after a lengthy exchange of questioning glances, a round robin of pointed fingers and pointed refusals, one of the cowboys rose from his seat, opened the door a crack, and peeked out.

Three steps back from the entryway there stood a man. A small man, slight of frame and short in stature. His attire was homespun and threadbare. His shoes were wrinkled and worn and run over. In hands raised at his chest, he held a hat. A hat the man might call a *txapela* or *bonita,* but what the cowboys would call a Basque beret. That, and the dog—the Euskal Art-zain Txakurra, or Basque Shepherd—that sat alert and attentive at his side engendered the realization in the cowboy that the man was, most likely, must be, a sheepherder.

Fearing for the safety of the visitor, owing to the traditional animosity between those who handled cattle and those who cared for sheep, the cowboy eased the door open only wide enough to slip through, stepped outside, and shut the door behind him. He did not speak to the sheepherder, questioning him only with his eyes—eyes that, at the same time, spoke of suspicion, skepticism, and mistrust.

The Basque cleared his throat and spoke. "Greetings. I am

Unai Etcheverria. I—"

"Speak up, mister. I can't hear a word you're sayin'."

Again, the sheepherder cleared his throat. He took a tiny, tentative step forward, crushing the beret in his hands. "I am Unai Etcheverria. I have come to see a man called Ben."

"Ben Colton? That who you want? Ben Colton?"

Unai nodded. "*Sí*—yes. That, I think, is his name in full. Ben Colton."

"What for do you want him?"

The sheepherder ducked his head, further crushed his hat, and shifted his weight from one foot to the other and back again. The dog whimpered. Unai looked up. "It is a personal matter, señor—mister."

The cowboy thought it over, pondered the nature of the request, considered the consequences. "Well, son, I don't think that's goin' to be possible."

Unai's eyes widened, his eyebrows arched, his forehead furrowed. "Señor?"

"Well, you see, Ben—he ain't well. He's a mite under the weather. He's not feeling too good."

As the pair talked, other cowboys, overcome by curiosity, had come outside. Before long, the entire crew was in attendance. They stood or squatted or leaned against the bunkhouse wall, and looked on and listened in.

The sheepherder was downcast. Disappointed. He looked heavenward, as if seeking assistance from on high. He sensed a change, or maybe detected a movement, at the bunkhouse door. He looked. He smiled.

There, in the doorway, propped against the doorframe, stood—sagged, rather—Ben Colton, head hung low. After a time, a long time, he raised his head and looked at the sheepherder. He spoke, his voice coarse and raspy. "Howdy, Unai."

Surprise was palpable among the members of the cowboy crew. Did Ben Colton, a cowboy among cowboys, know this man? This Basco? This herder of sheep? Could it be?

"*Kaixo,* Señor Ben! Hola! Hello!"

"What is it you want?"

Unai cleared his throat, held his beret to his chest. The dog stood up and barked—a single "woof," as if in greeting. The sheepherder spoke. "I have come to thank you."

Again, the cowboy crew stirred. The same unspoken question percolated in each and every mind: What on earth could Ben Colton, cowboy of cowboys, have possibly done to merit the gratitude of this man? This Basco? This sheepherder?"

"Oh, that ain't necessary, Unai. It weren't nothin'. De nada."

"Oh, Mister Ben! It was something! A kindness one cannot forget. Made more unforgettable for the unexpected . . . unexpectedness? . . . of the deed."

The cowboy crew exchanged wondering glances.

Unai continued. "A lost sheep may seem of little moment to a man such as yourself. But a sheep, a ewe, is of much value to a man like me. For the ewe, if lost as this one was, represents the loss not only of herself, but of her wool from year to year. As well as the many lambs, and the much meat and wool they represent, as the case may be, from year to year for many years. For this reason, I have come to express my thanks to you. It has only been the pressure of work that has kept me from coming to you sooner, and I express my regrets for the delay."

Then Unai, red-faced from embarrassment at the length of his address before a crowd of strangers, and in a language not native to his tongue, smiled and placed his beret atop his head and tugged it into place.

And, again, the shepherd dog at his feet emitted a single "woof," as if to punctuate the oration from his master's mouth that he, along with the others there assembled, had heard.

It had become clear, then, to the cowboy crew. Now, they knew.

Ben Colton, while riding herd one day on the ranch's range, must have encountered a sheep. A lost sheep. A sheep that had wandered away from home and herd. A ewe, as it happened. A mother, and a mother to be.

Perhaps he had attempted to herd the sheep toward home. But, as all cowboys know—not from actual first-hand experience, but from rumor and hearsay—sheep are intractable and unlikely to respond to such guidance with the same acceptance as would a superior species such as a cow.

So, they imagined, Ben would have soon given up the game as a lost cause. Then, determined to remove the woolly from the home range but unwilling to dispatch it with a well-placed shot from his six-shooter, he may well have hoisted the ewe with his bare hands, draped it across the forks of his saddle, and carried it back to its rightful place among others of its own kind, where sheep belonged. (Or, in the opinion of all who rode after cattle, did not belong, as sheep had no business being anywhere within sight or smell of cowboys.)

So, now they knew.

Now, they understood.

Now, all had become clear.

But it was up to Ben to put a nail in it.

He swallowed hard. "Well, I guess now you've found me out, boys," he said. "Now you know. Now you see why my life ain't worth livin'. There just ain't no comin' back from what I done. I . . . I . . . well, hell, boys—I ain't no better than a damn sheepherder."

He shook his head, pushed himself upright, turned away and shuffled, all but staggered, back to his bench at the bunkhouse table and sat, as if nailed to the spot.

GOOD HORSES

"That's a pretty good horse you're riding," McCarthy ventured, the first words out of either rider's mouth since leaving camp a quarter of an hour ago. Joaquin ruminated on the comment for a hundred yards or so.

"*Sí*. He is a good one. But that caballo you are riding, my friend, *that* is a horse," he finally replied.

"Oh, he'll do. Sure enough the best in my string. But I've watched that dun you're aboard all the way up the trail and I don't think this sorry roan compares," McCarthy countered.

For three months and more, the two had helped push a herd up out of Texas but this morning's exchange represented more conversation than they'd shared in all that time. Each cowboy's days and his piece of the nights were spent riding herd and, outside of cussing cattle, the work offered little opportunity for talk. Evenings around the fire, each man, by nature, kept his own counsel while other hands swapped stories in the nightly lying contest.

Now, the herd was bedded down a few miles outside Ellsworth, waiting for a train. By lot, this was Joaquin's and McCarthy's day to pursue a little recreation in town. The sun had yet to make an appearance above the horizon. Such days were rare, and the pair intended to not waste a minute of it.

"Shoot," McCarthy continued. "This pony pitches every time

I climb aboard, and has tried to pile me since the day I met him." Each man's thoughts drifted 700 miles south.

The Crazy Heart Ranch spreads over a sizable chunk of the Texas plains southeast of San Antonio. Spring roundup starts tomorrow, the result of which will be a herd of market steers to be trailed north. Working cattle was fine with McCarthy, one of the dozen or so hands hired on by the outfit, but this day was more to his liking. The horse herd had been run in, and today the boss would pick out a string of maybe a dozen horses for each cowboy to ride on the gather and as a remuda for the drive. Getting on horses was why McCarthy was a cowboy. He relished the thought of forking a string of unfamiliar mounts, getting to know them during the roundup, and spending long days in the saddle on the trail.

He watched the wrangler drop a loop around the neck of an ordinary-looking roan horse, and stepped up when the boss called his name.

"McCarthy!" the boss hollered. "This one's yours. See if you can get him saddled."

Most of the horses were green broke—they'd been ridden enough not to be strangers to the saddle, but were far from what you could call trained for cow work or even riding. Noting how the roan trembled, McCarthy figured he could be trouble. Nonetheless, he slid the split-ear headstall over the horse's head, wedged the curb bit between its teeth, and put the blanket and saddle in place as the animal sidestepped away from him. Giving the cinch an extra tug, he tied off the latigo, picked up his reins, grabbed the left ear of the quivering horse, and swung into the saddle. McCarthy found his right stirrup, released the ear, and squirmed into the lowest seat he could find.

Much to his surprise, the horse didn't explode. The roan just stood there, all atremble, front legs stiff and hind legs in a slight squat. *Well hell*, McCarthy thought. *Here goes nothing.*

He touched rowels to the horse's belly. The result, those in attendance would later say, was the stuff of legend. The horse leapt into the air, swapped ends, and landed stiff-legged with bone-crunching, teeth-rattling force. Almost before he had time to feel the impact, McCarthy was airborne again, the result of a spring-loaded skyward lunge of the horse's front end, followed by a high kick that put its hind legs well over its head. Shaken and surprised at the violence of the roan's attack, McCarthy was still aboard, but barely. He weathered the next few jumps and found his balance, but knew he was far from having this horse rode. The animal knew all the tricks. It sunfished, dropped shoulders, walked on its front feet, sucked back, jumped one direction and kicked the other, twisted and spun, anything and everything in the equine repertoire. But it couldn't unseat the determined McCarthy. The rider never raked or quirted the horse, partly because the roan needed no encouragement to work out the kinks but mostly because it wasn't McCarthy's way. He had never believed that antagonizing horses helped in the long run.

After what seemed to McCarthy to be about five minutes less than forever, the horse finally lined out into a lope. The pair of them, breathing hard, made a wide circle across the plain; the man, for now, still in the saddle and in control.

"Man, that was some bronc ride," Joaquin said, admiration in his voice.

"Yeah, I guess I lucked out that time. You'd think after all that pitching, one or the other of us would have learned something, though," replied McCarthy. "If I was any kind of cowboy, I'd have realized right then that this jug-headed roan would never make much of a mount. And if he was any kind of a horse, he'd have realized he wasn't going to buck me off and would have quit trying."

"Oh, my friend, the trail is at its end. The time for tall tales is over."

"Why, Joaquin, whatever could you mean by that?"

"I have seen many caballeros, and you are one of the best. I think you know that. I think, too, that your horse knows it."

"So?" McCarthy asked.

"So, you should save your lies for the campfire, and confess that the bucking is a sign of your horse's spirit. He wants to make sure you are awake when you ride him, so the fine horseman will appreciate the fine horse."

"Joaquin, mi amigo, you've gone loco. Now, that horse you're aboard—compared to him, this one I'm on can't tell a steer from a tree stump."

"It is true, this one understands the cattle. I think maybe it is because he is as stupid as they are."

"Be that as it may," McCarthy said, "if it wasn't for you and that little dun horse this whole outfit would still be sorting steers at the Crazy Heart."

Once again, their thoughts turned back down the trail.

"Joaquin!" the boss shouted as the wrangler led the dun forward. "Try to teach this one which end of a cow to chase!"

The horse didn't look like much, even among this herd of scrubs. Maybe thirteen hands high on his tiptoes, and light enough that Joaquin figured it would be as easy for him to carry the horse as the horse to carry him. He was a claybank dun, roman-nosed and paddle-footed. His ears were bigger than average and a bit floppy, tipped by fuzzy tufts of black hair. But it soon became evident to Joaquin that what the little dun lost in looks he more than made up for in cow sense.

He had a long, easy stride riding circle and ate up the miles with unflagging energy. Almost automatically, he headed into the thorny clumps of brush where cattle hide, knowing where to look better, even, than the cowboy on his back. Let a calf or mossy-horned steer or ornery cow cut and run and the dun was always a step ahead, turning them back into the herd without effort.

When it came time to road brand the steers, there wasn't a horse on the outfit that could keep up with the dun. He'd slide quietly into the herd, ease a critter to the fringes and then cut it out and move it toward the desired bunch, pivoting quick as a cat to block its path should it try to turn back. His every move was so precise it seemed effortless. Joaquin proved to be a poet with his reata, due to the combination of his skills and the ability of the little horse to put him in perfect position for the toss, whether a horn or heel shot.

Those days on the drive when Joaquin rode the dun were pure pleasure. The other drovers could only watch the pair in wonder. The horse and cowboy seemed to always know what the cattle were thinking before they knew it themselves. Trouble was avoided more often than not because Joaquin and the horse were there to prevent it. The dun was tireless, and as eager to be under the saddle and working the herd as McCarthy's roan was to buck. And, much as McCarthy was a born caballero, Joaquin was a natural vaquero.

"Yep. That horse under you ain't much to look at, but he's damn sure a good one."

"You are right about one thing, friend," Joaquin replied. "He is not much to look at. If I could choose a name for him, I would choose 'Tequila,' I think."

"And why would that be?"

"Because looking at this horse is like taking a drink—it burns all the way down."

McCarthy, stifling laughter, offered, "Surely you'd agree,

though, that your ugly dun could outrun any horse in the cavvy. I'd bet a month's pay that you'd even outrun that big fancy eastern-bred stud horse in the boss's string."

"I think not. I think that horse runs faster for sure, and maybe a couple of others. Your roan, too, will beat us. That is what I think."

"Well now I know you're plumb loco, Joaquin! This sorry bag of bones might out-buck yours, but he couldn't keep up on the run on his best day."

"Ah, but I know different, McCarthy. Have you forgotten the day we all raced for our lives?"

McCarthy knew well the incident of which Joaquin spoke.

The herd was at the crossing of the Canadian River in Indian Territory. With a storm on the horizon, the boss wanted to be on the opposite bank before rain swelled the stream and caused a delay. It took a lot of whooping and hollering, but the crew got the animals across by midafternoon and bedded them down to wait out the storm. The boss didn't expect that the steers, tired from the crossing, would stampede, especially in daylight. But with clouds rolling in and lightning flashing, he opted to keep every hand horseback and take no chances.

It's a funny thing about a stampede. One second the herd is lying quiet and the next they're on the run. Without communication any human ear can detect, they rise as one and take flight. And the only sound in a stampede is rumbling hooves, rattling hocks, and clattering horns; not a beller or bawl is heard. The stampede at the Canadian was true to form.

Quick as a lightning bolt, every cowboy was on the run, racing for the front of the herd. The only way to stop a stampede is to turn the leaders, and keep turning the herd back on itself until the cattle mill. It's a dangerous race. A false step, a wash, a prairie dog hole, a tangle of brush, a spot of slippery mud—all this and more can upset a horse, the result of which is almost-certain death for horse and rider since the stampeding cattle, running blind, pound everything in their path into the ground.

Joaquin watched as McCarthy, aboard his usually skittish roan horse, outpaced everything on four feet to gain the lead. His pressure to turn the herd slowed things just enough to allow other riders on fast horses—including Joaquin himself—to reach the fore and get them turned. The stampede was over sooner than most. Neither man nor beast was killed or unaccounted for. And the outfit's esteem for McCarthy's competence in the saddle and the speed and agility of his roan bronc climbed a notch or two.

"I saw how your horse runs, my friend. We all saw," Joaquin continued. "You left my little dun and every other horse in the dust—or mud, that day."

"Oh, that was nothing but luck. I just happened to be practically in front of the herd when the excitement started. Besides, you were stuck over there on the side closest to the river."

"*Qué?*"

"Well, you know, Joaquin! All those little washes and arroyos leading down to the bottoms made for a rougher ride. More dangerous, too. That dun picked his way through there like a night horse, only twice as fast. If my roan hadn't of been on smoother ground, you'd have run circles around us."

"I do not think so, my friend. This poor little crooked-legged horse can barely walk, let alone keep up with your roan."

"You really think so?"

"That is what I think."

"Hell, this sorry excuse for a horse is as likely to light into bucking as look at a man."

"Perhaps what you say is true, McCarthy. But I believe your fine *caballo* could cover the country faster while bucking than my dirt-colored, big-eared pony can at the run."

The cowboys rode on in silence for a time. Eventually, a grin spread across McCarthy's face and he burst out laughing.

Joaquin looked at McCarthy.

McCarthy looked at Joaquin.

Without a word, each rider spurred up his mount and the race on the road to Ellsworth was on.

THE TURN OF A CARD

The Carson River is a stream too lazy to announce its presence. The soft flowing sound came instead from breeze-rattled cotton-wood leaves on trees that shaded the watercourse.

Joshua Lonigan was only slightly more active than the river, perched as he was on a dry deadfall log massaging bare feet recently cooled in the stream. As he pulled on a sock the end gave way and two toes poured out the hole.

"Damn."

"Six bits says the same thing happens with your other sock," came a voice from under a dusty, oily, wide-brim hat shading the face of a long drink of water sitting with legs a-spraddle and a cottonwood for a backrest. The voice belonged to Seth "Six Bits" Slater, a longtime saddle pal of Josh's.

"Keep your damn bet. And shut up."

"There ain't no need to be testy," Six Bits said.

"Oh, I know it. I'm just tired of being here is all."

The two were shaded up from the heat of the day, keeping casual watch over a herd of trail-weary beef cattle and waiting their turn to partake of the pleasures available up the hill in Virginia City. They had bedded the herd here yesterday and the trail boss and owner of the beeves, Texas Red McIntyre, had given the rest of the crew liberty after instructing a pair of them to return to the herd this afternoon and relieve Josh and Six Bits.

The man knew from long experience with those two that had

he given them the first shift in town, the designated second shift would never set foot on Virginia City's boardwalks.

Lonigan and Slater had come north from Texas with McIntyre some half dozen years ago. They had pushed a mixed herd of cattle to California in 1856, McIntyre having liquidated in Texas hoping to strike it rich in the gold country selling beef rather than mining ore. But they arrived on the heels of more than seventy thousand Texas cattle driven to California over the few years past. Finding prices so cheap and cattle so common you could hardly give them away, McIntyre opted instead to take up ranching, selling the steers for what he could get and turning the cows and bulls out to pasture to eat grass and reproduce and await a better market.

Texas Red established his California ranch in the Sonoma country, squatting on what he considered free range but which was, in fact, part of a Spanish land grant held by Mariano Vallejo. But the Spanish, then the Mexican, sun had set in Alta California and McIntyre's claim, along with many other such tenuous claims, went largely unchallenged.

Now, the influx of thousands of men to work the Comstock mines across the mountains in Nevada had created what Texas Red hoped would be a lucrative market for beef. He had visited the Great Basin on a few occasions and was of the opinion that meat would yet be in short supply there since the Comstock country offered few prospects for raising cattle—grass being so scarce that a cow was forced to graze at a high lope just to find enough to fill its belly. He did not even consider the country suitable for raising sheep—never mind the fact that those animals could probably be convinced that graze was plentiful, sheep being the only critters so stupid that their intelligence was not affected in any significant way by being killed and eaten.

So McIntyre and his two top hands, Josh Lonigan and Six Bits Slater, gathered a few more drovers and a herd of steers and lit out on the Overland Trail across the Sierra. Having arrived, Texas Red had ridden off to negotiate a sale, leaving the two cowboys behind with nothing to do but keep the herd from quitting the country.

And wait.

"See them two steers laying over there? Them ones just off from the bunch a bit?" Six Bits asked after holding his silence for a suitable interval.

Josh said, "One of them red with a brockle face and the other one yellow?"

"Them's the ones."

"What about them?"

"I got six bits that says the yellow one gets up first."

"Covered."

As if on cue, the brockle-faced steer shook his long-horned head, shifted his grass-fat belly, hoisted up his hind legs and paused for a moment on the props before levering up the rest of his body.

"That's one more you owe me," Josh said.

"That it is. I trust you're keeping a tally. As you well know, I am not a man to welch on his bets."

He was a man, however, who would wager on anything, anytime, and offer a double-or-nothing bet when he lost. Josh had long since given up keeping track, figuring that Six Bits owed him more money from lost wagers than the cowboy would earn in wages in two lifetimes. But indulging your best friend's gambling habit is all part of the deal, isn't it? That, and keeping him from getting in too deep when the stakes were higher than six bits and the others in the game less forgiving.

Two of the other drovers eventually made it back, worse for wear but feeling no pain, to give Lonigan and Slater their chance at the town. The eager pair reined up at the edge of Virginia City just at sundown and commenced staggering back and forth across C Street in their intended attempt to visit every saloon along its length.

C Street slashed across the steep face of Mount Davidson, creating Virginia City's main boulevard. Cobbled-together shacks tumbled down from the slope above; downhill sprouted headframes of the richest silver mines ever known. In between, C Street rollicked day and night. Drinking establishments, opium dens, gambling houses, music halls, mercantiles, billiards parlors, haberdasheries, whorehouses, barber shops, restaurants—any and every appetite itching a man could be scratched several times over along this chaotic, raucous, decadent dirt road.

Before the night was finished—but not long before—Josh and Six Bits had made the circuit, ending their quest in the crowded, noisy, smelly C Street Saloon and Entertainment Emporium. The ramshackle saloon sat at the northern reach of C Street, the first or last place anyone coming to or leaving town on the main road north would encounter. Josh swayed gently against the bar, grateful for having it there to hold up himself and the considerable load of whiskey he carried.

The bar graced the north wall of the saloon, staggering back from the front doors along most of the building's narrow length. An out-of-tune piano, whose saving grace was its ability to jangle loudly if not melodically, filled the space from the end of the bar to the back wall. A battered door hung over a passage cut through the center of that wall, behind which were three narrow curtained-off cribs where saloon girls served up their own brand of intoxication.

Front-to-back along the south wall marched three scarred tables surrounded by rickety chairs. Next came a faro layout, abandoned at the time in favor of the game at the poker table in the back corner.

Here, Six Bits Slater was engaged in his favorite pastime.

Granted, the man would gamble on anything and play any game. But the ever-more-popular card game called poker was his preferred means of disposing of any money he happened to have. Faro, he often told Josh, was a fool's game where you played only against the house and the house held the odds.

Poker, though, that was different.

Slater liked the fact that every player at the table played against every other, with no one, including the house, having an advantage. Hell, you didn't even need the house to play poker. But the house was in tonight's game, in the person of Calvin Wiley, proprietor of the C Street Saloon and Entertainment Emporium.

He was a man gone soft and fat, given to perfumed hair oils and barbershop shaves and suits more suited to the elegance of a riverboat than the dingy environs of the Nevada desert. Still and all, his pretensions in dress and grooming could not disguise the fact that he was but a crude Missouri Puke belching and scratching and hacking and spitting his way down the social ladder he wanted so desperately to climb.

Tonight, he was financing his affectations at the expense of Six Bits Slater. Through the course of the night and a run of luck the length of C Street, Slater had managed to turn his forty-dollar wages into the princely sum of eighty-four dollars. But two hours across the table from Wiley had reduced him once again to poverty.

Slater considered the cards in his hand. His three-card draw had helped the pair of queens he got in the original deal. The king of clubs was worthless to his purpose so he pulled it from the center of the filled-out hand and placed it behind the other cards. But the other two drawn proved more useful—a pair of threes.

Queens and threes. The way the cards had been falling on this table, that ought to be a winner, Slater thought. So when the bet made its way around the table, he raised the stakes just enough to let the players know he was serious but not enough to scare them off. The next player saw the raise and the bet came to Wiley.

"Here's five," he said, tossing a gold piece into the pot for the call. Then he counted out a stack of coins and slid it to the center of the table. "And here's fifteen more."

You could almost feel the breeze from the poker hands hitting the table as every player in the game folded.

Except Six Bits Slater.

He scraped together every coin he had and borrowed a gold eagle from Josh to see the bet. Wiley could have raised again and forced Slater out of the game, but, being a sporting man, he said, instead, "What you got, cowboy?"

Six Bits fanned his two pairs onto the felt and reached confidently toward the pot.

"Hold on there," Wiley said.

He closed up the fan of cards in his hand and placed the stack face up on the table. Then, with his index finger, he slid the cards aside one by one to reveal a full house—sixes and tens.

When both of Wiley's hands hit the tabletop to rake in the pot holding the last of Slater's money, Six Bits took the opportunity to shove the barrel of his pistol under the gambler's well-trimmed moustaches, drawing back the hammer as he did so.

Slater said, "Now you hold on there, you sonofabitch."

"What the hell's the matter with you, cowboy?" Wiley said as Slater rose to his feet. "Can't stand to lose?"

"Oh, I can stand losing, all right. It's part of the game. What I can't stand is being cheated."

The word "cheat" prompted a wholesale scraping of chair legs across the plank floor as the other players vacated the table.

The commotion drew the attention of the crowd and silence rippled across the saloon until the only sound in the room was the tick-tock-tick of a wind-up wall clock above the bar and the noise of C Street seeping in through the swinging doors.

Wiley appeared unruffled but beads of sweat on his forehead betrayed his anxiety.

"Holster that gun and get out of my saloon, you sorry bastard," he eventually said, prompting the exhalation of so much held breath you'd swear the flames in the lamps flickered.

"I ain't no bastard," Six Bits said. "I just can't locate my folks."

That prompted titters from a few patrons, but the laughter was soon swallowed by the tension.

"Get out."

"I won't do it. Not before I kill you."

"You'll hang if you do."

At that, Six Bits laughed. "Hell," he said, "nobody would convict a man who killed a card cheater and you know it."

"I am not a cheater, and you know it."

"You're not only a cheat, you're a liar. You've got so much pasteboard stuffed in your sleeves and cuffs and pockets you'd likely catch fire if you got too close to a flame."

Wiley's only response was that the beads of sweat on his forehead grew so heavy they succumbed to gravity and commenced rolling down the fat gambler's face.

Six Bits cast a glance toward his friend at the bar.

"Come over here and clean him out," he said, and Josh Lonigan pushed himself away from the bar and walked over to the poker table, his footsteps ringing hollow through the saloon.

Josh peeled back the gambler's jacket cuffs and shirt sleeves, revealing hidden cards up both arms. Cards were pulled from Wiley's watch pocket and another was revealed when Josh jerked the vest open, popping off buttons in the process.

Six Bits said, "You said you ain't been cheating, you lying sonofabitch. What do you say now?"

Wiley sat and sweated in silence.

"Kill him," one of the other card players said, triggering assenting murmurs through the crowd, many members of which had come to the realization that Wiley had likely been skinning them right along.

"I ought to. But being a betting man, I got a better idea. You game for an honest wager, Wiley?"

"What's the game?"

"Five-card stud poker. That way we can keep your grimy mitts off the cards. One hand. He deals," Six Bits said, inclining his head toward the card player who had encouraged Wiley's death.

"What's the bet?"

"Well, here's how I see it. About the only thing I hold just now is your life in my hands. I'm willing to bet that against something you got—the title to this hell hole."

"You crazy?" Wiley sputtered. "You want me to risk my saloon on a poker hand?"

"That's up to you. Worthless as your life is, it ought to be worth more than this place."

"I guess I got no choice in the matter."

"I guess that's right."

Six Bits asked Lonigan to cover Wiley, holstered his pistol, sat down, then waved the designated dealer toward an empty chair.

"Deal," he said.

The man gathered up all the cards from the table, including Wiley's holdouts, and pitched the lot into a spittoon. The crowd pressed close to the table, forcing the bartender to elbow his way through with a fresh, sealed deck. The dealer unwrapped and shuffled the cards three times, then slid the stack toward Six Bits for the cut.

"Let Wiley cut them," he said. "I don't think he can sully the cards just by cutting them."

Wiley lifted off the top two thirds of the deck and set it aside. The dealer put the bottom stack on top with the comment, "Cut 'em deep, sleep in the street," which drew a nasty stare from the still-current proprietor of the C Street Saloon and Entertainment Emporium.

Hole cards hit the felt, followed immediately by a face-up ten of diamonds to Wiley and the ace of hearts to Slater.

Six Bits did not peek at his hole card.

Wiley cupped his hand around his and rolled back a corner to reveal the jack of clubs.

"Now you've looked, get your slippery hands away from them cards," Six Bits said.

Wiley complied.

"Ace bets," the dealer said.

"There ain't no bets but the one, you dumb shit!" Wiley said, stress evident in his voice if not his demeanor.

"Queen on top of the ten," said the dealer of Wiley's growing hand, "possible straight."

Then, "Eight of spades to go with the still-high ace."

The players contemplated the cards for but a second before the next addition lit on their respective piles.

"Nine of hearts to Mister Wiley. Straight still possible," the dealer said.

"Six Bits gets the three of spades. Ace high still the betting hand."

Wiley knew he had the jack of clubs in the hole and wished to hell he could somehow slip a king or an eight onto the deck to complete the straight. Were he the dealer, it could be done. But this, damn it all, this was an honest game and he felt himself at a disadvantage.

Then, "Nine of clubs. Busted the straight, but a pair of nines showing."

And then, "Seven of clubs to Six Bits. Pair of nines the high hand. Anything better?"

Wiley flipped over his hole card.

"No help from the jack. Pair of nines still on top."

Six Bits Slater made no move to turn his hole card, choosing instead to watch runnels of perspiration creep down Calvin Wiley's face. After ten seconds that stretched into eternity, he reached down without averting his eyes and slowly overturned the card. From the crowd's reaction, he knew it was a good one.

The dealer said, "Ace of diamonds—pair of aces wins!"

Wiley sagged in his seat, not knowing whether to be sorry at the loss of the saloon or happy to still be drawing breath.

"To quote the previous owner of this handsome establishment," Six Bits told Wiley with an insincere smile, " 'Get out of my saloon, you sorry bastard.' "

With surprising speed given the man's girth, Calvin Wiley vacated the premises.

"Drinks on the house!" Six Bits shouted.

The party was on.

Memories crept up slow on Josh Lonigan and he didn't rush things. He lay as still as possible for a time, trying to make sense of the noises. A clangy piano fought for dominance over a crowd of rowdy voices.

He lifted one eyelid ever so slow, using all his concentration to keep the other closed and saw sunlight streaming through gaps in a warped greenwood wall. Lonigan allowed the other eyelid to lift, despite the fact that the air on his eyeballs was the consistency of crushed glass, and glanced slowly about.

Finally, he realized, remembered, where he was, but had only a fuzzy notion of how he came to be there. Where he was, was on a cot in a crib in the back of the C Street Saloon and Entertainment Emporium.

One by one, he activated his extremities and since none of his motion was hindered, concluded he was alone.

Except, that is, for the loud snores leaking through the curtain from the next crib. He knew the source of the snorts and wheezes and whistles was Six Bits Slater, Josh having spent more nights trying to sleep through that same racket than he cared to remember.

"Six Bits," he called weakly.

No response. Not even a change in rhythm.

"Six Bits!" he said, louder.

Same result.

Lonigan got himself upright, took a moment to accustom himself to the change in position, and shuffled slowly around the end of the curtain. There, in the next crib, Six Bits Slater was sprawled across the cot in every possible direction. One spurred and booted foot was on the floor, the other bent awkwardly and dangling off the opposite side. His arms were flung to the sides, palms upward and fingers twitching with every snort of every snore.

"Slater!" Josh said, grabbing Six Bits by the toe of his boot and shaking vigorously to punctuate the call. At that, Six Bits sat upright as if stung by a lightning bolt.

"What!? What the hell?"

"C'mon, get up. It's burning daylight."

"So?" Six Bits said, lapsing halfway back into whatever fog he had just been startled out of.

"Get up."

"What for?"

"Don't you remember? Hell, Six Bits, you've got responsibilities."

"Huh?"

"Why, you're the new owner and operator of the C Street Saloon and Entertainment Emporium."

"Oh. That. Oh, shit!"

Josh said, "What's the matter?"

"What you said—responsibilities."

Lonigan looked perplexed.

"Hell's bells, just think of it, Josh. I got this here building to worry about, and that ain't the half of it. I'm responsible for at least one barkeep I know of, that raggedy-ass piano player jangling away out there, and three whores."

"So?"

"So! Don't you see Josh, I'm the one that's got to see that all these people get paid, and come up with the money to do it. I don't know thing one about buying whiskey more than a bottle at a time, or how to put out a free lunch, how to take a rake from the card games, how to split the proceeds with the women—hell, I don't know nothing about a saloon except how to raise hell in one. I ain't never been nothing but a saddle tramp and never figured on being nothing but."

"But you're a businessman now, Six Bits! Hell, you could get rich."

"Not me. Not interested."

"What you gonna do?"

"Don't know. But I got six bits says I'll think of something by the time we hit them swinging doors on the way out of here."

The two cowboys slid through the door into the saloon proper and paused for a moment to survey Slater's recently acquired empire.

It appeared the party had been going nonstop since Six Bits called for drinks for the house. He had neglected to rescind the order before incapacitation set in, and it seems that word had spread far and wide across the Comstock mining district that drinks were on the house at the C Street Saloon and Entertainment Emporium.

So, in the absence of the boss, the piano man kept pounding. The barkeeper kept pouring. The saloon girls kept serving drinks to prospective customers who were more interested in free booze than anything else on the menu—which explains why Six Bits and Lonigan had slept undisturbed in the ladies' usual workplaces.

"Let's go," Six Bits said and set out through the crowd toward the batwing doors at the other end of the room.

They hadn't got far when someone in the crowd recognized Six Bits through the alcohol haze. Cheers, hurrahs, backslaps, handshakes, and all manner of drunken adulation accompanied them the rest of the way.

When they finally reached the front, Six Bits pushed through the swinging doors and said over his shoulder to Josh, "You owe me six bits. Be sure to mark it down."

"So what's your plan?"

"You'll see. Come on."

Six Bits, with his pal Josh in tow, scoured every nook and cranny of C Street asking after Calvin Wiley, erstwhile proprietor of the C Street Saloon and Gambling Emporium. They finally tracked him down, stabbing forlornly with a fork at a plate of chop suey in a three-table noodle parlor tucked between a barber shop and pool hall.

"What the hell you two want now?" he said, the words slurred by a recipe of flat beer and greasy cabbage. "Already stole the only saloon I got. Ain't you caused me enough trouble?"

"How about we end those troubles, here and now," Slater said.

"Whatever do you mean?" Wiley asked, to the accompaniment of a rattling throat hack and a misguided spit shot at a cuspidor.

Six Bits grimaced, his stomach too tender this day for such demonstrations, but he carried on. "Wiley, I woke up this morning—this afternoon—whenever the hell it is—realizing I don't want to be no respectable citizen nor a property owner nor a businessman."

"What's that got to do with me?"

"I propose to sell you back your saloon."

The fat man let go a disheartened laugh, then said, "How do you propose I pay for it? I ain't exactly flush with cash, you know. Every penny I got is tied up in that place already."

"Well, here's how I figure it. I walked through your doors after a pretty good run of luck in this town. More than doubled my month's wage—had eighty-four dollars in my pocket. If I was to walk away from the C Street Saloon and Entertainment Emporium with the same money in my pocket as I had when I walked in, I'd call it good."

Lonigan was too flabbergasted to do more than sputter.

Wiley was so dumbfounded he could only manage a single word: "Done."

"One other thing," Six Bits said.

Wiley waited, suspicion all over his face.

"I ever hear tell of you cheating at them card tables, faro or poker either one, I'll come back to this town and shoot your sorry ass. And I'll do it, too. I already got one killing coming to me where you're concerned. Don't make it two."

Wiley nodded his assent, then yanked out his shirttail to get at a money belt from which he extracted four twenty-dollar gold pieces and a five-dollar half eagle.

"Keep the change," he said.

Within minutes, Joshua Lonigan and Seth "Six Bits" Slater had fetched their horses from the livery and were heading back to the herd at a long trot. Once clear of the crowds of Virginia City, they slowed to a lazy walk along the downhill dirt road.

Ahead, a pair of magpies sat between the ruts pecking out bits of grain from a pile of droppings left lately by one of the well-fed horses that hauled freight wagons along the road.

"See them two magpies yonder?" Slater asked.

"I see them," Josh said.

"I got six bits that says the one on your side flies first."

THE TIMES OF A SIGN

The truth of it is, that advertising sign on my place of business ain't nothin' but bullshit. It says:

FOR SALE
MULES & OXEN
BREEDING STOCK

Now, anybody with a lick of sense knows mules can't breed. Leastways not so's it amounts to anything. Besides, most all of them that needs it is gelded, anyhow. And the only ox worth a damn is a steer, which as everybody knows can't breed neither— they just plain ain't got the tools for the job.

It all comes down to that fool sign painter I hired way back when to make the sign. Had he put a little flourish or fancy or some such between them last two lines it would've worked out fine. But when I complained, he said he was too busy for such nonsense and wouldn't do it 'less I paid to have the whole thing done over.

But with things the way they is in Independence, and as they have been since I first hung up that sign, I been sellin' every mule and ox I can get growed up enough to pull a wagon as quick as, well, I can get them growed up enough to pull a wagon. So, I guess it don't make no never mind about that sign.

You see, it's like this. Independence is the place where most folks wantin' to set out for the western territories—Oregon and

California and whatnot—gets outfitted. Then there's all them freight trains wheelin' down the Santa Fe Road like they been doin' for years. Fact is, that Santa Fe Road is why I'm in the mule business in the first place. I got into the ox business later, but that don't matter for now. What you want to know is how I came to be doin' what it says on that sign I'm doin', so that's what I'm a-goin' to tell you.

Before I go on, I reckon I had best clear up that sign business. See, we do sell breeding stock—brood mares that will birth baby mules if bred to a jack—but we don't sell jacks no how, no way, them bein' the very lifeblood of my business—and we sell cows that'll produce passable calves that might make an ox one day. And we don't sell no bulls, neither. Good Durham bulls that throw sizable calves ain't that easy to come by, so when we get a good one, he ain't goin' nowhere.

'Course I don't let on that the mares and cows we do sell is the ones that ain't quite up to snuff, but that's just horse tradin'.

I already told you my name is Daniel Boone Trewick. No relation to ol' Daniel Boone his own self, but my daddy thought him a hero and thus hung the name on me. Most everybody calls me Boone, save my wife, who calls me Danny—which I don't prefer, but it's what she called me back when we was young and I guess she can't get over the habit.

What I ain't told you is that I got a partner in this here business, his name bein' Juan Medina. Now, Juan, he's a Mexican from out in California I hooked up with, but that was before . . . Aw, hell, I guess I had best quit ramblin' and just start at the beginning of this here story.

What happened was, me and a girl name of Mary Elizabeth Thatcher was sweet on each other back when we was young—me bein' about sixteen at the time, and her bein' fourteen or maybe fifteen. This bein' back about '39. Her daddy was Reverend Thatcher, and he had no use for me—or any other boys, of

which there were plenty—sniffin' around young Mary Elizabeth. One day up in Liberty, where we all lived, we was in the
reverend's carriage house sittin' in a buggy gettin' to know one
another, you might say, when the reverend caught us at it.

Well, he yanked me out of that buggy and went to whalin' on
me, which was not to my likin'. So, with me havin' got my
growth up to where I was of a size where I didn't have to take
such from anybody, I returned the favor.

Hangin' there on a peg on the wall was a singletree, which
sort of fell right into my hand, and I walloped Reverend
Thatcher upside the head with it. He went down like a poleaxed
steer in the slaughter yard and Mary Elizabeth started in to
yowlin' like a scared cat and the reverend was layin' there with
blood pourin' out of his head like used grass and water out of
the back end of an incontinent cow and me seein' nothin' but
trouble to come from it all, I lit out of there and hit the road for
Independence and never looked back. Never even slowed down
to say goodbye to my ma and pa nor nothin', which didn't matter much on account of them havin' so many other kids
scratchin' around the place that they might not even notice I
was gone anyhow.

'Course, I didn't stay around Independence long, on account
of it bein' near enough to Liberty that the Clay County law
would certain sure come there lookin' for a murderer. Per-
chance, there was a freight outfit ready to pull out for Santa Fe
and they hired me on as a herder. So it was that I come to
spend day after day a-horseback on an old high-withered
swaybacked nag of theirs, chafin' my backside on a worn-out
Mexican saddle they found for me somewheres, followin' a
bunch of oxen they took along to take over for them that lamed
up or tired out and needed a rest from them big freight wagons
they pulled.

I had no notion at the time of my leavin' what I was to do

with myself once I got to Santa Fe—my only purpose was to avoid gettin' strung up for killin' Mary Elizabeth's daddy. But somewhere along the way, I took up thinkin' about them mountain men and free trappers that I'd read about and had seen from time to time in Missouri on their way to someplace or another, and thought to look into becomin' one of them. When we got to Bent's Fort out on the Arkansas, there was some of them mountain men hangin' around, and listenin' to their stories made me want to try that way of livin' for sure. 'Course, bein' young and dumb and all, I had no idea how to go about doin' such a thing, but it was in my mind.

Anyhow, after makin' it on out to Santa Fe and collectin' my pay—which amounted to more money than I ever held in my hand at one time before—I heard tell there was mountain men livin' up at a place called Taos. On account of them bein' up there and out of the way, the Mexican government left them alone.

So it was off to Taos I went. Once I got there, I met up with a fellow with a wooden leg named Pegleg Smith, who, I was told, was one of the best of the trappers ever there was. Him and some others let me know right off that the times when a man could make a decent livin' trappin' fur in the mountains was gone. Pegleg his own self was lookin' to keep his belly full in other ways, one of which was goin' partners with a man makin' whiskey that come to be called Taos Lightnin' by them that got struck by it.

But at present, Pegleg and Old Bill Williams and some others was outfittin' for a trip out to California to steal horses and mules and bring 'em back to Santa Fe and sell 'em at a handsome profit. They asked me along with the promise of a share in the takin's, and me havin' nowhere else to go and nothin' else to do at the time, seein' as my becomin' a trapper wasn't in the offing, I did so.

Even bein' in Mexico as I was, there was too many Mexicans in on that horse-stealin' deal to suit me. I could see right off it weren't so, but I could not get rid of the notion that those people was by nature lazy and shiftless. And then when we got to this place called Abiquiu, there was this black man name of Jim Beckwourth came along. Me and him ended up in a dispute when he told me to do some thing or another and I let him know that where I come from, white folks *give* orders to his kind, not *take* 'em. Near as soon as I said it, I found myself on my back with his foot planted in my middle. But it turned out all right on account of he was one of them—a mountain man and trapper, I mean—and he was one of them that cooked up this here foray to California we was settin' out on.

And if it weren't bad enough to be in cahoots with Mexicans and a black man, a ways up the trail we hooked up with a bunch of Indians—Utes, they was—and one of 'em, called Wakara, was as much in charge of things as was Pegleg or Old Bill or that black fellow Beckwourth.

I'll tell you, they got a whole different way of doin' things out there than what I growed up with here in Missouri.

Well, anyway, we went on out to California followin' a wandering road that Mexican traders used. That path has since come to be called the Old Spanish Trail, even if it ain't that old and it ain't Spanish. We stole thousands of horses and mules and jackasses from California ranches and brung 'em back, just as planned—save for leavin' what must've been a thousand dead horses layin' out in the desert from pushin' 'em too hard, so as to avoid bein' overtaken by a posse of them Californios. I'll tell you, I seen things on that trip I never even knew to dream about, and was involved in all manner of adventures.

But all that's a story for another time.

There is one part I got to tell, and that's how Juan Medina came to be here in Missouri in this business enterprise of ours.

See, Juan is a Mexican from California and he worked on one of them ranches we stole horses from back then. 'Cept he wasn't there at the time we did it on account of him bein' in jail owin' to a dispute he had with the brother of a girl he was sweet on, which ended up with him bein' locked up till they sprung him to ride with the posse that was chasin' after us.

For reasons he'd rather I not talk about, he left off with that posse when it give up the chase and he followed us and throwed in with our outfit. Him and me spent a heap of time together on the trail and he learned enough white-man talk from me to where we could palaver some. Him bein' a hand with horses and mules the like of which you ain't never seen gave me an idea. I took a notion to take my pay for that horse-thievin' trip in mares and jacks—*yeguas y machos*, Juan called 'em—and drive 'em back here to Missouri and raise mules.

There was always plenty of plowin' and whatnot to be done on Missouri farms, and some of the outfits headin' out the Santa Fe Road used mules, so I figured sellin' off what mules we could raise would be easy enough and make us a right smart of money besides. And I had seen right off that them California mules we stole was a hell of a lot better than what was raised here in Missouri back then, and it was all on account of them California *machos*. They was big, strong jackasses and they throwed big, strong mules.

Juan, he had nothin' else to do and nowhere else to go, so he allowed as how he'd come in on the deal. I wasn't all that sure about throwin' in with a Mexican, but I seen how good he was handlin' critters, and he knowed a hell of a lot more 'bout *machos* and mares and mules than what I did, so I reckoned it was worth the risk.

What I didn't know at the time was what was 'bout to happen back in the States. I'll tell you more on that later on.

Anyhow, by the time we got that herd back to Santa Fe, I had talked it all over with Pegleg Smith and Old Bill Williams and them, and we had come to terms on my share of the takin's. Juan, meantime, had picked us out a nice string of mares and *machos*—some of 'em he'd had a hand in raisin' back on that California ranch he come from. I ain't sayin' how many head I got for my share, as that ain't no man's business but my own. Juan, he didn't get nothin' as he wasn't part of the outfit, but I took him on as equal partner anyhow.

You will recollect that I had gone out west with a freight outfit on the road to Santa Fe. But, fact is, I spent the whole trip in a cloud of dust followin' the spare oxen and, besides, I wasn't payin' all that much attention. So, I didn't have but a smidgen of knowledge about the road, and sure as hell could not pass myself off as an expert. But I knowed it took them ox trains two, two-and-a-half months to make it out from Missouri and I figured it would take them about as long to get back here. But we had no oxen and wasn't pullin' any wagons, and horses that ain't under harness or saddle can travel at a quicker pace, so I figured me and Juan ought to be able to get our herd back here to Independence in somethin' less than two months. We sold off some of our stock to buy supplies and pack outfits to haul 'em. We sure as hell didn't buy no pack animals, as we had horses and jacks enough to carry what we needed and then some.

We strung the critters carryin' packsaddles together head to tail and let the rest run loose, as we knowed they would stay in a bunch and not wander off 'less somethin' spooked 'em. Headin' southeast out of Santa Fe, the road winds through the mountains and over Glorieta Pass till strikin' the Pecos River and some fords called somethin' like San Jose del Vado and San Miguel del Vado. Don't know what them Mexican names mean, but I recall Juan sayin' it was somethin' about them namin' them crossings after some Mexican saints.

Juan and me decided to lay over in Las Vegas for an extra day, that bein' about the only town that amounted to much between where we was and where we was goin'. We fed up good in them bean parlors there, not knowin' when we'd again have occasion to eat food cooked by someone who knew what they was doin'. See, neither of us was much of a hand at the cookfire. Oh, we could put the scorch to enough provisions to keep ourselves alive, but it ain't like what we fixed was worth eatin' otherwise.

Whilst we was havin' dinner the day before pullin' out, a trail-worn old man—I say old, but lookin' back, he likely hadn't more'n forty years on him—stepped inside the door and looked around in the dim light in the place till he seen us.

He wandered over to our table. "You the young fellers got that bunch of horses and jackasses out yonder?"

I nodded.

He stood, waiting for more, shifting his weight from one foot to the other. I sliced off another forkful of meat and went to work chewin' it. He watched me, looked at Juan, and back at me. He shifted his weight again and cleared his throat. "Mind my askin' where you-all are takin' them?"

I watched him as I chewed and swallowed. "Why might that be of interest to you?"

The man shuffled for another moment. "Mind if I sit down?"

I nodded toward the empty chair he stood behind and set down my knife and fork. It didn't look as if he was goin' away anytime soon, so I figured I might as well pay him some attention. "Well?"

Again, he cleared his throat. "I'm lookin' to get back to the States."

"There's plenty of freighters on the road most anytime," I said.

"I know it. Thing is, I been a bullwhacker and mule skinner

195

on them trains more times than I care to remember, and I've had my fill of 'em."

I could see how that could happen. It's a hell of a long road, and the monotony and drudgery of it all can wear on a man. And that ain't even takin' into account the risk of mishaps of one kind or another, or a run-in with Indians.

Turned out the man had family up in St. Joseph and wanted to get back to 'em. Leastways that's what he said.

"You ever drove any loose stock?"

"Oh, hell yes. I was a herder on a couple trips out and back years ago, 'fore I got a place on a wagon. I can pack a mule or horse and throw a passable hitch. Ain't no expert at it, but I get by."

"Me and Juan, we can handle all that. The drovin', too. It ain't like we need any hired help."

"I ain't askin' for no job. All I'm after is a way to get home. Travelin' that road alone ain't smart. You-all take me along, I'm more'n willin' to pull my weight with the work to be done. Keep me mounted and fed is all I'm askin' you to do. I'll even do the cookin' if you-all want."

After talkin' it over with Juan, we decided to take him on. Come the morning, we rustled up an old saddle and bridle at a wagon yard and added some extra supplies in the way of foodstuffs. After a last café breakfast, we readied to leave. Our new man was leanin' against a tree out where the herd waited when me and Juan rode up leadin' a packhorse. I led it over to where he sat, untied a knot, and tipped the saddle off to where it landed at his feet.

"Pick yourself out somethin' with four legs to cinch that onto," I said.

He had already made his choice, as he walked right over to a leggy sorrel mare and slipped the bit into her mouth and slid the headstall over her ears. After getting her saddled, he helped us finish packing and loading.

We pulled the last diamond hitch snug and strung out the pack animals and swung aboard our mounts, with Juan holdin' the lead rope for the string.

The new man squirmed into his saddle, lookin' for a comfortable seat. Then, "You boys decided where you-all are goin'?"

"What do you mean?"

" 'Fore long—I'd make it about twenty miles—we'll come to a place called La Junta de los Ríos. Get there, you got a choice to make. The road branches there and you-all can take what's called the mountain route, or the Cimarron route."

I pulled off my hat and scratched my head. "I don't know nothin' about that. Only thing I know is when I come out here, we followed the Arkansas River and went by a place called Bent's Fort."

"That'd be the mountain route."

"What's the difference 'tween that and the other'n—what'd you call it, Cimarron?"

"That's right. Cimarron route. It's a good ways shorter, save you some time. Cuts off a big loop up through the mountains. Meets back up with the Arkansas not too far from where the road leaves that river."

I thought it over. I looked to Juan, but he only shrugged. Could be he didn't savvy all what the man said, or could be he had no more idea than what I did.

"What would you do?"

The man slid his greasy hat up his forehead till it perched on the back of his head. " 'Twas me, I'd go the mountain way. It be longer, but there's good graze and water most all the way. They call the Cimarron the 'dry route' and it's for a reason. Plenty of times out that way there ain't no more water than what a man could spit."

That decided it for me. "We take the mountain road, then.

197

These critters has already had more'n their share of goin' without enough to drink. I thank you for the information." I nodded at Juan and he set out with the pack string in tow. "By the way," I said to the man as we waited to push the loose stock onto the trail, "that boy's name is Juan. I go by Boone. What's your name?"

He looked at me and pulled his hat back down over his forehead. "You can call me Conley."

So that's what we called the man from then on. Don't know to this day if that was his first name or his last, or if it was his name at all, but it's the only name I know.

Things went along without much of anything happening. We just plodded along the road up through Raton Pass and on down onto the plains. Looking to the east, there wasn't a thing to see but empty. Now, I wasn't raised in no mountain country, but for the past many months I hadn't never been out of sight of mountains, and mostly in amongst 'em. Even them big ol' dry lakes out in the desert that the Mexicans call playas, which was the flattest places I ever seen, was surrounded by mountains. Anyway, the emptiness of bein' in a country without no mountains again was a mite strange.

We passed freight trains on the road to Santa Fe now and again, and overtook some on the way to the States. We'd share a camp on occasion with the freighters and there was a few men among them that seemed to know Conley. But no one of them ever went out of his way to act friendly to the man. I had no notion of why that was and did not ask.

Conley, he turned out to be the kind of man who didn't do a thing 'less he was told to. Oh, he would do pretty much anything he was told, and do a passable job at it, and whilst his cooking wasn't anything to brag on, it was way ahead of what me or Juan could've done. So, while havin' him along was a help in some ways, he wasn't the kind of a man you'd want to be in harness with any longer than need be.

I came to think that even more so when we laid over at Bent's Fort to let the horses rest for a time. And I came to know why none of the bullwhackers that knowed him wanted anything to do with him. One day I was sittin' in the plaza there at the fort listenin' to men tellin' stories—some of them the same old mountain men and same old tales that put me in mind to take up fur trapping—when a man who looked to be from a freight outfit squatted down beside me.

"You're the one herdin' horses, ain't you."

It wasn't really a question, so I didn't say nothin' to him. He knowed who I was, so I just waited to see what he wanted of me. He waited a bit as I looked him over, then invited me to find someplace quiet to talk. We walked over to where the powder house was, as there wasn't anyone hangin' around there, and I leaned against the wall listenin' to what he had to say. He allowed as how he was wagon master on a bull train, and had run several such outfits out and back on the Santa Fe Road.

"You got a man name of Conley with you, ain't you."

Again, it was not a question, so I waited.

"Was I you, I'd keep an eye on that one. See, I've had him in my employ before, so I know him."

"What might it be that I should watch out for?"

The wagon master glanced around to make sure no one was near enough to overhear. "Conley's a thief."

"A thief? What's he steal?"

"That's the thing. He ain't like no other thief I ever seen. It's like he can't help himself. He'll steal anything. Even trinkets and such that won't do him no good at all."

I thought over what he said. Then he said more.

"He stole money and such, like you might expect. And we caught him pilfering out of the stores on the wagons. But he'd steal about anything. Take little keepsakes and doodads out of another's man's baggage. We booted him out first chance we got, soon as we could run him off where he wouldn't starve to death." He scratched his beard and kneaded his chin. "Like I said, sometimes it's like he can't help it. So was I you, I'd watch him, for it is my notion that a man who'll steal when he don't even have to will steal for sure when he sees it to his advantage."

I extended a hand to the wagon master and, as we shook, thanked him for the information. I allowed as how we would watch Conley extra careful. Then I looked up Juan and passed along the caution.

Things went along just fine for weeks as we trailed them mares and *machos* along the Arkansas. We come to several places where Conley said there was crossings for them that took the Cimarron way, and after that there was more freighters on the road. We chose to stay clear of them most times, and kept a close watch on our man Conley whenever we camped with them.

After a time, we reached the Great Bend, where the Arkansas takes a more southerly course and the road leaves the river and goes on east towards Independence. The country was startin' to look more like home, what with more and more trees a-growin'. We laid over at Council Grove, where I was told there'd been a treaty of some kind made with the Indians there. There was one big old tree folks called the Post Office Oak on account of there bein' a hollow place at its bottom where you could find letters and messages and such left in there. Some had names wrote on them and was undisturbed by others, and some was just messages of a general sort meant for anyone who cared to read them. Some told about bein' on the lookout for someone who run off, children that got carried off from their folks, news about weddings on the trail, Indian troubles, and all manner of things.

I pawed through the stack of letters there and was nearly

surprised right out of my boots to find a folded-up page sealed with wax that had wrote on it in a fine hand, if faded some, *Daniel Boone Trewick.*

It took some time to catch my breath and gather my wits about me. I could not fathom any reason why there should be a letter for me there, or who might have wrote it. I broke the wax seal and unfolded the crisp sheet. The writing inside filled a portion of the page. My eye went first to the name at the bottom, and again I was discombobulated to read *Mary Elizabeth Thatcher.* I went on to read what she wrote.

Danny,

I do not know what has become of you. It crossed my mind that you might have taken the Santa Fe Road in your haste to be gone from Liberty after the unfortunate circumstances of our parting. I hasten to tell you, should this missive find its way to your hand, that there was not then, nor is there now, any reason for your continued absence from Clay County. No doubt you were concerned for the well-being of the Reverend Thatcher, but I can assure you that Father is well. Any lingering difficulties between the two of you can, I am confident, be settled satisfactorily and I pledge my heart to see it so. If you hold any feelings for me, please return at first opportunity and with haste to me in Liberty.

Yours,
Mary Elizabeth Thatcher

That whole deal rattled my brain so that I ain't got much recollection of what went on the next few days. All I remember is that we kept trailin' them mares and jacks along the way to Independence. I had no firm notion of how to proceed with my plans once I got there, and that letter from Mary Elizabeth only addled my brain more. I reckon that's part of the reason why what happened next happened.

We was camped along the trail within sight of Blue Mound when things took a turn for the worse. We was all three rolled in our blankets sleepin'—or so I thought. We never posted a guard on account of the horses bein' content to graze and rest through the nights and us havin' no notion of any danger of any kind in that part of the country.

But when I rolled out of my blankets in the morning, it was a mite later than usual, there bein' no smells in the air of Conley cookin' breakfast or makin' coffee. I sat up and scoured out my eyes with my knuckles and looked around. The campfire had gone cold, without even a wisp of smoke risin' from the ashes. There weren't no sign of Conley. I stood up and hollered for Juan to wake up. We walked out to where the horses was pastured and there weren't but about a third of them there. There wasn't no other way to think about it, save that that sonofabitch Conley had made off with them in the night.

We talked over some what to do. We found the track where he took them out of there, and it appeared he was settin' a northern course toward St. Joe, but there was no tellin' how long he'd hold to that direction or if he'd only talked about St. Joseph now and then as a way to throw us off. What with Juan bein' a whole lot better tracker than me, we thought to put him on Conley's trail whilst I pushed on to Independence with what horses and jacks we had left. That was one thing—Conley hadn't stole a single one of them jacks—he only took the mares.

Then we thought better of sendin' Juan off in pursuit. What with him bein' Mexican and all, and his English bein' somewhat lacking, we decided he might find himself in more trouble than he could handle should he be accused—by Conley or on general principles—of bein' the thief.

Which brings up somethin' that might matter in the circumstances. Them horses was stolen by me and them others way back in California. But that was Mexico, and this is America, so it likely wouldn't matter. But I had tucked away a bill of sale wrote up and signed by Thomas L. "Pegleg" Smith, declaring me the rightful owner of them animals. He even had it attested to by some make-believe official of the government in Santa Fe. Still, even with that paper in hand, folks might not be inclined to believe Juan, him bein' Mexican and all.

So I set off after Conley and my mares and left Juan to wait where we was. Well, not exactly where we was—we determined to push a ways farther off the trail, where him and them horses would be less likely to be found by anybody. If he was found, well, all we could do was hope for the best.

It turned out Conley held true on a course towards St. Joe and he made no effort to throw me off the trail. But he was movin' fast, so I was glad to have brought along a spare horse on a lead, which allowed me to move at a good pace over the prairie, stopping only for a few hours' sleep in the dark of the night.

By the time I hit Fort Leavenworth, Conley wasn't but a couple of hours ahead. There was men at the fort—soldiers and civilians both—who had seen him with my horses, and said he could yet be gettin' them across the Missouri River on the ferry. With promise of a reward, I hired on two men who looked like they knew their way around a scrape. When we got to the river, the man who kept the ferry—name of Cain, as I recall—said Conley and the horses couldn't be more than half an hour gone, as he had just tied up after returnin' from the last trip haulin' him over. I don't know where Conley came up with the money to pay the man, but he had it from somewheres.

We caught up with Conley pretty quick. One man wrangling a herd of horses ain't no match for three men horseback. My two men stayed out of sight behind the herd and I hurried off through the woods to get ahead of the thief. His look of surprise when he saw me sitting horseback on the trail turned to fear before despair overcame him.

"Boone, I—"

"Shut up, Conley. I don't want to hear it."

He looked around like he was mulling over making a run for it. But then the men from Fort Leavenworth rode up and I could see he was resigned to his situation.

One of the men said, "This him?"

I nodded.

The other said, "Well, hell, we might just as well get on with it."

It sickened me to hang a man, but we left Conley dangling from a red oak tree and rode away. Hanging from his neck by a loop of whang leather was a piece cut from a saddle skirt with the words HORSE THIEF scratched on it.

We got the horses ferried back across the river and those two men offered to help me get the horses back to the Santa Fe Road.

"No, gentlemen. I reckon if that sorry sonofabitch Conley got them up here, I can get them back."

What cash I had been carrying was now in the hands of the ferry man, so I allowed my helpers to take a mare each from the herd. Pretty good pay for a day's work, I thought. Even if the job required stringing up a horse thief.

I found Juan without no trouble and we set off for Independence, which I figured to be two, maybe three days away. We made it in two.

Me and Juan spent a few days riding around the country and located suitable pasture that was there for the taking. It was a different deal in town, where I had to put the horse herd up as security for a bank loan to buy land in town for a barn and pens and an office.

As you might imagine, most all them mares had already been

serviced by them big jacks on the trail somewhere between here and California, and was carrying foals, so our first crop of mules was already on the way. Them *machos* did their job that year, and every year since. So did that herd of mares, as have them we've added since.

By the time we got that first bunch of mules raised up and Juan got them broke to drive, things had changed in Independence. What we figured to be a ready market among freighters was still there. But in the meantime, all kinds of folks from the East was headin' west, most bound for Oregon and some for California. We couldn't raise mules fast enough, and every team that left our barn left behind a hefty profit. That's when we got in the ox business, bringin' in some big Durham bulls from back East and breedin' them to lanky longhorn cows brought up from Texas, and whatever other cows of a suitable size we could find hereabouts. We been at it ever since, sellin' every mule and ox we can get raised up to a proper size for work.

Which brings us to that damn sign. I confess that slab of wood daubed with paint is right handsome, even though it's showin' its age all these years later. And it has sure done its job. But, like I said, the way it reads makes it look like we're sellin' mules and oxen for breeding and there sure as hell ain't no such thing. Sticks in my craw. I could have had a new sign made over the years but never did. Fact is, as much as the damn thing bothers me, I like the look of it. And plenty of folks stop in to ask about it, just like you did.

So that's the story about that sign, and I don't know what else I can tell you.

Well, there is one more thing. After we got settled in and doin' business, I made my way across the river to Clay County and on up to Liberty, where I made my peace with the Reverend Thatcher. It took some talkin', but I done it. It didn't take much talkin' at all to convince Mary Elizabeth to marry me.

The reverend allowed as how she was too young for it, but she was past sixteen and as stubborn as one of my mules, so he finally gave in. Hell, he even read out the rites for us. The passel of kids that's come along since has been to his likin' as well.

As for me, I've been content and have not ever once been tempted to take another trip on the road to Santa Fe. And, no matter how much I admire the horses and mules and *machos* out that way, I sure as hell ain't been back to California.

THE NAKEDNESS OF THE LAND

I thought I'd seen the last of my little brother the night I left him for dead in Cold Spring Draw. But here I am, fettered to a cast-iron stove in his house and having no idea what happens next.

At least it's warm, which is something I haven't been much lately. And the food's good. Which is something else I haven't been seeing enough of. The cook's culinary skills surpass her conversational abilities, if the fact that she hasn't spoken six words to me in all the days I've been here is any indication.

Being stuck in this room has given me plenty of time to try to figure Joey out, but I'll be damned if I can find any sign I can read. He looks to be well off, or at least living like it. There are books all over the walls and a big desk with papers poking out the cubby holes and a safe off in the corner bigger than this stove I'm chained to.

Of course, none of it's his.

He runs the ranch, but says it belongs to some rich man back East who only shows up in the summer. Nonetheless, I'd have to say my little brother has done well for himself these dozen years we've been apart.

"Joey, you better get started. It's a long enough ride and Ruben is probably needing these supplies by now. I hope you'll find him up on Blacktail Ridge but if the feed gave out, he probably pushed the herd over into that valley toward the Pyramid Peaks."

Looking more and more at seventeen like the man his father hoped he'd become, the boy checked the cinch one last time and swung into the saddle as the old man tightened the diamond hitch on the packhorse.

"You ride easy. This old mare's not as young as she once was," the man said. "And get back here soon as Ruben turns you loose. There's work to be done."

The boy nodded and rode out to find his brother. It was hard to think of Ruben as his brother. Ruben was well past thirty, and had no use for a baby brother. He especially resented the favored treatment young Joey got from their parents.

The way Joey looked at it, he didn't ask to be a surprise—blessing, as they put it—in his folks' declining years. And he had to admit that they doted on him. Take the summer herding, for instance. Ruben hated being stuck out in the hills, far away from the town and the saloon and the dance hall girls, while Joey would have taken his place in an instant. But Dad—Ma, really—liked to keep him home at the ranch.

He knew Ruben considered him spoiled. To Joey, it seemed more like smothered. He craved long days horseback in the hills, tending the cattle and exploring the world inside his head. He was determined to enjoy this trip as long as it lasted.

Riding across the flatland, he looked with satisfaction upon the stacks of hay here and there in the grassy meadows that held the sagebrush at bay. He thought of how, when cold winds scoured the land and the cattle bunched up in the low places to shelter from snow blowing dry as sand, they'd undo the summer's work and dump the grass back on the meadows.

It was a delicate balance, ranch life on this high desert. Without the mountain pastures and hay patches, cattle would be forced back to the green, humid country they came from.

Through the clear air, the plateaus in the distance seemed near enough to touch but Joey knew the sun would be well up in tomorrow's sky before he started his climb.

From before he had a tooth in his head, the kid could do no wrong in Ma and Dad's eyes.

I was mostly grown when he was born, and it was bothersome to be out working my tail off and come home to see them fawning all over the little brat. Truth be told, he was a good kid. And me being such a disappointment, looking back I can see where they'd put all their hopes in Joey.

After all those years of watching him grow up smarter than me, better with cattle and horses, more willing to work, I guess I'd had a bellyful.

Still, I doubt I'd have done what I did if I hadn't been looking at the world through the bottom of a whiskey bottle for three or four days straight. But being out in those mountains with nothing or no one for company but a bunch of mangy cows for weeks on end, who could blame me for trying to improve my outlook with a little liquid?

Riding along the spine of Blacktail Ridge toward the divide, Joey could see the cattle had been gone from here for several days. He topped out and set his course toward the Pyramid Peaks, figuring to cover most of the distance by nightfall and hook up with Ruben sometime the next day.

Ruben would for sure be needing the supplies, more so than Dad suspected. But what the packhorse was carrying wasn't what needed replenishing so far as his brother would be concerned.

Joey knew Ruben had dumped one of the sacks of flour Ma had packed for him back into the barrel and refilled the bag with bottles of whiskey from his stash. No matter how far from town he got, Ruben wasn't one to deprive himself of the thing he enjoyed most.

Shadows lengthened and clouds stacked up against the horizon. Joey rode through stands of quakies and across parks painted with lupine and yarrow. Dark evergreen trees climbing the slopes provided contrast for the glowing sun-struck colors of the alpine meadows.

Joey found it hard to imagine a better time or a better place.

All the same, he had this gnawing feeling that all wasn't as it should be. From the scattered sign he'd seen, it looked more like the herd had merely wandered through here, rather than being moved. And even though cattle tended to roam and disperse across the hills by nature, as many cows as they had up here ought to have left more trace than he could see.

As he unsaddled and unloaded and made camp near Cold Spring Draw, he figured he'd be taking up the subject with Ruben soon enough.

When I saw the fire down at the other end of the valley, I hoped—hell, I don't know what I hoped. But it had to be another human and I hadn't seen one in a spell.

So I pocketed a bottle of hospitality, saddled up and rode down there.

I stopped a good ways off to study the situation and saw it was Joey—wide awake and dreaming. While not exactly my choice of company on a summer evening, I figured I'd have to see him sooner or later so decided to go ahead and get it over with.

Firelight reflected off Joey's face as he stared into the flames, lost in thought. He didn't hear the horse's approach. Was unaware of advancing footsteps. So when the man stepped between him and the fire, a startled Joey scrambled to get up.

A heavy hand halted his progress, pushing him back to the ground.

"Sit down, you little turd," a voice growled. "No need to get up on my account."

"Ruben?" Joey sputtered. "Is that you, Ruben?"

"Yeah, it's me," he replied as stepped past the boy and squatted at the edge of the fire's glow. "And, sad to say, it's you. I was hoping for some worthwhile company when I saw the fire."

"I brought supplies."

"Yeah, little brother. But you ain't supplying what I'm needing."

Joey studied Ruben's haggard appearance and figured he was pretty well supplied already. His eyes were so red, Joey suspected they'd glow without benefit of the fire. And the way his face sagged, it appeared gravity—or lack of sleep—was about to get the better of him.

"Where are the cows, Ruben?"

"Oh, they're around. Here and there. They haven't wandered too far."

"You let them stray like this, it'll take too long to gather them. And we'll likely not find some of them at all. Dad ain't going to like that."

Ruben finished off the bottle he carried and threw it across the fire at Joey.

"Yeah, well, I'm sure he'll have confidence in you to get the job done." He staggered to his feet and started for his horse.

"Where you going, Ruben?"

"Back to my camp. I don't care much for the company here."

He missed the stirrup. He got it on the second try and heaved himself into the saddle.

"You best just leave the grub here and head on back at first light. We don't want Ma and Dad to miss you. It'd be pretty hard on them if they thought something bad happened to their baby boy."

"Dad will want to know about the cows."

"Well, you can just tell him they're fine."

"Ruben, it appears they're scattered from hell to breakfast and I'll tell him so."

"You'd be well advised to mind your own damn business, little brother."

"It is my business. Dad's, too. He ain't going to be too happy about you laying around up here drunk."

Without thinking, Ruben unstrung his lariat and shook out a loop.

"That's a piece of news he won't be hearing anytime soon," he said as he cast a loop over Joey, jerked the slack, took a turn around the horn, wheeled his mount and spurred him madly into the darkness.

As the boy bounced and caromed off rocks and bushes, the horse veered sharply to avoid plunging over the edge of the draw. Joey, cracking at the end of the whip, dropped into empty air. The tail of the rope burned through Ruben's hand as his dally gave way.

To tell the truth, I didn't even think about what I'd done to Joey. I rode to my camp, all but fell off my horse and collapsed.

It was late in the day when I finally woke up. The next day, I guess. Maybe the day after. Hell, I don't know.

I rolled over and raised up on my hands and knees. My horse was grazing a little way off, still saddled. As the fog in my aching head thinned, a wave of sickness washed over me, either from all the liquor or the realization of what I'd done.

I hauled my sorry self into the saddle and rode toward Cold Spring Draw, my backbone stabbing my brain with every step that horse took. I couldn't find any trace of the boy. Maybe he walked away.

Then again, I could have been looking in the wrong place altogether.

His camp was pretty much as we'd left it. Ashes gone cold in a ring of rocks. Bedroll on a mattress of pine boughs. Horses—thirsty by now—staked out. Supplies strung up in a tree.

It struck me that even abandoned, that campsite was a lot better organized than my thoughts. I had to figure out something.

With the one arm and leg that still worked, it was all Joey could do to push himself backwards downhill. Which, with the box end and steep sides of the draw through there, was the only way to go.

For parts of two nights and days—the parts when he wasn't passed out from pain or blacked out from the aftereffects of the blows his head had absorbed—he crawled down the draw.

Some ways below, a trail from the plateau above wound into and out of the draw. The small stream from the spring above spread into a shallow pool at the crossing and it was here the boy gave up. Lying in the cool water, he was barely breathing when the prospector found him.

Doubting it would save him but feeling obligated nonetheless, the old man bound up the boy's arm and leg, then lashed together a travois to drag him down to the flat land. He figured if no one could help him, at least someone might know where the boy ought to be buried.

The first stop was the Dream Ranch. The prospector was afraid it would be the boy's last.

Sooner or later, I'd have to face the music with Ma and Dad and I figured on sooner, if for no other reason than to get it over with. Besides, leaving the herd to bear the news might be explanation enough for the cattle being scattered hither and yon.

I strung together Joey's saddle horse and the old pack mare and headed for the ranch, concocting a story along the way.

The way I figured it was this: Joey never did make it. While riding out to check the herd one morning, I came across his horse, wandering free and dragging a lead rope from a halter. The packhorse was staying close and was spooked. When I found the camp, it looked like hell had been through it, scattering goods and groceries to the four winds.

Bears got it, I figured.

And while I never found any trace of the boy, I figured they must have got him, too.

It was worth a try.

Only eighty or so miles as the crow flies from Joey's home place, the Dream Ranch might as well have been across the sea.

The only wagon roads through the rugged plateaus required a long drive to mountain passes far to the north or south, so there was little travel and no commerce to speak of between the regions.

The land itself little resembled the high desert Joey came from. The Dios del Sol Valley was a greener, wetter, and altogether gentler country.

The ranch, centerpiece of the valley, was the result of a rich Eastern gunmaker's dreams of being a cattleman. A few long weeks horseback each summer was the extent of the owner's involvement, so operations and the big house fell to a hired manager.

Joey's care fell to the ranch cook. She tucked him into a back bedroom and nursed him until a doctor was fetched from town. He set the broken leg and arm as best he could, wrapped the banged-up rib cage, and did all he could for the battered head—

which was hope for the best.

Then, as doctors are wont to do, he pronounced Joey young and strong and likely to survive, took up the lines and headed back to town.

So it was back to the cook. She spoon-fed the boy, changed his dressings, and slowly but surely coaxed him out of bed and back to life.

Once Joey was up and around, he started helping out with chores around the place and it seemed natural somehow for him to stay on to do some cowboying when the offer was made.

He had no idea what Ma and Dad knew of his fate. And although he worried about them, months had passed and he felt no urgency to return to his former life. Spending his days riding over the ranch's vast range tending cattle seemed an ideal way to spend time for the time being.

Bad as it sounds, losing my little brother was the best thing that ever happened to me.

I swore off the sauce. I took an interest in running the ranch. And I tried, through being a better man, to fill at least a piece of the hole losing Joey left in Ma and Dad's lives.

And things did seem to get better after a while. I settled into my lot as a rancher and took as much of the burden off Dad as he'd allow.

Still and all, life does have a way of catching up with you.

The years on the Dream Ranch were good to Joey. The ranch manager came to rely on him. The owner liked riding with him summer days. Through hard work and savvy, he worked his way up to cow boss.

But there was a fly in the ointment, and one summer the Dream Ranch seemed more like a nightmare.

For starters, the owner found out his manager had had his

hand in the till for years and sent him packing.

Then one evening Joey stopped by the big house to report to the owner, who was still out riding. While waiting in the shade of the side porch, he and the man's pretty young wife flirted like they always did.

But this time, she wanted more than talk.

She parked her pretty little backside on Joey's lap as he sat in the porch swing, swept his hat aside and planted a kiss on him.

Scared near to death, the young man did the only thing he could think of on short notice.

He ran.

And, as he rounded the corner on his way to the steps, practically ran over the owner.

"What on earth is his hurry?" the man asked his wife.

She blushed in reply, on top of the flush that already colored her face.

"What's been going on here?" he asked, angrily.

He'd had occasion to suspect his wife more than once. Then, seeing the hat on the swing, he assumed he had reason to suspect Joey.

"I don't know," she said. "Nothing. We were talking. He just came at me. Oh! Thank goodness you got here when you did! I don't know how much longer I could have held him off."

The owner found it hard to believe. He felt like he knew Joey from the hours they'd spent together horseback. He knew his wife, too.

But what could he do? What could he say?

"Well. I suppose I better talk to him," he finally said. "At best, it'll be a matter of sending him down the road. At worst, I might have to call him out."

Her "Thank you!" was muffled as she threw her arms around his neck, face pressed to his chest. "Oh, thank you!"

"Now," she said shakily, "if you don't mind, I'm going to my

216

room. I'm in such a state!"

She left him alone, hat in hand, deep in thought. He stood as if rooted for several minutes, mulling over his options.

"Sir?" a voice asked tentatively, breaking the spell. He looked around and saw the cook standing in the kitchen window.

"Sorry. A bit preoccupied," he said. "What is it?"

"Well, sir, it ain't my place to say anything and you know I seldom do. But I've known that young man from the day he showed up here all busted up. And I've gotten to know him right well since. And I'll just say this. If you sack that fellow, or shoot him, or anything else, you'll be punishing an innocent man."

With that, she turned away from the window and back to her work.

And with that, the owner realized he'd found a man he could trust as his new ranch manager.

All that first spring, we kept supposing it would rain any day.

Nobody worried much through the summer, because other than an occasional thunder bumper, it seldom storms then anyway.

But when fall passed without the usual rain, Dad saw cause for concern.

Very little snow fell in the high country that winter, which didn't bode well.

And when the seasons repeated themselves the next year with little relief, it was real trouble.

The cattle were poorer than usual coming out of the hills, and throughout the fall they cropped what little grass there was right down to dirt. The hay meadows hadn't even greened up that summer, so hay was scarce. Any blade of grass that dared to rear its head was fought over by hungry cattle.

But things sure changed that winter.

Overnight, the brown, denuded landscape was turned into a white wasteland, empty as the naked thigh of a crib girl.

Snow. Deep snow. Accompanied by cold that cracked your spit before it hit the ground.

What little hay we had was soon gone.

Snow kept coming and the cold never let up and our sorry stock started dying. Cattle drifted in close to the houses and barns and bellered night and day as if begging could produce fodder. The racket was enough to drive you crazy.

We skinned out what dead cows we could to try to get something out of them in lieu of the calves that would never be born, and frozen stinking hides piled up all around the place.

With no hope left and nowhere to turn, Dad and I hatched a desperate plan.

We'd hire as many wagons and drivers as we could from town and I'd try to lead them across the desert and over Crooked Canyon Pass to the Dios del Sol Valley. The thinking being that conditions there had been better, and there might be hay for sale.

We knew we could never haul enough to save all the cattle still standing. But we could save some.

If I'd known how the trip would turn out I'd have never set out on it. But we got here.

The sound of wagons rolling into ranch headquarters woke Joey from a dead sleep. He pulled on his pants and boots, lit a couple of lamps in the house, slid into a coat and stepped onto the porch.

He recognized Ruben the moment his brother pulled the scarf from his face and spoke. Sensing an advantage, he stayed where he was, silhouetted against the open front door.

"We left a herd of starving cows on the other side of the mountains. We're looking for hay to take back," Ruben offered for openers.

"It's a long way to haul hay."

"That it is," Ruben said. "But we didn't see any choice in the matter, other than letting the rest of the herd die off. That whole country is covered with snow—and the only thing under that snow is dirt. Naked as an innocent babe."

"What ranch you come from?"

"The Compass"

"Wasn't that Jacob Stone's place?"

"Still is. Although he's along in years to the point that giving advice is about all he can do. Jacob's my dad. I'm surprised you know of him."

"Used to have dealings over that way. But it's been years," Joey said. "We've got hay enough to fill your wagons. Stable your horses in the big barn. You men can put up in the bunkhouse tonight. We'll fix you up come morning."

Before sunup, when the only other thing stirring on the ranch was the cook—who somehow knew she had extra work this morning—Joey huddled with his foreman.

He outlined the terms of the sale, which the foreman thought were too favorable to the buyers given the circumstances, but Joey held firm. He followed up with detailed instructions on how the first wagon—the one on which the man named Ruben held the lines—was to be loaded.

Several hours later, Joey watched from the shadows of the porch as the laden wagons rolled away.

Once they were well out of sight, the foreman and a couple of hands took up their trail, soon overtaking and halting the procession.

"What's the trouble?" Ruben asked, unnerved at the display of weapons.

"It seems you gentlemen are hauling away more than just

hay," said the foreman.

"I don't know what you mean."

"Maybe we'll just have a look at your load."

Much to Ruben's shock and surprise, the foreman found the wallet full of the money that purchased the hay tucked into the supply box.

Ruben, bound with a catch rope, started back toward the ranch afoot, the two cowboys following along. Saying he saw no need for the cattle to suffer any longer than necessary, the foreman sent the wagon train on its way.

"We'll keep the law out of this if we can," he told the departing drivers. "But tell the ranch owner he'll have to come fetch Ruben himself. If he wants him back."

Even in broad daylight, we were well into our conversation before I realized who it was I was talking to.

Knowing I hadn't taken that money, I suspected little brother was up to something. But I couldn't figure out for the life of me what it might be.

We talked some as the days passed. For the most part, though, he's left me rattling around this living room chained to the damned stove. Waiting.

For what, I do not know.

You could see the lone horseman coming from a long way off.

Joey went inside and watched through the window as the old man covered the last little way. He slid cold and stiff from the saddle, looped the bridle reins around the hitching post, and climbed the porch steps.

Invited into the house, he removed his hat and blinked and rubbed his watery eyes to rid them of snow glare.

Jacob found his focus. And found himself face to face to face with his sons.

DROWNING IN RICHES

The banker closed the door behind him, turned toward the street, and looked both ways up and down the thoroughfare as he tugged the tails of his vest to smooth the wrinkles rippling over his ample belly. Satisfied that all was in good order in his town, he set out toward the café two blocks up the street, where he routinely took his midday meal. The common word—walk—does not adequately describe his gait. His important strides landed somewhere between *strut* and *swagger* as he moved along the board walkway. The people he encountered stepped out of his path. Women offered a tip of the head and a timid smile; the men, lips tight, touched fingers to the brims of their hats. The banker wore no head cover, save a snowy crown of hair rising above his forehead, sweeping backward in swells and waves as if blown by a gentle wind, covering the tops of his ears and collar.

Across the street, Lew—short for Lewellyn—Turnbow turned and spat in the general direction of a tarnished brass cuspidor, adding another filmy layer to the stain surrounding the spittoon and marring the whitewashed boards flooring the porch. He sat in a rocking chair in the shade on the hotel veranda, as he had for most of the past four days. The hotelier knew him as a traveling cattle buyer, as did the hostler at the livery stable, the clerk at the bank, and the serving girl at the café where he took his meals—the same eatery patronized by the banker. Otherwise, he had kept to himself while in town.

As the banker entered the café, Lew eased himself out of the rocker, fingered out his cud and flung it toward the cuspidor, hitched up his britches, negotiated the steps down to the boardwalk, stepped down onto the street, and angled across to the bank.

Inside, he stood in the small lobby, testing his memory of the layout. A man wearing an eyeshade and sleeve garters stood behind a barred window counting and stacking coins slid across the shelf to him by a woman as she plucked them from a small clasp purse. The only other person in the bank was a man seated at a desk, separated from the lobby by the cap and balusters of a wooden rail. The banker's empty office lay beyond, behind a wainscoted half wall topped with panes of frosted glass.

When the woman left, Lew stepped up to the teller window. As the clerk slid the stacks of coins from the shelf and jangled them into the cash drawer below, Lew refreshed his memory of the safe tucked into the corner—a black metal affair like many he had emptied over the years; some at the point of a gun, others with the aid of explosives. This one he intended to relieve of its burden by persuading the clerk, with the aid of a shotgun, to empty its contents into his saddlebags.

But not today.

The clerk looked up, recognized Lew, and said, "Welcome, Mister Turnbow. How are you today?"

Lew smiled. "Holding it together, Albert. Barely. Any word on that draft I'm expecting?"

Albert slid the cash drawer closed and pushed until the latch clicked. "Not that I have heard, Mister Turnbow." He cleared his throat and raised his voice. "Nigel!"

The man at the desk looked up from his ledgers. "Yes?"

"Any deliveries from the telegraph office this morning?"

The man called Nigel put his pen in its holder, picked up a sheaf of papers and envelopes from the corner of the desk, and riffled through them. "No, sir. I'm afraid not."

Lew asked if any of the envelopes carried a postmark from Miles City, Montana, or the imprint of a bank there.

Nigel said not.

Lew sighed and shifted his weight from one foot to the other. He pursed his lips and kneaded his chin with a thumb and forefinger. "Damn!" he whispered. He looked at Albert through the bars. "You know, Albert, if that draft don't come through soon, I'll lose this deal I been workin' on. I can't afford to miss out on that herd."

Albert smiled in sympathy and shook his head. "I'm awful sorry, Mister Turnbow. I'll send Nigel down to the telegraph office later to see if anything has come in. And there's the afternoon mail delivery. If what you are waiting for arrives, I will send Nigel right over to the hotel to fetch you."

Lew looked at the bookkeeper, who smiled and nodded his assent, then back at Albert. "Is he in?" he said, tipping his head toward the banker's office.

Albert stretched to his maximum height. "Oh, no, Mister Turnbow. Mister Baumann always takes his dinner at this time. However, I am assistant manager of this bank, and I can assure you there is no service Mister Baumann can accomplish in your behalf that I cannot provide just as well."

"Sorry, Albert. No slight intended," Lew said with a smile. "I'm just a little antsy, is all." He gave a nod to both men. "Thanks, gentlemen."

Lew smiled as he crossed the street. He had never been to Miles City, Montana, and knew nothing of any bank there. Nor was there any deal in the making for a cattle herd. He lowered himself into his accustomed rocking chair on the shady porch and cocked one leg over the other. Tipping his hat back, he fetched a plug and a jackknife from a vest pocket and shaved off a chew. He worked the tobacco around with his tongue and jaws and turned his attention back to the bank.

He drummed the tips of his fingers against the arms of the rocker. Soon, the roller shades came down over the front windows. A shadowy figure behind the front door—Albert, he knew—turned the sign from OPEN to CLOSED and pulled down the shade behind it. *Right on time,* Lew thought as he flipped open the face on his pocket watch, a keepsake from an earlier encounter with the conductor on a railroad train.

Behind the walls of the bank, Albert and Nigel would be dragging the day's express box or pouch out from below the counter under the teller cage. The safe would be open, and Albert would be counting out gold coins and bundles of currency and small change as Nigel credited the proper amounts to the appropriate columns in his ledgers. When finished, the door of the safe would close and the men would eat a hurried meal from bags and baskets brought from home. If all went well, there would be time for a few minutes of shuteye before getting back to work.

In any event, both men would be awake and at their stations, the sign turned back to OPEN and the window shades lifted before Baumann paraded his way back down the street from his leisurely repast at the café. If the pattern held, the banker would pause before the front door and cast his gaze up and down the street to assure all was in good order in his town before entering the bank. Inside, he would find all in good order as well.

That would not be the case tomorrow.

Days before checking into the hotel, Lew had ridden the hills and canyons around the town. In an isolated little valley some twenty miles out, he found an abandoned homestead. The cabin roof had collapsed, and the window and door frames were empty. The outhouse lay on its side, tipped off the hole it once stood over. But a few repairs to the fence made a small pasture secure. A carpet of grass covered the enclosure, and a corner of the fence crossed and recrossed a shallow spring-fed stream.

The place would serve his purpose well.

Lew stowed a supply of food—no more than filled a sack lashed behind the cantle of his saddle—and turned his spare horse into the pasture. Then, working his way back toward the town, he scouted a serpentine trail through timber lining the ridges. He found a stretch of water with a firm bottom flowing through a narrow valley. Where a branch of a deer trail scrambled through a narrow gap in an outcropping reef on a steep hillside, he cut a scraggly young pinyon tree and stood it in the gap. And he plotted a course across a sandstone mesa where his crossing would leave little trace.

Satisfied with his planning, he rode toward town. The place lay at the foot of a mountain range pockmarked with mines, with a mile-wide sagebrush flat cut by dry washes and gullies for a front yard. The road from the wide valley and big cow outfits below skirted the mountains, and after passing through town entered a long canyon through the range to reach another settled valley beyond. There was talk of a railroad, but it was only talk so far.

As his mount covered the ground with a mile-eating single-foot gait that rode smoother than the usual trot, Lew mapped his exit from the town. He would avoid the road and ride hell for leather through the brush to the hills opposite, counting on speed and surprise to put distance between him and whatever pursuit would come. By the time the posse followed his path into the hills, he expected to be well up into the higher country on the way to the cabin. His other ruses—the blind trails through thick timber, the trackless stretches through water and over stone—would further confuse and delay the pursuers if all went according to plan.

Most towns like this one, he knew, had trouble mustering a posse. The services of an experienced tracker were even harder to come by. There was little a man on the run could do to fool someone with a history of cutting sign and reading trails other than slow him down as he ferreted out the track. But, most times, outlaw tricks could confuse and dishearten an inexperienced posse.

Lew hoped that would be the case on this adventure.

The shadows lengthened and the spit stain spread through the afternoon as Lew sat in the rocker on the hotel porch. Right on cue, the window shades in the bank came down and the sign in the door turned to CLOSED. Nigel came out and stepped off the boardwalk, hurrying through the alley beside the bank to the streets beyond and home. Albert came through the door on Nigel's heels, but stopped to lock up. After removing the key, he tried the knob and gave the door a good shake and rattle, testing its security.

Baumann the banker had long since left the premises, bankers' hours apparently too trying for a man in his position. As was his wont of an afternoon, the old man with the flowing, well-coiffed mane crossed the street from the bank, on the opposite angle from where Lew sat, to reach the town's other hotel in the middle of the next block. Fancier and dearer in price than Lew's lodgings, that establishment featured a high-minded bar where the town's high and mighty congregated to rub elbows, chart a course for the future, and conspire to further entrench themselves in power.

All for the good of the town, of course.

Lew poured the last half-glass from the bucket of beer on the side table, drawn from the taps of the humble bar at his hotel. When the glass was empty, he dropped it into the bucket, stood and hitched up his britches, lifted his hat and raked his fingers through his hair, then settled the hat with a tug on the front and back of the brim. He stepped off the porch, ambled up the sidewalk, and crossed the street when opposite the café. An early supper—or late dinner, if you will—and a late, but substantial, breakfast served as his only occasions to put his boots beneath a table these days, as his appetite was not what it was in his younger days. Whether an effect of age, or a result of persistent hunger over days and weeks and months on the run when following the outlaw trail, he could not say.

The cowbell dangling from a leather strap pegged to the top rail of the door clanged when Lew pushed it shut, announcing his entry into the café.

"Well! Hello, Lew," Ingrid, the serving girl, said with a toothy smile. "Good to see you again. You're gettin' to be a regular around here."

Philo, the cook and owner of the eatery, stood in the kitchen, looking out through the wide pass-through window. The only other person in the place was an old man sitting at the counter nursing a cup of coffee—perhaps the same mug he had in his hands when Lew was in earlier for breakfast, refilled countless times from Ingrid's pot. The lack of busyness this time of day played into Lew's reasons for choosing his hour to dine.

"Afternoon, Ingrid." Lew removed his hat and hung it on the post of a ladderback chair, then pulled out an identical chair on the opposite side of the table and sat. Ingrid carried out a coffeepot and mug and filled it without being asked as Lew studied the daily specials, chalked on a slate hanging on the wall. Hand-lettered signs of various sizes posted all over the walls listed the regular bill of fare. "What's good today?"

"That venison stew on the board is right tasty." Ingrid leaned in and said in a low voice, "I wouldn't bother with the liver, or the chicken fricassee."

"Fine. Bring me a big bowl of that stew, then. And some bread rolls, if you've got them."

"Dinner rolls ain't out of the oven just yet. But I can slice

227

you some bread from a loaf that was fresh yesterday."

"That'll be fine. Slice it thick and bring plenty of butter."

Lew watched through the windows the comings and goings on the street, sparse as they were, while he waited. He did not wait long.

Ingrid set a big bowl of stew in front of him, and laid down a spoon and napkin next to it. Another trip brought a bowl of butter and a plate stacked with bread. "I'll be back directly with a butter knife." And she was, along with the coffeepot, from which she topped off Lew's mug.

Lew looked up at her and smiled.

"When you plannin' on leavin' us, Lew?"

"Can't say for certain. Once I've done my business at the bank. Soon, I hope."

"Well, I'll sure miss you once you're gone."

Lew smiled again. "I'll miss you, too, Miss Ingrid. Not to mention old Philo back there's cooking."

She glanced over her shoulder toward the pass-through window to see if her boss was looking on. "Yeah, he does pretty good." She glanced back again, then leaned in to whisper, "Long as you got somebody to tell you what's off." She returned to her counter, wiping it down with a damp rag for the umpteenth time, leaving Lew to eat in peace.

That girl was sure right about this stew, Lew thought as he spooned up mouthfuls, and tore off chunks of buttered bread to dip in the gravy. Ingrid kept his coffee hot and brought out a second bowl of stew when she saw Lew scraping the last of the gravy from the bowl with a crust of bread.

By the time he finished his meal and lingered over a last cup of coffee, the early supper crowd was trickling in. He fished out a gold dollar and a Liberty half dollar and laid them on the table. The sum would more than cover his bill, leaving a generous amount of change for Ingrid's apron pocket. He stood and retrieved the hat hanging from the chair post and started for the door. Before leaving, he caught Ingrid's eye as she bustled about behind the counter and she acknowledged his wave with a smile.

The seat in the rocking chair on the hotel porch seemed to have conformed to his backside. He lowered himself to sit. He watched until the whole of the street lay in shadow as the sun dipped below the high mountain peaks. Still, at this time of summer, dusk would last a good long time before fading to darkness.

Lew looked to be idle, but his mind was at work, rehearsing over and over the events of tomorrow. A lone man robbing a bank was an unusual—and somewhat daring—crime. But Lew had carried out many a robbery with one or two partners as well as with entire gangs, and he had concluded that the only man he could count on in a pinch was himself. While he had run with some of the best outlaws, most of the rest were either foolhardy, excitable, trigger happy, slow and sleepy headed, or just plain dumb.

Lew knew who to trust: Lew.

Besides, when he worked alone there was only one slice of the pie, and it was all his.

Come morning, Lew shaved, then indulged in a hot bath. He had no idea when the next opportunity for a thorough cleaning might present itself. He gathered his few belongings into a saddle roll and stowed them with his saddlebags at the hotel desk after settling his bill. At the café, he made short work of a stack of pancakes slathered with butter and drizzled with maple syrup, along with a rasher of bacon, some fat sausages, and lots of hot coffee.

The same old man sat at the counter drinking coffee, but there were no other patrons during the lull between breakfast and dinner. Lew pushed back from the table and put on his hat.

With Ingrid nowhere in sight, he stepped over to the counter to wait. Philo saw him through the pass-through window. He turned away and said something, and Ingrid came bustling through the kitchen door, smiling and toweling dishwater off her hands.

"How was your breakfast this morning?"

"Just fine, Ingrid. Thank you. And thank old Philo back there."

"I surely will. Did you get enough? And enough coffee? Sorry I didn't keep your cup full as regular as you might've wanted. There was more dishes to do today than most mornings."

"Don't you worry none about that, young lady. I'm about to float away, truth be told. Any more coffee and I'd slosh when I walked."

Ingrid smiled. Lew handed her two gold dollars. "Why, Lew! That's way too much money for your breakfast." She handed back one of the coins, but Lew refused it.

"No, Ingrid—you keep that, and whatever other change I'm due. I've sure appreciated your taking care of me these days I've been in town."

Ingrid's smile disappeared. "Lew! That makes it sound like you're leavin'!"

Lew nodded. "I believe so. I got a feeling I'll get the money from the bank today. If things work out the way I figure on this deal, I'll have money enough to last the rest of my life."

"Well, I'll miss you, Lew Turnbow."

Again, Lew nodded. He hesitated a moment, then left the eatery. He looked in as he passed the front windows, saw Ingrid watching, and waved.

The livery stable was around the next street corner and down the block. He did not look for the hostler, but took down a halter from a peg on the wall and went back outside to the pen his horse shared with a few others. The horses stood hipshot in the corral, their tails swishing flies, and did not move as he walked among them. Lew patted his horse on the shoulder, rubbed its neck a time or two, then slipped the halter over its muzzle and buckled it around the horse's throat.

Back inside, the hostler was waiting. He had fetched Lew's saddle and it sat atop a sawhorse-like rack. Lew tied the horse to a wall ring and went to work on its hide with a currycomb and brush.

"I'll take care of that for you," the hostler said. "All part of the service."

"No, that's all right. I've been ignoring this horse these days he's been in your care. This way, he might remember who I am."

The hostler laughed, and slid his backside onto a feed box to watch as Lew laid on the saddle blanket and swung the saddle onto the horse's back, then walked to the offside to straighten the straps and cinches, and to make sure his rifle was secure in its scabbard. Back around the horse with a pat on the rump, he buckled the back cinch, threaded the latigo through the front cinch ring and pulled it snug, then gave an extra tug before slipping the prong into a hole on the leather strap. He slid the short-barreled shotgun partway out of the sheath hanging beneath the stirrup fender and shoved it back in, assuring it was secure.

"That's a lot of hardware you're carryin' there."

Lew looked over the seat of the saddle to where the hostler sat on his feedbox against the wall but said nothing. He took down the bridle hanging from the saddle horn, slipped off the halter, thumbed the bit into the horse's mouth, slid the headstall over its ears and buckled the throat latch.

He looked again at the hostler. "I spend a lot of time alone on the road in my line of work—sometimes carrying a goodly

231

amount of cash money. A man's got to have protection, times like those."

The hostler nodded. "I see."

Lew settled his bill, then untracked the horse by leading it out through the stable door into the alley. He checked the cinches once again, then swung into the saddle and heeled the horse into motion, stopping at the hitchrail in front of the hotel. He stepped down and looked across at the bank in time to see the banker come out the front door, tug on the tails of his vest as he surveyed the street, and start for the café. Lew gathered his belongings from inside the hotel and tied the bedroll behind the cantle. Rather than tie on the saddlebags, he slung them over the seat.

Leaving the horse tied, he stepped onto the porch, sat down in the rocking chair, and whittled himself a chew. He spat at the cuspidor but missed, starting afresh another puddle on the stained porch floor. Lew opened his pocket watch to check the time, and looked across at the bank. *Won't be long now.*

Lew sat and spat for a few minutes before again consulting his watch. He stood, hitched up his britches and gun belt, then left the porch and made his way down the steps and across the sidewalk and onto the street. Unwrapping the reins from the hitchrail, he double-checked the saddle cinches, then led the horse across the street to the bank. He did not use the hitchrail there, instead dropping a rein to leave the horse to stand ground tied, trained to stay put. Looking up and down the street for anything untoward, Lew eased the shotgun from its scabbard, then draped the saddlebags over his shoulder.

He walked into the bank just as Albert pulled down the first window shade. "Oh! Mister Turnbow!" the clerk said. "I'm sorry, but we're just closing for the noon hour."

"That's all right, Albert. I won't be but a minute."

Nigel sat at his desk; ledgers open before him. Albert noticed the gun pointed at him and looked confused.

"Just go on about your business, Albert." Lew stepped aside and watched Albert pull down the other window shade, turn the sign in the door to CLOSED, and unfurl that shade. With the short barrel of the shotgun, Lew directed Albert to his place behind the counter, and told Nigel to abandon his bookkeeping to join them there. Lew followed the bankers behind the counter. "Just like always, Albert."

Trembling, the clerk reached below the counter and pulled out the express box delivered on that morning's stagecoach, then opened the lock with a key from the cash drawer. With one eye on his work and the other on Lew and the shotgun, he managed, after two tries with a shaking hand, to open the safe. Nigel stood by, face pale with sweat beading his forehead, hands raised above his head although he had not been asked to do so. A smile twitched the corners of Lew's mouth.

Lew pulled the saddlebags off his shoulder and tossed them to land in front of the safe. "Fill them up. Start with the gold."

Albert started emptying the safe of its cache of eagle, double eagle, half eagle, and gold dollar coins.

"Even 'em out," Lew said, and the clerk alternated handfuls into one bag then the other. With the safe emptied of gold, he followed suit from the express box. Each pouch of the saddlebags was topped off with bundles of currency, starting, at Lew's instruction, with the larger denominations.

With the saddlebags stuffed and tied shut, Albert stood. "You won't get away with this. Mister Baumann will pursue you to the ends of the earth."

"We'll see about that. Turn around."

Cradling the shotgun in one elbow, Lew pulled a pigging string from his waistband and bound the clerk's hands. He pushed Albert out of the way, and kept watch on him while he tied Nigel's hands behind his back with a second short length of rope. He hefted the saddlebags with a grunt and slung them over his shoulder. Then, with the shotgun barrel, he prodded the men out from behind the counter and into the railed-off enclosure, then through the doorway into Baumann's office.

"It has been a pleasure doing business with you, gentlemen."

Nigel said nothing. Albert started to speak, but stopped when Lew raised the barrel of the shotgun. He closed the office door, walked through the bank, and went out. He figured he had a good fifteen or twenty minutes before the bank was due to reopen, and a half hour or more until Baumann would reappear. Sliding the short-barreled shotgun into the scabbard, he draped the heavy saddlebags over the seat, checked the cinch, gathered up the dangling rein, stepped into the stirrup, swung aboard, and rode up the street as if nothing were amiss.

Lew had not traveled two blocks when he heard the shout.

"Stop! Stop that man! Stop him! He's a thief!"

Lew turned to look and saw Albert standing on the walk in front of the bank. He had managed to open the office door and front door of the bank, despite his bound hands, and raise the alarm.

Shit. Lew pulled a pistol from the holster on his hip and fired a meaningless shot in Albert's direction as the clerk continued hollering, raising the attention of the few people on the street. *Shit,* Lew thought again. He happened to glance over at the café as he rode past and saw Baumann, brow furrowed and eyes questioning, looking out the window. With surprise already gone, and just for the hell of it, he shot again and watched the window shatter and rain glass down on the banker, adding sparkle to his glowing coif.

Lew holstered the pistol, tipped his hat to the frightened banker, and spurred his mount into a run. At the edge of town, as planned, he abandoned the road and rode headlong into the brush, across the swales and gullies toward the hills beyond.

Once across the irregular flat, he slowed the horse to its single-foot gait, following a well-worn cattle trail into the hills. As the trace gained altitude, oak brush lined the bottoms of the draws, with cedar and pinyon pine on the slopes, later giving way to fir, spruce, and clusters of quaking aspen. Lew kept to his planned route, abandoning game trails to weave through the thicker timber. He topped out on the plateau and followed a windswept sandstone outcrop for a time, then dropped off the other side of the mesa into a shallow canyon, the horse picking its way among rocks and boulders in the stream along its bottom.

Farther on, Lew reined the horse uphill again, nearly doubling back in direction, until he reached the outcropping reef near the top of the steep rise. He dismounted and pulled aside the scraggly pinyon tree he had stood in the narrow gap through the low cliff, led his horse through, and dropped the tree back into the slot. With a bit of scrambling, towing the horse along as it humped up the incline, Lew soon reached the summit. He loosened the cinch and pulled the bit from the horse's mouth, leaving the bridle hanging but allowing the horse an easier time of cropping at the grass while they rested. Walking back toward the rim, Lew sat in the shade with his back against the trunk of an aspen tree to watch the backtrail for any sign of pursuit. Seeing none after several minutes of watching, he rode on to the abandoned homestead and a fresh horse.

Lew sat in the shade of the wall of the derelict cabin, all his worldly goods between his outstretched legs. The thick money belt he had taken out of his bedroll lay across his legs as he stuffed its pockets with gold coins, filling most of it with double eagles, using the $10 eagles to take up the remaining space. Bundled currency and leftover gold coins he left in the saddlebags. He stood and pulled his shirt over his head, then strapped the money belt around his waist, pulling the double set of buckles taut. He twisted back and forth, working the leather and the fabric of his underwear into an agreeable position.

The money belt was heavy, and Lew knew it would rub him sore as a cinch-galled horse. But a little discomfort was a small price to pay for the wealth the money belt carried.

Wasting no time, Lew saddled the fresh horse, tied the saddlebags and bedroll to the back of the saddle, stepped into the stirrup, and set out at a long trot across the little valley to the narrow canyon that would lead him down to the big valley where he would ford the wide river and ride on to the city, there to catch a westbound train he would not leave until the tracks ended at the Pacific Ocean. He felt the money belt with every footfall of the pounding hooves as the horse trotted along, and he longed for the smoother single-foot gait of the tired horse left behind to fend for itself. Still, *a small price to pay.*

Heavy gray clouds crept into the mountains, relieving the heat of the sun. But that comfort soon gave way to the discomfort of pounding rain as lightning shredded the air and thunder pounded again and again, rolling and echoing through the canyon. The lightning storm passed, but the rain continued long into the night. In the darkness, Lew could find no shelter. The tired horse between his legs plodded along through puddles and rivulets, leaving the treacherous trail at times for firmer footing but found no relief there, having to pick its way along boulder-strewn slopes.

Finally, long past what must have been midnight, the rain let up and the clouds broke apart. By the light of a full moon and blanket of stars, Lew reined up near a narrow overhanging ledge. He pulled the saddle, the leather wet and spongy, and draped the soggy saddle blanket over it to dry. Knotting his catch rope into a makeshift halter, he relieved the horse of the bridle and staked it out to find what food it might among the rocks and brush. Once he had seen to the horse, Lew stretched out along the narrow band of dry ground under the ledge, and, using a rock for a pillow, drifted off to fitful sleep.

Direct sunlight had yet to reach the canyon floor when Lew awakened, stirred from sleep by the growing daylight and accompanying warmth, as well as the squawking of a magpie that, for whatever reason, objected to the man's presence. Lew sat upright and spent a few minutes stretching his muscles and flexing his bones. He filled his jaw with tobacco and sat watching steam rise from the wet earth in the growing heat.

Lew's clothing was still rain-damp to the skin, and the saddle and saddle blanket had yet to dry. But there was nothing for it except to move on. Still, he took his time getting on the trail, believing the storm had surely hindered any pursuit, even, perhaps, making it impossible. He followed the canyon—dry in normal circumstances, but now with a small runoff stream flowing along its bottom—down to the big valley, then angled off in the direction that would lead him to a place to ford the river. The ford was seldom used nowadays, with most traffic using a bridge several miles upstream. He considered riding to the bridge and the small town that had sprouted there, but opted to avoid it. Even if not hot on his trail right now, sooner or later a posse, or at least a lawman or bounty hunter, would come looking for him and he did not care to leave any hint of his having passed this way.

Lew leaned out of the saddle and spat, the syrupy stream barely missing the toe of his stirrupped boot. He sat up straight, hands stacked on the saddle horn, and studied the river as he worked the chew of tobacco in his jaw. It was much wider than he remembered. Lew wrote off the increase in the size of the river to storm runoff. The current looked faster as well, probably for the same reason. He contemplated waiting it out, but decided to risk the crossing. For a man on the run, there might be greater risk in waiting.

He dismounted and loosened the saddle cinch a notch, checked the buckles and ties securing his accoutrements and weapons, then snugged down his hat and remounted.

The horse was reluctant to step into the stream, testing the water with pawing hooves, then snorting and blowing and backing away. Lew kept prodding with the spurs, and after more false starts, used the tail ends of bridle reins as a quirt and lashed the horse across the rump. The move surprised the animal, and it leapt into the river.

The water was no deeper than the horse's hocks. Its hooves skated on the bottom, firm yet slippery, and it scrambled to keep its feet. Lew tugged on the reins and spoke to the horse, leaning down to rub its neck. After a moment, the trembling stopped, and the horse snorted and blew and tossed its head. Tapping his spurs to the animal's belly and clicking his tongue, Lew encouraged the horse to move farther into the stream. The mount's hesitant steps moved them out into the flow and Lew could feel the increased pressure of the current, even though the water did not deepen much.

Without warning, the stream bed dropped away. The horse went under, drenching Lew to his hat brim as he clung to the saddle. Its head breaking the surface, the horse's legs and hooves churned at the water. Lew kicked free of the stirrups and allowed the water to float him out of the saddle. He kept hold of the reins and grasped the saddle horn, struggling to keep his head in the air. The current was slow but strong. Lew pushed his mount's head upstream, angling across the flow as it pushed the pair downstream.

The horse worked, but made little progress and Lew could feel its strength waning. He grabbed the butt of his rifle and tugged until it came free of the scabbard, then dropped it into the flow. He caught a glimpse of his hat floating away and wondered why, not recalling its coming loose. He dallied the reins loosely around the saddle horn and, gripping the horn with one hand, used the other to free the bedroll and supplies tied behind the cantle. His cramped fingers tugged at the sodden saddle strings, but the knots in the wet and swollen leather held firm. He managed to find the jackknife in his vest pocket, pried the blade open with his teeth, and used it to saw through the ties. He watched the bedroll and all that was wrapped in it float away, roll in the water, and sink.

Still wielding the knife, he sawed through the lashings holding the saddlebags. Underwater, he worked his feet as well, alternating between kicking to stay afloat and using the toe of one boot to pry against the lever of the spur shank on the opposite foot in an attempt to free himself of the heavy, water-logged boots.

Just as he cut through one of the saddle strings binding the saddlebags, the horse pounded against him, almost jarring him loose. The horse jolted him again and slowly turned in the current as a floating log scraped and shoved them out of its way, nearly rolling the horse over Lew as it went. The half-free saddle bag now dangled deep in the water, its weight further unbalancing the laboring horse. The animal still thrashed against the stream in an attempt to stay above water, but both it and Lew were under the surface as often as above it.

Lew managed to free the saddlebag, and felt it thump against his leg as it sank under the weight of the gold it held. He went to work on the money belt, pawing at his vest and shirttails to get to the double set of buckles that held it tight. He felt fight leave the horse. Its legs stopped thrashing and it rolled on its side, pushing Lew's head under. Reaching toward the surface, he took hold of some part of the saddle and pulled himself upward, his head clearing the river just long enough to take in a gasping breath of air.

Now with both hands free, he pawed his way through the clothing covering the money belt and felt for the buckles. He could see little in the murky water, only bubbles and bits of debris floating past. Even that faded as the water deepened and darkened around him. His mind clouded. His fingers numbed. And then he was sitting on the bottom of the river, slowly, slowly sliding downstream.

He fumbled at the money belt that held enough gold to last the rest of his life.

Lungs bursting, he gasped and opened his mouth to suck in one last breath.

A BORDER DISPUTE

The walls of the gorge lit up briefly in the lightning flash. Although it was but midafternoon, heavy clouds and high cliffs blocked enough light that it was dark as late evening along the river's course in the canyon's bottom.

Knowing it was a matter of minutes until the clouds burst, the man in the canoe started watching the walls for a place to put ashore.

Not that he minded getting wet. But the tons of water the storm was dumping on the desert were already pouring down feeder gorges and into the river, and the coming high and white water was more than he cared to tackle in a cheap open canoe. His cargo was much too valuable to risk. And so he scanned the shore as he slid along on the current.

Not that there was shore to speak of. But that was why he was on this stretch of the Rio Bravo—Rio Grande, the gringos called it. Smuggling drugs across the border wasn't the cakewalk it once was, so the commerce was forced into ever more inventive avenues and isolated places.

The so-far successful method that brought him here was simple. Get to a place on the Mexican side of the river where you can get yourself, your cargo, and a cheap canoe over the rim of one of many canyons downriver from the Big Bend country and float lazily downstream for a few days or even a week to reach another semi-accessible pre-arranged place on the American side, set the canoe adrift, and climb out of the

241

canyon with the cargo.

So far, it had worked. The buffoons in the Border Patrol and the DEA idiots could not comprehend this offset fashion of fording the river and so concentrated on more conventional crossings. But, he feared, the *Rinches*—the derogatory border Spanish term for the Texas Rangers—were wising up and he might soon have to come up with a new and equally devious plan or he could wind up in some Texas *juzgado*.

His eyes picked out a dark cleft in the cliff's face just a few feet above the water and he backpaddled to slow and turn the canoe, pushed himself back upstream a few yards with a dozen deep strokes, then pivoted again and allowed the canoe to drift downstream as he used the paddle to force it against the wall.

When he again spied the slender opening, he grasped jagged rock and stopped for a closer look. The canyon hereabouts was riddled with caves, but not many were accessible without serious climbing, and he had neither the time nor inclination for that. So he sought shelter that was above the high-water mark and no higher.

This should do fine, he thought.

With a couple of lengths of bright yellow plastic braided rope, he lashed the canoe securely fore and aft to rock outcroppings. He rummaged through one of the watertight plastic chests that filled the canoe and selected a blanket, a battery-powered fluorescent lantern, a water bottle, and a lunch sack full of cold tamales and tortilla-wrapped frijoles. He fashioned a makeshift sling from the blanket and with the food and lantern in its pouch scrambled the few feet up the cliff to the narrow opening.

Once through the crack, he sat back against the wall for a moment to catch his breath. As he sat, a thunderclap rolled through the canyon, shattering the sky, knocking the storm loose into the gorge. The sound of heavy raindrops splattering off rocks and pocking the river made him glad he was out of it.

Even in the dark he sensed the cave was a small one and sang a few lines of a favorite corrido to see if the echo agreed. It did.

The smuggler slid a few feet further into the mountain before unslinging the blanket. He set the lunch sack aside, stowed the lantern between his thighs, and wrapped the blanket around his shoulders before punching the button to activate the lamp.

He did not realize how accustomed his eyes had become to the dimness until the painful glare of the light. His face wrinkled in a squint and he raised a hand instinctively to shield his eyes. Then his vision cleared and an inadvertent gasp, nearly a scream, filled the cave when he saw what he saw.

Sitting next to him, no more than a foot away, was a rack of bones and stack of litter that had once been a man. Another skeleton lay on the floor nearby. The smuggler, whose line of work had occasioned his seeing no small number of dead bodies, and even watching a goodly number who were alive become dead, was nevertheless startled and shocked and left temporarily lacking the ability to breathe.

Calderón died instantly in a powder flash and since he saw it coming, it would be incorrect to say that he never knew what hit him. Another cliché often applied to such instances may, however, be true: he never felt a thing.

That cannot be said of the other man, Butts, whose death was both lingering and painful.

And although it violates the order of their dying, it is yet true that Calderón killed Butts, and then Butts killed Calderón.

The smuggler considered bolting the cave and braving the storm, but curiosity got the better of him once composure returned. He studied the bodies—corpses—skeletons—and wondered how they came to be dead in this out-of-the way place.

It was clear they had been dead for a long time. A long, long time. Little remained in the way of flesh—the odd strip of jerky clinging here and there the only evidence that meat and skin once covered the bones.

Since the skeletons were largely intact, the place must be protected from predators, at least large ones. He assumed bugs and worms and rodents had done the scouring.

A sizable chunk of bone was missing from the upper forehead and top of the skull of the man seated beside him. The side of the head of the other man, the one curled on the floor next to the black smudge that must once have been a fire, was dented and cracked. *That says something,* he thought.

Butts knelt next to the small fire, kindled from rats' nests and twigs and a few pieces of driftwood he'd collected from where they'd been lodged in the rocks near the cave's entrance. The fire would never burn long enough to dry them, but the spindly flames provided a bit of light and took the edge off the chill.

It wouldn't matter if they were still wet come morning, anyway, he thought, since it would be back in the river for the both of them until they could find a place on the left bank to climb out of the canyon. He fed the fire a few more twigs and turned toward Calderón in time to see the rock in the Mexican's fist the instant before it smashed into his head with a dull crack like a stick of wood snapping underwater.

The blow rattled Butts to the soles of his boots, but as his eyes blurred and his ears buzzed and his brain bled, he managed to unholster his Colt and with the last remnant of strength in his arm and hand bring the weapon to bear and fire. Calderón, weak from the flight and the fight and the fall and the float, had barely managed to lift the rock, no bigger than the crown of his lost sombrero, for a second swipe at the fallen Butts when the heat of the muzzle blast withered his eyelashes and the bullet ripped a peso-sized chunk out of his head.

As soon as Butts fired the shot, the weight of the gun carried his hand to the cave floor and he instinctively curled into a fetal position. The noise inside his shattered head drowned out the sound of his whimpering. Pain squeezed at his skull and the blood poured both into his head and out of it, eventually washing away all awareness and finally life itself.

Not much left in the way of clothing, the drug runner noticed. Practically all the fabric, it appeared, had been unraveled and hauled away string by strand. Most likely, he thought, to line rodent nests. Dried and cracked remnants of leather boots remained. Rusted spurs said both had been horsemen.

Other metal objects survived. Corroded buckles and tarnished brass cartridges in a gun belt around the body on the floor. A rusty old revolver wrapped in finger bones. And, still surrounding the thin bones of the men's wrists, a pair of handcuffs.

The cuffs linked the right wrist of the man leaning against the wall to the left wrist of the man on the ground. That, and the fact that the downed man held the gun, led the smuggler to the obvious conclusion that the one seated next to him had been the prisoner of the other.

But what the hell were they doing here, in this miserable cave in the bottom of a river gorge with no way out? As he mulled it over, his eye caught something else. There, wedged in the dust under a rib bone, was a dull metal disk. He wiggled it out of the dirt and brought it closer to the light.

He could see, after rubbing off a layer of grime, that it had once been a silver peso. But its face had been crudely hammered smooth and a series of wedges punched out to create the shape of a star within a circle, around which was stamped the

Rod Miller

words TEXAS RANGER.

Rinches! he realized. This dead *pendejo* was one of the *Rinches!*

Butts clung to the rocks with one hand while the other fist held a twisted handful of Calderón's shirt collar. He was further encumbered by the Mexican's heavy mochila, an oversized set of saddlebags, slung over his shoulder. Both men sputtered and spat volumes of water back into the river where it belonged. Calderón had the worst of it, in turn hacking water from his lungs and spewing it from his stomach.

"Stay afloat, Calderón. I can't keep you from drowning by myself."

"Why don't you just let go?"

"You ain't getting off that easy, you thieving sonofabitch. I'll watch you rot in a jail cell and enjoy every minute of it."

The Mexican made a half-hearted attempt to tread water while the Ranger looked over the rocks above. The canyon walls were rough and jagged, nearly vertical. Caves and shelter rocks were visible in the cliffs, but he could not see a way to get to them. Then, just before casting off to float downriver and try again elsewhere, he spied a dark cleft in the rock a few yards upstream. Maybe, just maybe, he thought, it was within reach and might offer shelter from the coming night.

"Come on. Upstream," Butts said.

"*Qué?* What do you want?"

"There," the Ranger gasped, pointing out the cave. He hacked up and spit out another gob of slimy water. "Climb. Get out of this damn river."

Butts pulled Calderón through the water and spun him toward the rocks. The Mexican clawed for holds and between the two of them pushing and pulling they reached the spot below the cave. The Ranger jerked upward on Calderón's shirt, lifting him higher in the water.

246

"Up," he said. "Arriba."

The Mexican barely had the strength to struggle the few feet up the face, and it was almost more than Butts could do to pull himself along behind and prod the prisoner at the same time. As Calderón disappeared into the narrow crevice, the Ranger called out to him.

"Calderón!"

He waited a moment, stuck to the rock like a lizard, then called again, louder this time.

"Calderón! Poke your ugly face out that hole!"

The Mexican's face slithered out the crack like a tortoise poking its head out of its shell.

"Qué?"

"Here. Grab these."

Butts pulled as many sticks and twigs of driftwood as he could find out of the rocks and shoved them upward one at a time. Calderón took them and pushed them into the darkness behind him. Having scavenged all the wood at hand, Butts scrambled the last few feet up through the rocks and followed his prisoner into the cave. Before he even sat down, he clamped handcuffs around Calderón's wrist and fastened the other end to his own.

"What the hell, man?" Calderón said. "You think I'm going somewhere?"

Butts did not reply, merely dropped to the ground in a heap of fatigue and sucked in a few ragged breaths.

"Unhook these bracelets. I don't want to spend the night chained to no damn Ranger."

"Shut up. It ain't like you got any choice in the matter."

"Where am I going to go? I been chased halfway across Tejas. I been beat up. Fell off a cliff. Nearly drowned. I ain't got the strength to break wind and you think I'm going somewhere? Besides, you know I can't hardly swim anyhow."

Butts ignored Calderón. Or pretended to. He did not believe for a minute that the Mexican was anywhere near as bad off as he let on. Besides, the Ranger had experienced all the same troubles his prisoner had and doubted he himself had the strength to stop an attempted escape.

After a brief moment of blessed silence, the prisoner piped up again. "Hey, Ranger—what's your name?"

"Butts."

That drew a chuckle. "Butts? What kind of name is Butts?"

"My name. The one I got from my daddy. The only one I've got."

"What, gringo, you don't got a first name? Everybody just calls you Butts?"

"That. Or C.W."

"*Qué?*"

"C.W. Them's my initials. I go by C.W. Butts."

"What's that stand for, C and W?"

That drew a chuckle from the Ranger. "Clarence. Clarence Winthrop. Clarence Winthrop Butts."

Calderón laughed. "*Madré de Dios!* No wonder you like C.W. How come you know my name?"

"Hell, you're famous, Calderón. Either a hero of your people or the most hated man in West Texas, depending on who you ask. I've known your name these ten years since I been with the Rangers."

A fruitless chase after the Mexican had, in fact, been the first assignment Butts was given as Ranger. Butts was detailed to the Rangers' Frontier Battalion, which had just a few years earlier captured the notorious murderer John Wesley Hardin and killed the outlaw Sam Bass. The day of his enrollment in July of 1882, the tenderfoot Butts was sent out with a posse to chase down Calderón and his bandido gang after they had robbed an express shipment out near Marfa.

But the robbers won a long hot miserable race across the desert and crossed the border before the Rangers could overtake them. Butts had spent a goodly portion of the intervening decade trying to stop the Calderón gang's robberies and killings across West Texas, but the Rangers always seemed to be a day behind the bandits.

"I been on your tail now and again over all that time."

Again Calderón laughed. "You must not have got too close, Butts, or I would know who you are."

"Maybe so. You are a slippery little bastard, I'll give you that."

"*Claro.* But outsmarting gringos is no big thing. It has been an easy life, robbing those who stole our country. It is like— how do you say it?—taking candy from a baby. Beating you people is almost too easy."

"That maybe was true once, but those days are over now. You make the same mistake my daddy said caused the Confederacy to come out in second place—thinking that winning battles is the same as winning a war."

"What are you talking about, Butts? I have good English but I do not understand what you say."

"I'm saying you may have won some battles by getting away up till now. But now you're mine, and that means you done lost the war."

Both men sat quietly for a time. Then Butts unslung the heavy saddlebags from his shoulder and tossed them back into the cave, where they lit with a soggy clink. As his eyes adjusted to the dim light, he spied a wad of grass that had once been a nest for rats or mice and picked it apart into a small pile in front of him. Other, similar wads were within easy reach and he retrieved a few of those and piled them nearby.

Finding a likely-looking piece of rock, Butts next pulled his pistol from its holster and glanced the stone against the metal at the bottom of the grip to see if he could raise a spark. He could.

Soon, the dry grass sparkled and smoked and glowed and a few gentle breaths coaxed out a flame.

"Thank God for Samuel Colt," Butts said, holstering his revolver as he added progressively larger twigs to the fire. He knew the fire would be short-lived. But he did not know that within minutes, more than a fire would die in this cave.

Curious about the rest of the story, the smuggler hoisted up the lantern and cast his eyes into the dark corners of the little cave. At first he saw only evasive movements of rodents and insects hiding deeper in cracks and crannies, but in due course his eyes picked out a curled and cracked hunk of leather in the shadows.

Stepping gingerly to avoid splintering the bones on the floor he followed the lamplight to the discovery and dragged the heavy bag away from the wall and into the cave's center. It looked to be of the same vintage as the bodies and about as intact. It was, he decided, a mochila of the type he still saw used occasionally by the vaqueros of his homeland on the opposite shore. Smaller than a kyack for a packsaddle but bigger than the saddlebags of Texas cowboys, a mochila was cut to fit over a saddle horn and cover all or part of the seat. Pockets or pouches were sewn on the sides for carrying whatever the rider wanted to take along.

And what, exactly, the smuggler wondered, was this one carrying?

The mochila was dried out and some of the leather strings that stitched it together had rotted through. Parts of it were gnawed away. But the pouches still held whatever they held. He shifted it around to get to one of the buckles and find out what, and as he tugged the strap to free the buckle prong, it broke in his hand. Peeking in through the lifted flap, he caught the dull glint of metal.

His heart skipped a beat and his lungs involuntarily gasped

for air. In the exuberance that followed, he tore loose the other pocket flaps and shook free a trove of tarnished silver and glowing gold coins that clinked into a pile on the floor of the cave, followed by the dull thud of a quartet of shiny good-as-new gold ingots.

Butts knew the bandit was his when he saw Calderón abandon his spent horse, leaving the broke-down animal quivering and dripping sweat and sucking wind at the rim of one of the many rocky canyons hereabouts that dropped into the bigger canyon of the Rio Grande.

From a distance, he watched the robber strip the mochila and head down the deepening gully afoot. Calderón attempted to spook the horse away, but the scrub had hit bottom and stood unfrightened, spraddle-legged with head sagging. The Ranger's horse was also tired, but being accustomed to better feed, had held out just enough longer to run the Mexican mount into the ground.

Turning his horse in the downhill direction of the gully, Butts pushed hard along the rim for better than half a mile, figuring to get ahead of the bandit before dropping into the canyon for a surprise attack.

The plan worked. Concealed behind a rock outcrop at the side of the narrow draw, Butts watched for some minutes as Calderón hustled downhill, dodging boulders and scrambling over drop-offs into the shallow hollows at their bases where storm runoff would puddle and churn before heading again downhill to the next short fall.

Having been the object of the Ranger's pursuit for several long hours and many hard miles, Calderón assumed Butts was still coming after him, so he spent as much time looking behind him as ahead. And so it was unnerving when Calderón turned from one such backward glance to find himself stood up by the barrel of a revolver mere inches from the end of his nose.

Too startled to react, the Mexican did not even breathe until Butts spoke.

"Don't you move, you greaser sonofabitch, or I'll shoot you dead sure as you're born. Get them hands up, real slow."

As Calderón complied, Butts pulled the bandit's pistol from its high-riding, cross-draw holster and threw it into a jumble of rocks on the steep side of the canyon.

"Now, sit down. Drop right straight down on that skinny butt of yours and don't try anything cute."

Keeping his pistol trained between the man's eyes, Butts squatted before him and patted around for the knife he knew would be concealed in the Mexican's boot tops. He found it and tossed it away.

Butts then holstered his pistol and looked to where he had tucked a pair of handcuffs under his gun belt, his brief inattention prompting the prisoner to reach behind his head and slide a thin-bladed knife out of a scabbard concealed between his shoulder blades.

Calderón's sudden movement caught the Ranger's notice and he instinctively took a backward step. The resulting accident is the only thing that saved his life. Butts stumbled and tripped when his heel caught on a rock and he fell flat on his back. Unable to stem or shift the momentum of his thrust, the bandit's blade sliced only desert air as he followed its path over the top of the fallen Butts, likewise stumbling and landing half in the dirt and rocks and half atop the lawman.

Quick as spit on a hot griddle, Calderón scrambled off Butts and onto his feet and looked around desperately for the knife jarred loose in the fall. Butts saw it first, and grabbed it up from where it had landed almost in his hand. He flipped quickly to his knees and braced for the Mexican's next attack, but Calderón instead turned and loped off downhill. The knife clattered in the rocks as Butts flung it away and took after him.

Even with the heavy mochila Calderón carried, Butts figured he must have a thirty-pound advantage over the outlaw, who, while short and skinny, was likewise wiry and cagey. And had it not been for dumb luck, he knew the Mexican's knife would already have cut him to ribbons. So while his pursuit was vigorous it was not without caution.

It took another accident to again stop the chase. An unfortunate step wedged Calderón's foot between boulders, impeding his stride just enough to stretch him out face first among the muddle of rocks in the bed of the dry watercourse. Butts was upon him before he could recover and, with all the force he and gravity could muster, dropped a knee into the middle of the man's back.

Rather than disabling the desperate bandit, the capture inspired him. Calderón flipped to his back and unleashed a vicious knee that landed swift and square in the Ranger's crotch, expelling his breath more effectively than the Ranger's knee to the Mexican's back had.

Calderón exploited his advantage by crabbing out from under the Ranger and landing another ferocious kick to his ribs. Butts automatically reached for his pistol as the blow rolled him, but could not accomplish the draw as he had affixed the safety strap over the gun's hammer to secure it during the chase.

Now it was his turn to scramble out of the way on elbows and bootheels as the Mexican attempted to brain him with a rock. Again, Calderón's momentum carried him to the ground and again Butts took the opportunity to leap astraddle his back. He grabbed Calderón by the wrist and wrenched his arm behind him, forcing the hand painfully upward. Then, for good measure, he landed a few kidney punches.

The Ranger relaxed slightly when the Mexican sagged limp below him and again he reached for the manacles. The instant he loosened his grip on Calderón's wrist to replace it with the grip of a cuff, the bandit exploded upward and again scrambled out of his grasp and down the draw.

Calderón did not get far, soon skidding to a stop. His next step would have carried him into empty air with nothing between him and the river below but a sheer drop of some thirty-five feet. Lacking the Mexican's knowledge of their current situation, Butts did not stop as Calderón had, instead launching himself with a mighty leap, the force of which barely diminished as he wrapped his arms around the bandit and carried them both out into the chasm.

Although Calderón knew what was coming and so his scream came first, Butts soon overcame the disadvantage and his yell surpassed the Mexican's on all counts—length, intensity, and the quality of the profanity. He did not stop the scream until it was replaced in his mouth by river water.

The shock of the landing tore the pair apart. When Butts surfaced he saw that Calderón was in a bad way, his slight frame lacking the buoyancy to keep himself and the heavy mochila above water. Besides, the bandit evidently lacked swimming skills beyond the ability to thrash around enough to break the surface from time to time and gasp a breath as the river pushed them along downstream.

A few powerful strokes carried Butts across the current to where the Mexican floundered and he wrapped his arm around Calderón's neck to hold his head above water. Calderón, of course, misinterpreted the action as another attack and objected violently. Butts increased pressure on the bandit's throat to dampen his struggling and yelled into his ear instructions to hold still. Either fatigue or lack of oxygen or the Ranger's yelling finally calmed Calderón, and he relaxed and allowed Butts to keep him afloat.

"Damn it, man, here I am trying to save your life and here

you are trying to drown us both. You're going to have to shed them saddlebags or they'll drag you down."

"Are you *loco*? This mochila is why I have been running from you and why you have been running after me. And now you want me to dump it in the river?"

"No, you fool. I'll carry it. It won't weigh me down near as much as it does you, you skinny little bastard. Give it over, then we can figure how to get out of this damn river and back on dry land."

Quarter eagles. Half eagles. Eagles. Double eagles. Spanish reales. Silver dollars. Gold dollars. Silver pesos. Other curious coins the smuggler had never seen nor heard of. But he knew enough to know that the metal the coins contained far exceeded their worth as minted currency.

And then there were the gold ingots, whose value he could not, dared not, even imagine.

He passed the time stacking, restacking, dividing, subdividing, combining, separating, shuffling the coins.

There were worse ways to pass a rainy night, he thought.

All the success Calderón had enjoyed eluding the Rangers over the years ended by sheer happenstance; one of those ugly coincidences life throws at one from time to time in order to keep one humble.

Butts and a couple of other Rangers happened to be laying over in the railroad town of Sanderson on a trip from Fort Stockton to Langtry. Word came down while the men were enjoying a rare hotel breakfast that a bandido gang had waylaid the morning eastbound a few miles outside of town and made off with a bank shipment—not a tremendous haul, but a significant one. Even before their abandoned breakfasts had gone cold, the Rangers were armed and mounted and on the trail.

Calderón did not imagine that pursuit would come so quickly, so the Rangers surprised the bandits squatting around empty money sacks dividing the take for easier transport. Had they done so in concealment, the lawmen likely would have captured them then and there. But the Mexicans had stopped on a wide and dusty dry lakebed and so saw the Rangers coming from a good way off.

They quickly stuffed the loot back into bags, into pockets, into pouches, into saddlebags, into mochilas, even inside shirts and the crowns of sombreros, and clambered aboard their horses and lit out across the flat. But the Rangers were better mounted and the gap between the three of them and the five bandits closed with every stride.

Pursued and pursuers started exchanging optimistic gunshots while still outside pistol range, and kept up the fire as the distance closed. Whether the Ranger riding next to Butts meant it or whether it was a fluke—a subject of much discussion in Ranger circles for years to come—the fact remains that he placed a bullet directly through the back of the neck of one of the retreating bandits, evening the odds some by making it three after four.

Shortly after the bandit fell, the group split in two, with three of the *ladrones* staying together and the other striking off alone. Butts signaled the other two Rangers to continue after the group of three, knowing they could improvise in the likely event the bandits split up again later. He veered sharply southward following the lone rider. Already, he sensed victory—sensed, at least, that the chances of catching the bandit were heavily in his favor. What his chances might be once he caught up with him, Butts could not say.

Off the flats and onto more rugged terrain, the pace of the

pursuit slowed. But still Calderón drove his mount furiously. He knew the river was ahead. And he knew it cut through one deep gorge after another throughout this country, most likely putting it and the border beyond reach. But if his horse held up, the off chance that he would hit the river at a place he could cross was the only chance he had.

The rain had stopped sometime during the night, and by midmorning the worst of the gullywasher had passed and the Rio Bravo was back to its normal flow.

The smuggler was nervous, tense, wound tighter than his usual state of alertness while at work. Which is to be expected, perhaps, given that yesterday's unlikely events had made this far and away the biggest payload of his career—even if he jettisoned the contraband drugs. So, even though the chances of someone in law enforcement spotting him on this rugged, lonely stretch of river were practically nil, he nonetheless kept a sharp eye on the cliffs above the left bank. He did not think he would spot a Border Patrol officer up there, or a DEA agent.

But those *Rinches*, he thought. Those damn *Rinches*. It's hard to get the best of the *Rinches*.

LOST AND FOUND

Half of my right thumb is somewhere in a patch of shadscale at the mouth of a scrub-oak draw on the west face of the Swasey Mountains. I reckon maybe some magpie or maybe a kit fox has ate it by now—a morsel so small likely wouldn't interest a buzzard or a coyote.

I ain't afraid to say it hurt like hell when I pinched off that thumb when takin' my dallies. It was a heifer calf, weighed maybe 500 pounds, on t'other end of my rope. I was a-huntin' strays we'd missed in the fall gather—which ain't hard to do in that country—off the government lease the old man's family has run cows on since before there was government leases. I been takin' wraps for more years than I care to admit to and not once in all that time had I had such a misfortune. But my horse ducked off to dodge a rock just as I was takin' the turn and kind of upset the balance of the whole deal. Be that as it may, there ain't many dally ropers of my age that's still got a full set of fingers, so I reckon I was overdue.

Anyways, right after that sudden shock of pain, it sort of quit hurtin' but that stub of a thumb was bleedin' like a stuck hog. Not havin' no other ideas, I broke loose the drawstring from my Bull Durham sack and with the fingers of my left hand—which ain't none too agile—and what teeth I got left, I somehow managed to twist it around there and fashion a tangled knot and tie it off tight enough to where the blood was only seepin' out 'stead of squirtin'. A passin' thought said rollin' a smoke would prove a real adventure from then on.

That heifer in the meantime had skedaddled back up that draw I'd choused her out of. So I climbed into the saddle and went after her. Hell, she was draggin' a reata I had only just barely got stretched and tallowed, and I'm damned if I was gonna ride away and leave a brand new gutline behind. And, anyways, that critter'd likely get it all snarled up in the oak brush and not be able to get to water and maybe die 'fore anybody'd find her.

Besides, I don't reckon you could put a price on half a cowpuncher's thumb, but the old man could sure as hell name the cost of a lost heifer calf.

I had not got far uphill 'fore I could hear that calf thrashin' around. Just as I figured, she'd ducked in and out of the oak brush on those cow trails and strung that rawhide twine through branches and limbs and forks and trunks till it was so bound up it wouldn't drag no more. I rode up to where she was and managed to reel her in a ways and get enough slack to tie off to the saddle horn. I dismounted and told that horse in no uncertain terms to keep the rope taut no matter what, then waded into that tangled scrub oak to find the end of that skin string that bit my thumb off and work my way back up the length of it to get it all unsnagged. Which I did.

It didn't take but a few rods of draggin' that heifer downhill till she realized hangin' back and bawlin' wouldn't do her no good. We bottomed out and I reined that horse to where I'd parked the truck and trailer by a little corral there. The morning wasn't but half over, but I figured I'd load up and haul for the ranch anyway on account of half my thumb bein' missin' and all.

Workin' the door latches on the trailer was a whole new experience, but I managed to open it up and jump the horse in, then back up to the gate and load the heifer out of the pen. I was easin' the truck along the two faint tracks that served as a road when I noticed a rooster tail of dust out on the flat where the county road was.

Now, you gotta understand there ain't a whole lot of traffic out that way—a few ranchers and cowboys from time to time, rock hounds once in a while, and, now and then, one of them university folks doin' one thing or another with them cosmic ray outfits they got scattered all around. I kept creepin' along, watchin' that pickup comin' up the road toward where I'd be meetin' up with it after a mile or so. I seen it was a pickup. No ranch outfit, though—one of them jacked-up trucks with big tires and spotlights like town kids drive. The road left the flat and climbed into the foothills and I'd lose sight of the pickup now and then, but the dust trail pointed to right where it was.

'Fore it got to where I would meet the road, it came a-tearin' around the side of a little ridge and skidded to a stop, stirrin' up more dust. It stopped right where there was a big steel culvert where rain and runoff—what little there was of it—could run on down a dry wash. That pickup made about a six-point turn to get back around the way it come. By then, curiosity got the best of me and I stopped to watch.

The driver, he jumped down out of the cab, dropped the tailgate, and dragged somethin' heavy out of the back. I knowed it was heavy on account of he had to tug and pull on it to get it out of there, and when it hit the ground, it kicked up dust. It looked like a rolled-up tent or some such, but I couldn't tell more than that. That kid—I knowed he was a kid on account of his ball hat bein' turned around backwards on his head as if he was fixin' to milk a cow or play catcher in a baseball game—hefted and yanked on that bundle and rolled it off the edge and down into the gully. He dusted off his hands, climbed back into the truck, revved up the engine, and spun out of there flingin' dust and gravel like the devil was on his tail and about to bite him on the butt.

My throbbin' thumb—what was left of it, that is—had slipped my mind altogether, what with every workin' part of my brain wonderin' what the hell was goin' on down there. But it come back to me in a flash when I reached up to put the truck in gear and whacked it on the shifter. Hurt so bad I damn near puked. That started the stub into bleeding again, too, so I decided I better take a minute and see to it. But the knots in the string was too tangled to tighten, so I rummaged around in the mess in the truck for somethin' that might help and come up with a bottle of iodine we used for doctorin' cows, and a ripped-up shirt that didn't look too dirty.

So I set in to tearin' strips from that old shirt with my teeth and left hand. Then I stepped out of the truck so as not to spill iodine in there—like a new stain would show—and poured a dollop on the wound and wrapped my hand up good with them cloth strips. There wasn't no way to tie that bandage on that I could think of, but I found a bundle of feedstore receipts held together with a rubber band and used that elastic, and it worked pretty good. I held that hand up high as I eased the truck along and it felt a little better.

A few minutes later I got to the place where I'd seen that truck stop, and I did too. Whether he meant to or not, that kid had found a pretty good place to hide that bundle. I stood there on the edge of the road lookin' down into that dry wash where he'd dumped it and couldn't see anything for a minute or two. Then, down there under some greasewood and rabbit brush, I spied what looked like canvas, but bein' as it was near the same dun color as the dirt it didn't hardly show.

It took some hikin' to get to a place where I could slide down into that wash. I waded through the brush in the bottom till I got back up to where I'd seen that canvas. I soon seen what it was—a canvas dam from an irrigation ditch. It was water stained and splotched with dried mud.

The bundle was tied off near each end with some of them orange plastic hay strings that was faded and frazzled enough to show they'd been layin' out—maybe hangin' from a fence post— for a while. With curiosity gettin' the best of me, I fetched out my pocket knife and managed to unfold the blade with my teeth and sliced through them wraps of twine.

I had a suspicion what might be in there, but it was still a shock to peel back that canvas and see a human bein'. Other than a gray, pasty-colored face, the kid looked peaceful enough, like he was only asleep 'stead of deader'n hell.

Along about then I wondered if maybe gettin' one of them cell phones was a good idea. But I soon thought better of it and found me a place to scramble out of that ravine and walked back up to the truck.

There was no sign of dust from that pickup truck out on the flat anymore, but you can bet I made plenty of my own. I crossed the blacktop highway and kept on the county road to the ranch gate, and laid on the horn as I rolled into the yard and skidded to a stop.

The old man's wife came out the kitchen door wipin' her hands with the tail of her apron. Her eyes went wide when she saw that bloody bandage on my hand, which wasn't hard to see, what with me holdin' it up in the air like I was wavin' hello.

"Where's Raymond?"—him bein' the old man—I said as I walked over to the porch.

"Land sakes, Vic, what have you done?"

"Nothin' much—just a little wreck. Is Raymond here?"

"He's putterin' around out in the barn somewhere, or maybe cleanin' out the water trough in the south pasture. I suppose he'll be along to see what all the racket's about."

"Can I use the phone, Lila?"

"Sure. Come on in." She swung open the screen door and

stood aside to let me pass.

I dialed 911 and after some doin' got hooked up to the county sheriff's office. I told a deputy there what I'd found and what I seen. It took some explainin' on how to get out there—some of them deputies know that country pretty good, but this wasn't one of them. He asked could I lead someone out there, but I told him I had best see a doctor, and that started up another bunch of questions.

"You sure your injury isn't related to the body you found?" he said.

"Hell no, it ain't. Listen, I gotta go."

"Wait just a minute. Give me those directions again. I want to make sure I've got them right."

"Look, Deputy, if you ain't found the place by the time the doc's done with me I'll take you on out there. That kid sure ain't goin' nowheres, but I am. I'll stop by your place while I'm in town."

The screen door slammed just before I hung up the phone. I turned to see Raymond there on the rug workin' his feet out of a pair of rubber boots.

"What the hell, Vic," he said. "I only see one calf in that trailer. That all you found? And what're you doin' back here at this hour?"

He said all that without never once lookin' up. When he did look at me after gettin' out of them boots, he didn't notice my hand as it was hangin' down by my side like normal.

"Raymond, I need to go into town. Right away."

"The hell you say!"

I raised up my hand and his eyes got wide like Lila's had. I guess the sight of blood is a surprise to most folks.

"Can you help me unhitch the trailer and see to that heifer calf? I'd best be goin' soon as I put up the horse."

"C'mon," he said. "I'll drive you."

Unsaddlin' a horse with a hand and a half proved quite the task, and by the time I got it done and turned the horse into the corral the old man was waitin', revvin' the truck engine like it would hurry me along.

"You lose much blood there?" he said with a nod toward the hand I had propped on my knee and leanin' against the truck door.

"Not enough to matter, I don't think."

He asked me and I told him about the wreck. Then I told him about seein' that other pickup truck and about the dead kid that got dumped down the wash. By that time, I was gettin' a mite edgy so I asked if he'd roll me a smoke.

"Hell, Vic, you know I don't use tobacco. Never have. I seen you do it a thousand times, but I still wouldn't know how to make one of them roll-your-owns you smoke."

"Pull on in here, then," I said, as we come up on a crossroads gas station.

The young girl runnin' the counter got me a pack of factory-made cigarettes and tapped her multi-colored fingernails on the counter while I fished in my hind pocket for my wallet with the fingers on my hurt hand. She kept up the drummin' when I laid the wallet down and fumbled around with my left hand pullin' out enough bills to pay for the overpriced smokes.

The old man was grinnin' when I climbed back in the truck, havin' watched the whole circus through the window. He laughed out loud drivin' along as I fussed with the cellophane wrapper to get the pack opened, then tried to light a match holdin' the book in between the fingers of my hurt hand and strikin' it with my left. I admit I looked about as handy as a cub bear wearin' mittens, but I finally got lit up.

"Them damn cigarettes look like more trouble than they're worth," the old man said.

"I reckon so."

" 'Sides that, they'll kill you.

"Prob'ly."

He smiled and shook his head but said no more. Nor did I. We made it to the little hospital in town and Raymond dropped me off in the driveway where the ambulances bring sick folks and I moseyed on in. There wasn't a soul in the place but me and a girl at a desk punchin' on the front of one of them cell phone things with both her thumbs. I took off my hat and looked around for a minute, then went and stood next to the desk. Without sayin' nothin' or even lookin' at me, the girl opened up a drawer and slapped down a pen and a clipboard with some sort of form on it.

I stood there a minute lookin' at the papers and finally sat down. She poked at the phone a few more times, then set it down.

"You need to fill out this form," she said.

I looked at her for a minute, then held up my right hand. She was the fourth one to see that mess, and the third to go all wide-eyed.

"Well," she said, with a big long sigh like she was facin' a job that couldn't be done, "it looks like I will have to do it for you."

It took quite a while for her to ask all manner of questions that had nothin' to do with catchin' a thumb in your dallies, and by the time we was finished I was feelin' that stump throb all the way up to my eyeballs. She picked up a phone—a regular phone, not that little flat box that sat there on the desk and buzzed from time to time—and in a couple of minutes a doctor come out through a pair of swingin' doors. Leastways I expected he was a doctor on account of he had one of those stethoscope things slung around his neck. But the fact is, he weren't no more than a kid and looked and talked like he come from India or Pakistan or some other place over there.

He led me back to a room and sat me on one of them bed affairs and made a lot of "tsk-tsk" and "hmmm" and "my, my" noises as he undone my bandaging handiwork. He left and came back in a minute with a nurse and she went wide-eyed on seein' my hand. She stuck me with a shot needle and after that I don't remember much about what went on till I found myself walkin' out the door with the old man guidin' me by the elbow. My hurt hand was hangin' in a sling and was all wrapped up so's it looked like I was wearin' a white boxin' glove. I wasn't feelin' no pain, and Raymond had ahold of a little white sack he said had some pills in it that would keep it that way.

"County sheriff came lookin' for you," he said when we got to the truck. "Told him I'd bring you by."

Lawman said they'd found the kid's body all right. Asked about what I'd seen, about the truck and the driver and all. I told him what I knew about it, which wasn't much. It was pretty clear to me, even in my addled state of mind on account of the drugs the doc had give me, that the sheriff thought maybe I knew more than I was sayin' or maybe was even in on it, whatever it was. He asked again and again about my hand, as if that had anything to do with what happened to that boy. The old man heard enough of it and swore at the sheriff some, told him I'd stuck my thumb in my dallies, that I wasn't the first cowboy what done it, and damn sure wouldn't be the last.

The sheriff was kind of taken aback at Raymond's impertinence and my ignorance and sat for a while just lookin' at us. It was kind of like what some of those cops on the television say— folks'll get uncomfortable with the quiet and end up confessin'. That wouldn't work with us, on account of we didn't have nothin' to confess about.

I did decide sittin' there with no one sayin' nothin' was a waste of time so I said, "Do you know what killed that kid?"

"Not yet. We've got a doctor—a specialist—on the way to look at him. There were no visible signs of trauma. He hadn't been beat or shot or stabbed or anything like that. My guess is a drug overdose."

"Drugs?" Raymond said. "I didn't know kids around here was into drugs like in the cities."

"Oh, they're around, all right. There's a bunch of town kids mess around with it some. They'll get to partying, drinking and such, and someone will start passing around drugs of one kind or another."

"Well, I'll be damned," the old man said.

"It's mostly marijuana, sometimes ecstasy. Usually not the real hard stuff—but we do run across some meth and heroin, now and then." With that, he stacked up the papers spread in front of him on the desk and tapped the edges to get them all tidy and tucked them into a folder. "I guess that's all, gentlemen." He looked at me. "You're free to go, Victor. Leave a phone number where we can reach you with Pearl out at the desk in case something comes up and we need to talk to you."

I told him, "I ain't got a phone of my own. And there ain't one in the bunkhouse. Just call out to Raymond's place and I'll get the word sooner or later."

"You don't have a cell phone?"

"No sir."

His office chair squeaked when he leaned back in it and he give me a funny look. "No shit? I thought everybody had cell phones by now."

I stood up and put on my hat. "I guess most folks do. But there ain't nobody needin' to get ahold of me in a hurry. Leastways no one I want to talk to." I looked at Raymond and give him a wink of my eye. "That," I told the sheriff, "and the cows don't seem to care if I got one or not."

When we got in the truck, I pulled out my store-bought cigarettes and shook one out of the pack.

"Here," the old man said, and handed me one of them cheap

little lighters you see for sale everywhere. "Got that for you while you was with that doctor. 'Fraid you might die of a nicotine fit trying to light them gofer matches with one hand."

"Why, thank you kindly, Raymond," I said. It took me four or five tries to master that gadget, but you got to remember I ain't all that handy with my left hand.

We call it the bunkhouse, but what it is really is an old ten by forty-two foot trailer house that the old man hauled onto his place years ago and has been rustin' away out by the barn ever since. Raymond dumped me out there and said, "C'mon up to the house in about an hour and Lila'll feed you. You ain't in no shape to be cookin'."

"Oh, I'll be all right," I said.

"Like hell. All them drugs that doctor's got you on, I'm afraid you'll burn down the bunkhouse. See you at the house," he said, as he turned the truck around.

Next day, I stayed pretty close to home doing what I could do with that mitt on my hand. I mucked out the bunkhouse some, tidied up the saddle shed, and spent the afternoon organizing things in the shop. Damn near went crazy. A man can stand that sort of work on a stormy winter day, but when the sun's shinin' in the fall he wants to be out horseback. So that evening I tossed aside the sling and unwound about forty yards off that bandage and put the pain pills in the medicine cabinet behind the mirror on the bathroom wall.

Lila wasn't too thrilled when I moseyed up to the house and told Raymond and her I was goin' back out to the lease in the mornin' and finish huntin' cows. The old man didn't say much—he knew somebody had to do it, and he would rather it was me than him.

It was still a chore hitchin' the trailer and saddlin' the horse and whatnot, but with the fingers of my hurt hand pokin' out of the bandage I managed to get it done. I didn't have no trouble and managed to collect one old dry cow, a yearlin' heifer, and two steer calves. By the time I got them corralled and loaded, I was wonderin' if leavin' them pain pills home was a good idea.

The sun was down as I eased the truck and trailer down the two-track to the county road. 'Bout the time I got there, I seen lights down the road a ways and when the outfit came around a bend in the road I'm damned if it weren't that same jacked-up truck from the other day. I hadn't turned on my headlights yet, and what with the noisy pipes on that fancy pickup truck they probably hadn't heard me up there either.

I stopped to watch for a minute. That truck was goin' slow and shinin' a bright spotlight around in them washes and gullies along the road. Puttin' my truck back in gear, I drove on down and turned onto the county road. I topped a little rise there just before the road dropped down to where that big culvert was and that truck was stopped, with the spotlight shinin' into the ravine. Even from where I was, I could see some of that yellow tape the cops strung around on the brush down in the bottom where that kid's body had been.

I pulled the knob to turn on the headlights, and that spotlight swung up and around and near blinded me when it hit. The tires on my truck and the trailer skidded in the dirt and gravel when I stomped on the brakes, even though I couldn't a been goin' more'n ten miles an hour. That light went off after a few seconds and I went on down the hill.

The road ain't hardly wide enough for two outfits to pass unless they slow right down and take it easy, and that pickup was pulled over to the wrong side of the road—so the driver could see down into the wash, I suppose. Creepin' along like that, I could read the license plate and I wrote it in the dust on the dashboard. I eased up beside the pickup and stopped. Besides the driver—wearin' his hat ass-backwards—there was a kid in the passenger seat. Big guy, looked like maybe a high school football player, wearin' a too-tight T-shirt that showed off his bulgy muscles. They was both starin' at me, tryin' to look mean but lookin' kind of sheepish at the same time.

"Howdy, boys," I said out the far window. The passenger looked at the driver, then looked back at me and they both nodded.

"Whatcha doin' way out here?"

They looked at each other again, looked back at me, and the driver said, "Spotlighting deer. Not shooting or anything, y'know—just seeing where they are for when the hunt comes."

I nodded in reply. Someone else said somethin' and they turned to look in the back seat and I seen there was a girl sittin' back there. Bein's she was outside the glow of the dashboard lights, I hadn't noticed her before. She looked to be about the age of them boys, but I couldn't get a real good look at her.

"Be careful." I let the truck start to roll, but pressed the brake and stopped. The boys looked startled, but relaxed when I said, "You got water, and somethin' to eat?" They nodded. "Good. The way these roads is, you might get stuck out here and end up spendin' the night. It's best to be prepared."

The kid in the passenger seat held up his phone with the front of it all lit up. "That's okay," he said. "We can call if we, like, need help."

"Them things work way the hell out here?"

"Not always. But, y'know, if you get to, like, a high place you can get service."

I nodded and drove away.

It was long past dark when I got back to the ranch. The old man must've heard me comin'—even though that time I wasn't honkin' the horn like the other day—and he was waitin' to help me with the stock.

"Lila, she was right worried. Ever'thing go all right?"

"Like a charm. I don't think there's any more cows out there.

If there are, they're hid up pretty good."

We put the cattle in a holding pen for the night and the old man threw them some hay while I unsaddled the horse. He climbed in the truck and backed the trailer to where we kept it and I unhooked it while he stood in the glow of the taillights watching.

"Say, Raymond," I said as I cranked down the tongue jack, "do you suppose I could come on up to the house and use the telephone?"

"Sure. Lila's figurin' on you comin' for supper anyway. She's got a plate stayin' warm in the oven for you."

I stood up and with both hands in the small of my back stretched out the kinks. "Oh, there ain't no need for that. Not that I'd turn down Lila's cookin'."

"Who you need to call? Not that it's any of my business."

"Oh, that's all right. I just want to call that sheriff. That pickup truck was out there again."

The old man asked and I told him all about it, and he agreed the law would be mighty glad to have that license plate number. Save them all manner of rootin' around in the dark tryin' to come up with a suspect.

After dialin' up the county sheriff's office and askin' whoever was answerin' the phone to have him call me, I sat down to Lila's dinner. About the time I was done eatin' the phone rang, and she answered it and handed it off to me. I told the sheriff what happened and he started in with the questions.

"No sir, I don't know what they was doin' out there. Said they was spotlightin' deer . . .

"Well, they was sure as hell nosin' around where that body was dumped, but it didn't look like they was too sure right where it was. When I come up on 'em that spotlight was a-shinin' right there where you people strung that yellow tape . . .

271

"If I was to guess, I'd say they didn't know the kid's body had been found . . .

"Can't say I'm a hundred percent sure, but it looked like the same truck, and the driver's bass-ackwards hat was the same color . . .

"Sure, I could identify him if I was to see him again. Same with the other kid . . .

"No. Couldn't see her very good—like I said, I didn't even know the girl was there at first . . .

"Yeah, I got the license plate number. Here you go . . ."

A man don't realize how much he uses his thumbs till he needs one and ain't got one. I figured that little stub I had left would be of some use, but not until I got rid of all them damn bandages. Anyways, it was three days later and I was tinkerin' around tryin' to patch together a busted bridle rein when the sheriff drove up. I ambled out into the yard where he parked his county truck, and he pushed a button somewhere and the window came whirrin' down.

"Well, we got him, Victor."

I nodded.

"Hell of it is, he ain't a bad boy. Plays football at the high school. Mother's a good woman. Daddy works at the bank—runs the place, all but."

I nodded again.

"Turns out that boy you found drowned."

"Drowned? The hell you say!"

"God's honest truth. Doc says there ain't no doubt."

I mulled that over for a minute, thinkin' how unlikely it was to find a drowned kid way the hell out in the desert, miles from so much as a mud puddle. "What happened?"

He tipped back his hat, turned off the engine, and squirmed his way into a more comfortable place in his seat before answerin'.

"You know the old Anderson place, down by the reservoir?"

I nodded.

"Kids use the place for drinking and partying and stuff. Been abandoned for years, and nobody lives anywhere nearby so they think no one knows what they get up to out there. We know, but we mostly leave them alone.

"Seems this boy we caught heard from some friends his little sister was out at the Anderson place with another kid from the football team. Says he figured they were at a party and went out to get her and take her home. Didn't want her getting into trouble.

"Turned out there wasn't a party—just the girl and that boy, and he was having his way with her and she didn't want no part of it. So, the brother dragged the boy off her and tossed him off the bank into the reservoir. Then he jumped in after him and held him under until he stopped bubbling."

He stopped for a minute to let that sink in. Then, "He dragged the boy out of the water and into a patch of willows on the bank and took his sister home. Sometime in the night he decided someone would find the body, so he went back out there in the morning. Wrapped him in the canvas from an old irrigation dam he found laying out there and trussed it up with baling twine. You know the rest."

But I didn't know the rest. Not by a damn sight. I asked, and he said the kid panicked again and decided to drive out and bury that boy and talked a friend into helping him. That's when they saw me out there. No good reason for the sister to go along, but she did. They didn't know the body had already been found and were surprised by the crime scene tape.

He said it would be up to the county attorney to decide what to charge the kid with, and whether he'd be tried as an adult or a juvenile. And what'd happen to the sister and the other boy, if anything.

The sheriff started the truck, then reached across hisself and stuck his hand out the window to shake mine. He was careful not to squeeze too hard. Then he put the truck in gear and before drivin' off, said, "Appreciate your help, Victor. Someone from the office will be in touch."

That's 'bout the end of it. Oh, there'll prob'ly be a court trial of some kind and the sheriff says I'll likely have to testify. I'm tellin' you this story now so's you can put it all down and it won't be forgot.

Me, I don't suppose I'll ever forget the day I lost half of my right thumb and found a dead kid out there on the west slope of the Swasey Mountains.

ABOUT THE AUTHOR

Writer **Rod Miller** is a four-time winner of, and six-time finalist for, the Western Writers of America Spur Award. His writing has also won awards from Western Fictioneers, Westerners International, and the Academy of Western Artists. A lifelong Westerner, Miller writes fiction, history, poetry, and magazine articles about the American West's people and places.

Read more online at:
writerRodMiller.com
RawhideRobinson.com
writerRodMiller.blogspot.com

The employees of Five Star Publishing hope you have enjoyed this book.

Our Five Star novels explore little-known chapters from America's history, stories told from unique perspectives that will entertain a broad range of readers.

Other Five Star books are available at your local library, bookstore, all major book distributors, and directly from Five Star/Gale.

Connect with Five Star Publishing

Website:
  gale.com/five-star

Facebook:
  facebook.com/FiveStarCengage

Twitter:
  twitter.com/FiveStarCengage

Email:
  FiveStar@cengage.com

For information about titles and placing orders:
  (800) 223-1244
  gale.orders@cengage.com

To share your comments, write to us:
  Five Star Publishing
  Attn: Publisher
  10 Water St., Suite 310
  Waterville, ME 04901